SNOW STRUCK

SNOW STRUCK

NICK COURAGE

DELACORTE PRESS

Text copyright © 2022 by Nick Courage
Jacket art copyright © 2022 by Mike Heath | Magnus Creative
Interior illustrations used under license by Shutterstock.com/Anton Malina and Shutterstock.com/Pipochka

Visit us on the Web! rhcbooks.com

Educators and librarians, for a variety of teaching tools, visit us at RHTeachersLibrarians.com

Library of Congress Cataloging-in-Publication Data
Names: Courage, Nick, author.
Title: Snow struck / Nick Courage.
Description: First edition. | New York : Delacorte Press, [2022] | Audience: Ages 10 and up. | Summary: "Three kids get stuck in a blizzard of epic proportions when they travel to New York City for Christmas"—Provided by publisher.
Identifiers: LCCN 2020051385 (print) | LCCN 2020051386 (ebook) | ISBN 978-0-593-303498 (hardcover) | ISBN 978-0-593-30350-4 (library binding) | ISBN 978-0-593-30351-1 (ebook)
Subjects: CYAC: Blizzards—Fiction. | Survival—Fiction. | Voyages and travels—Fiction. | New York (N.Y.)—Fiction.
Classification: LCC PZ7.1.C677 Sn 2022 (print) | LCC PZ7.1.C677 (ebook) | DDC [Fic]—dc23

The text of this book is set in 12-point Mercury Text G2.
Interior design by Andrea Lau

Printed in the United States of America
10 9 8 7 6 5 4 3 2 1
First Edition

For Rachel,
who snowboarded off an alp on a hang glider

Not only are severe snowstorms possible in a warming climate, they may even be more likely. . . .

—National Oceanic and Atmospheric Administration (NOAA Climate.gov)

PART

ONE

WASHINGTON SQUARE PARK, MANHATTAN

December 24, 2:30 p.m.

The tiny hawk shifted from one foot to the other on top of her cold marble perch, a thick crust of hail crackling beneath her talons as she peered into the wind. It didn't blow so much as scream, ripping down Fifth Avenue from the arctic tundra of Central Park and swelling the streets with never-ending snow. Tendrils of ice from ruptured pipes and water mains crept through fissures in the earth as the snow banked higher and higher against darkened windows and strained awnings, so deep that the city groaned beneath its weight. The hawk tilted her head against the storm, her red eyes staring—unblinking—at a shadow, gray and grainy behind a curtain of white.

Movement.

It had been twenty-four hours since the East River

had frozen over and more than twice that long since the Cooper's hawk had eaten. Over a million pigeons—plump and easy pickings—had disappeared at the first sign of frost, secreting themselves into rotting cornices and abandoned lofts while gray squirrels nestled deep in the hearts of hollowed-out plane trees. Even the rats had been driven underground, into the roots of the city: a tangle of sewers and subways where they huddled for warmth. Only the deer—who had traversed the thickening ice floes on the Hudson River from New Jersey in search of food—roamed the streets.

Shoulders taut, the little hawk leaned forward on her perch, talons flexing with anticipation as the shadow shuffled out from behind a half-buried cab. It was a squat, pigeon-shaped bird with wind-ruffled feathers so perfectly suited to the weather that it seemed to almost disappear into the shimmering wall of the storm. Snowy white and unaware, it pecked hopefully at its feet as the hawk's eyes narrowed, ravenously judging the puff of the smaller bird's chest while it scratched for grubs and other signs of frozen life beneath the ice.

So comfortable in the biting cold.

And so far from home.

The Cooper's hawk spread her wings, her rust-red feathers rippling atop the triumphal arch as she launched herself into the howling wind. In the half-second before she connected with the helpless ivory gull, the empty park looked almost peaceful. Somewhere beneath the snow and ice, Christmas lights still twinkled and thick, airy snowflakes swirled over the surrounding brownstones like a scene from a picture book. If it were any other year, a smiling Salvation Army Santa Claus would be ringing his bell as pink-cheeked carolers gathered beneath the arch with hot chocolate in mittened hands. But caroling—long-since canceled—was the last thing on anyone's mind. It had been days since the high end of the forecasts had dropped below zero and the trains had stopped running. Even without the citywide curfew, there was no one left outside to hear the startled cries of the ivory gull as Fifth Avenue erupted in an explosion of feathers.

No last-minute shoppers.

No tourists dodging snowballs.

In the hours after the governor declared a state of emergency, they'd jostled shoulders on overcrowded subway platforms and shouted into their phones from endless airport lines, waiting to board planes that would never take off as taxis fishtailed across black ice, slamming into parked cars and telephone poles. Blocking the plows. It was only after news of frostbitten evacuees spread throughout the tri-state area that stranded vacationers finally accepted the inevitable: there was no outrunning the historic blizzard. Their only options were to wait for the roads to clear . . . or for help.

Whichever came first.

The snow, so bright it was blinding despite the sunless sky, darkened where the little hawk struggled to subdue her prey, black talons squeezing with all of her might as the two birds sank into the rippling frost. Two thousand miles from his rocky nest, the ivory gull shrieked, pecking wildly at the little hawk's chest—his wings flapping frantically, beating against the side of her head. But the hawk's hold was too strong, and she was too hungry for sympathy. Tightening her grip, the little hawk looked away as she waited for the fight to drain from the visiting gull, her red eyes drawn to the thickening gauze of the horizon.

Before long, Washington Square Park was quiet again.

Quiet except for the unrelenting wind.

And then a shout, trembling and muffled by the snow.

"Hello?"

FIVE DAYS EARLIER

JOHN F. KENNEDY INTERNATIONAL AIRPORT

QUEENS, NEW YORK

December 19, 10:25 a.m.

Elizabeth tugged on the sleeve of her brother's shiny new parka.

"That's them," she said. "By the taxis!"

Even though Elizabeth's own jacket (also new) was still stuffed in her faded green backpack, she was overdressed and sweating in a hoodie and jeans. Neither she nor her brother had ever been north of Savannah, Georgia, and they'd been hoping for snow in New York . . . but it was so hot that even the air-conditioned airport terminal felt like a greenhouse. Elizabeth squinted through the glare in the floor-to-ceiling windows as she dragged her rolling suit-case past the baggage carousels and security guards, trying to remember if she'd packed a pair of shorts. They'd spent an entire week double-checking the daily forecasts and shopping for cold-weather clothes, but her arms were already damp with sweat and she couldn't imagine needing her long underwear or puffy thermal gloves anytime soon.

Not that the heat wave made the trip any less exciting.

After everything they'd been through, Elizabeth would have been happy to wear ski pants in a sauna— just so long as she was on vacation. She'd been living shoulder to shoulder with her family in Florida for half of the school year already, from summer vacation to winter break: cooped up in a cramped hotel room with her little brother while their parents waited for contractors to put a new roof on their house. There was no telling when their lives were going to get back to the way they'd been before the storm, but they'd logged so many endless hours in the Value Inn by the Waffle House that it was starting to feel like home . . . and the more normal their new life felt, the more Elizabeth wanted to scream.

It was still so hard to believe in the first place.

She knew there was always a hurricane or a wildfire happening *somewhere,* but to have one actually hit their house, where she'd lived since she was three years old—it felt like the kind of thing that happened to other people. People in the news, not regular kids like her. The entire neighborhood was still tented in blue tarps, gutted by the flood and abandoned until further notice, and it wasn't through lack of effort. Elizabeth had spent more than a few weekends helping her parents clean up the wreckage where their living room had been. She'd hammered through moldy walls until her hands were raw and dragged heavy trash bags out to the dumpster, but there was just too much to fix. Even the lights in the motel flickered on and off in the evenings, and the tap water still wasn't safe to drink—not without boiling it first. It tasted terrible, and Elizabeth fell asleep most nights praying for something to change.

But Christmas with their cousins in New York City?

It was so much better than anything Elizabeth would have even thought to ask for, and she still couldn't believe her dad had suggested it. Seventh grade was supposed to have been her big year: new school, new friends, new *everything* . . . but taking online classes in the aftermath of Florida's biggest storm had been about as much fun as it sounded—and with more than five months' worth of lost time to make up for, Elizabeth was so bursting with pent-up excitement that she felt like she was going to explode. Spotting her cousin struggling with a small fluff of a dog, she smiled and waved through the sliding glass doors instead. The dog circled her cousin's legs, tripping over its jewel-studded leash and then scrambling as her cousin picked it up, its nails catching on her shirt as she hugged it against her chest. Inconsolable, the puppy barked—so sharply that it cut through the din of the airport and the double-paned glass.

"C'mon, Matty," Elizabeth said, spinning on her heels.

But her brother was trailing behind her so slowly that he was barely even moving. Elizabeth walked backward so she could watch him scroll through his phone—completely entranced, like usual, with his forehead wrinkling in nervous concentration.

"It's way too hot for this time of year, isn't it," he said.

It was more of a statement than a question.

Elizabeth tried not to roll her eyes.

While she'd been bored half to death ever since they'd moved to the motel, Matty had just been worried. He was two full years younger than her and small for his age, so she didn't blame him for being scared every time it rained. Elizabeth had been a little scared, too, if she was being honest with herself . . . but while she'd spent most of her days trying not to think about the storm—or all the fun she was missing out on because of it—her brother had funneled every anxious minute into research. His phone was packed with every weather app he could find, from radar trackers to air-quality charts, and she'd even caught him signing onto an earthquake alert network while they'd waited for their plane to take off in Tampa Bay.

Elizabeth was pretty sure his research only made him worry more.

But it was easier to let Matty be Matty than to try to change him.

"Nothing bad's going to happen to us on this trip," she said, trying to sound reassuring—and not exasperated—as she pulled her brother into a sweaty hug. "I pinky promise, okay? This city's been here for literally hundreds and hundreds of years and it's still here."

Matty squinted up at her.

"Something bad *might* happen," he said.

"Will you let me know if you think it's going to?"

Matty blinked twice, considering, then nodded.

"Then it's a deal," Elizabeth said.

She gave her brother one last encouraging squeeze, then jogged ahead while he buttoned his phone back into an insulated pocket, her suitcase skittering behind her as she crossed out of the air-conditioning and into the hottest winter day on record in New York City. As annoying as he could be, her brother wasn't wrong about the weather. Even the newscasters—reporting from every television in JFK International Airport—couldn't stop talking about it. The high had already climbed past eighty degrees, almost twice as hot as it had been when they'd boarded their flight in Tampa.

Adjusting for humidity, it was so far from sweater weather that the ever-present Christmas music warbling forth from tinny speakers felt almost funny.

Like a joke without a punch line.

Elizabeth smiled as she dropped her suitcase to the sidewalk.

She'd texted with her cousin every once in a while, sharing funny videos and birthday GIFs, but it had been years since they'd spent a Christmas together in the same city. Now that they were reunited, Ashley seemed so much older than Elizabeth remembered. Seeing her in her faded ringer tee and scuffed combat boots, it was hard for her to believe that they were almost the same age. Or in the same family. If she didn't know her so well, Elizabeth would've even said that she looked cool—like an actor who was playing a teenager in a movie.

"You made it," Ashley said, grinning ear to ear beneath a flip of brown hair.

"We made it!" Elizabeth said.

Ashley pulled Elizabeth into a tight, sweaty-armed hug and Elizabeth laughed as her puppy squirmed, wriggling its way down to the sidewalk while Ashley's mom sideswiped them into an even tighter hug. "What you kids went through," Aunt Charley murmured, squeezing Elizabeth's shoulders up against her ears. Her big round glasses fogged as a hot tear formed and fell behind them, running down her cheeks and onto

Elizabeth's neck. Elizabeth tried to shrug an arm free to wipe it away, but her aunt just gripped even harder—oblivious to the curious looks from the cab line and the puppy weaving its thin pink leash between their knees.

"It's okay, Mom," Ashley said. "Everyone's okay."

She gently untangled herself from her mother's arms while Aunt Charley dried her eyes in the curve of her wrist. Finally free, Elizabeth tied her hoodie around her waist as she scanned the sidewalk for her brother. He was standing quietly next to their baggage in his shiny red parka, waving awkwardly with one hand and shielding his eyes with the other.

"Hey, Aunt Charley," he said. "Where's Uncle Jack?"

"*Matty,*" Elizabeth hissed.

But it was too late—the damage was done.

She could feel her cousin sagging next to her, deflating at the fresh memory of her parents' divorce. Elizabeth silently shouted at her brother. *SHUT UP,* she screamed wordlessly, her eyes popping out of her head, while Aunt Charley pushed her oversized glasses back up onto the bridge of her nose, ignoring his question. "Oh, honey," she said, fighting a smile as she surveyed Matty's winter ensemble, from his heavy boots to the warm knit cap peeking out from the back pocket of his blue jeans. "You're gonna cook right up underground."

Ashley sighed as Matty unzipped and carefully folded his jacket.

Elizabeth sighed, too.

But it was hard to stay mad at her brother while a steady stream of travelers surged around them, racing from the baggage claim to the long line of yellow cabs snaking around the airport. It felt so good to be someplace new and exciting. Someplace other than the double bed in front of their motel television or the weirdly green community hot tub. A cab beeped, and then another answered—setting off a chain of shouts and grumbles as Aunt Charley tugged the loose end of Matty's scarf from their puppy's jaws and zipped it into his suitcase with a flourish.

"All right," she said, tousling the part from Matty's hair. "Let's do this."

Their new apartment wasn't far on a map—it was less than the length of a dollar, if that—but between the airport shuttle and the subway, it was nearly twenty stops away. And as Aunt Charley had predicted, it was even hotter underground—at least at first, in the crush of commuters funneling through a squeaking turnstile and down worn tiled stairs, feeding one by one into the sweltering heart of New York City. If there had been time, Elizabeth would have stopped to roll up her jeans.

To twist her hair up with a rubber band and take it all in.

But there *wasn't* time, not with everyone in such a rush.

Passersby knocked against Elizabeth's suitcase, sweeping her along with the current on the subway platform as she jogged after Ashley and Aunt Charley, who was already motioning them onto a waiting train. "You can make it!" her aunt shouted, standing between the doors to keep them from closing. Elizabeth sprinted across the last few feet of the platform in time to duck beneath her outstretched arm. Red-faced and breathless, Matty joined her—and he almost looked like he regretted it as he pushed his way into the packed subway car.

There was nowhere left to sit, and barely room to stand.

Elizabeth gripped a cool metal pole, leaning against her brother for support as they lurched and then hurtled beneath the city streets. Lights from a passing train strobed through the darkened subway windows while someone played the opening riff of "Rudolph the Red-Nosed Reindeer" on a battered saxophone. "Don't forget to tip!" he shouted, interrupting his own melody and starting over from the top. Wide-eyed and whimpering with excitement, Ashley's puppy tried to sing along. Ashley laughed, scratching beneath his rhinestone collar as she listed everything she had planned for them on her free hand, finger by finger: the record stores and the skate parks. Their impossible-to-find tickets for a big Broadway musical.

"My mom's work friend knows one of the producers," she explained.

Elizabeth nodded and smiled, but with the saxophone wailing and the ground racing beneath her feet, she was too distracted to really listen. It was like balancing on a skateboard, and her knees wobbled as the train squealed to a stop, emptying and filling again before lumbering on. There were hundreds of people in their subway car alone, and thousands on the train—thousands of strangers swaying together beneath rivers and restaurants, entire neighborhoods over their heads. More people than Elizabeth had ever been around in her entire life . . . and they were still a few stops away from the hustle and bustle of Manhattan. Elizabeth stared into the smudged windows as Ashley talked, straining for a shadowy glimpse of the massive steel beams holding the city above their heads.

It was like nothing she'd ever seen before. . . .

And she hadn't seen anything yet.

WASHINGTON, D.C.

December 19, 11:00 a.m.

Joy frowned as she bit into a piece of red licorice, her first of the day.

Candy never tasted good after coffee, a lesson she was destined never to learn. Not when the readouts on her monitors were always so distracting. She twirled the licorice noncommittally, letting the flavors settle on her tongue as she scrolled down through the latest reports from the field. She knew she had to lay off the sweets, but Joy couldn't help it. She was a nervous snacker and watching the feeds, day in and day out, at the National Climatic Research Center was a good way to make anyone nervous. There was always something terrible happening, wildfires in Southern California or flooding on the Gulf Coast, and it was Joy's job—along with the rest of her team, all highly trained scientists—to keep one step ahead of disaster. They weren't saving the world, not exactly . . . there was nothing they could do to stop an earthquake. But if they were lucky, they could save lives.

It was easier said than done.

The fresh streak of white in Joy's otherwise black hair was a constant reminder of that.

She took another bite of licorice, leaning back in her chair as she scanned projections from the NCRC-3, a hundred-million-dollar satellite that fed atmospheric data into the National Climatic Research Center's predictive modeling program. The result: the next ten days of weather swirling across global maps in oranges and blues. Their best guess at it, anyway. It all looked more or less normal to Joy. She wasn't a meteorologist—her specialty was emergency response, not the emergencies themselves—but she took note of a dark purple band of heavy precipitation in the Pacific Northwest. It wasn't a red flag, not by itself, but if the heat wave that was climbing the Eastern Seaboard pushed any farther west, it could lead to snowmelt and swelling rivers in the flatlands south of Seattle. Nothing that would set off any alarms at the NCRC . . . but with weather, Joy had learned to expect the unexpected.

It was a lesson she wasn't likely to forget, not anytime soon.

Not when she still saw crumbling sinkholes every time she closed her eyes.

Joy sighed, pulling an oversized pair of headphones over her ears to drown out the hum of the air conditioner and the ever-present drone of cable news. There were televisions mounted on every wall of the NCRC's offices, a windowless warren in the basement of a nondescript government building, and they were always on—side by side and tuned to different channels, so the hallways echoed with cross talk. Spending every day underground, surrounded by worst-case scenarios and breathless reportage, it was easy to forget that the sky outside was a clear robin's-egg blue and the air was crisp and fresh to match. That not everything was as dire as it sometimes felt sitting at her desk, beneath the flickering fluorescent lights.

She turned up the volume and stared at the ceiling.

Burnout was common in her line of work.

That's what Joy thought was happening at first.

She was only a few years out of graduate school, but for the past couple of months she'd felt about a hundred years old every time she logged into her computer. As much as she loved her job, the long hours were taking their toll and Joy was starting to worry that she'd lost her touch. It wasn't until she dug through the NCRC's databases and filing cabinets, leafing back through forty years of dusty records, that she realized that it wasn't *her* that was changing. It was the world around her, the change creeping up so gradually that it felt almost normal. The proof was right there, in black-and-white and colored graphs, its truth etched clearly in numbers: the frequency of billion-dollar disasters had doubled and then tripled since her first days on the job, jumping up to twelve and almost twenty every year. It was a major break-through, hiding in plain sight.

And it was a reason to keep working.

To keep pushing through the exhaustion.

So Joy stayed put, her music playing loud enough to mute her worries while she rested her eyes, waiting for the caffeine and sugar to kick in. It never did. Not before someone knocked on the wooden frame of her open door, hard enough to get her attention. Startled, Joy fumbled with her headphones as Dr. Abigail Carson strode into the room. There was nowhere for Dr. Carson to sit—the chair across from Joy's cluttered desk was draped with her scarf and coat, her bicycle helmet and messenger bag crowning the pile. "I can, um . . . ," Joy said, sweeping empty candy wrappers into an overstuffed drawer with the back of her hand as Dr. Carson stood, tapping a manila folder with man-icured nails. "I can move those if you want."

Dr. Carson shook her head, then nodded at the maps on Joy's monitor with the sharp wedge of her chin. "The most recent projections," she said. "What'd you think?"

Suddenly unsure of herself, Joy turned back to her computer.

She didn't mind being caught napping at her desk.

That was just part of the job when you worked eighteen-hour days, but the last thing she wanted was to embarrass herself in front of the director. "It's . . . a wet week in Seattle?" she mumbled, her mind racing as she scanned the swirling colors for any patterns she might have missed. Dr. Carson absentmindedly batted the manila folder against her jeans in a burst of nerves that betrayed her cool exterior, then straightened her blazer. "It's not Seattle I'm worried about," she said, frowning. "Scroll up higher, to Quebec. They're under two feet of snow right now, but we're saying it's going to be sixty degrees next week."

Joy blinked, then squinted at the maps.

She'd been so focused on extremes that her eyes had slid over the thick bands of sunshine cutting through North America, as if they weren't even there. For the NCRC, good weather was rarely bad, but Dr. Carson was right—it was disconcertingly temperate, and so far out of the ordinary that Joy should have seen it as soon as she sat down. Even for a rookie, it would've been obvious.

But Joy was slipping.

You're not slipping, she thought. *You're just tired.*

Dr. Carson was too distracted to notice either way.

"Something's happening," she said, her phone suddenly alive with the buzz of incoming messages. They started out slow, like the first snow of the season, and then quickened until she had to excuse herself. Joy could hear them accumulating as Dr. Carson stepped into the hallway, her phone ringing as she walked. *Something's happening,* Joy thought, repeating Dr. Carson's parting words as she bit into another stick of licorice and stared into her computer screen. She felt suddenly awake now, her eyes widening as adrenaline coursed through her veins. It was always this way at the beginning—the excitement and the danger. The flurry of phone calls and the fear of the unknown. "But what?" Joy whispered, clicking back through the projections.

Looking for clues.

UNION SQUARE, NEW YORK CITY

December 19, 11:45 a.m.

Matty struggled up the narrow subway stairs, clutching his heavy suitcase against his chest as he staggered toward a square of clear blue sky. They'd been in Manhattan for less than an hour and he was already managing to get lost, stuck behind a tour group while Ashley and his sister climbed ahead—two laughing silhouettes disappearing into a churning sea of strangers. If he'd had a free hand, he would have reached for the silver dollar in his pocket and worried the ridge of it with the pad of his thumb. A nervous habit, and one he was trying to shake . . . but it was hard to convince himself, after so many months sharing a suite with Elizabeth at the Value Inn, that he didn't need a little extra luck. Matty squinted into the light as he crested the last of the grimy steps, scanning the street for Ashley and his sister—hoping he hadn't fallen too far behind. The sun was shining so brightly aboveground that it was almost blinding, and he dropped his suitcase to the sidewalk to shield his eyes.

The stairs had led him directly into the heart of a winter market, a seasonal maze of peppermint-striped awnings and tables brimming with homemade cookies and crafts. "Watch it," someone said, pushing past him into the subway entrance. Startled, Matty sidestepped out of their way, knocking into a man in a well-tailored suit. He was carrying an armload of pine cones that had been spray-painted gold and dipped in glitter. "Sorry," Matty said, cringing as the man cursed into his graying beard. But there was no good place to stand and look for his sister while the lunch hour crowd tripped over his suitcase and jostled his shoulders. Matty felt for his phone—his pulse quickening until he remembered: it had been repacked into his suitcase, tucked safely inside a pocket of his shiny new parka. "I'm just gonna be a second," Matty mumbled, apologizing to passing ankles as he knelt to open his bag.

"Hey," Elizabeth shouted, waving excitedly. "Over here!"

Matty jumped up at the sound of her voice, his suitcase still open at his feet.

"Wait up!" he shouted back, his voice breaking in frustration—but his sister had already stopped walking. It took him three long Mississippi seconds to spot her anyway. She was standing with their cousin in a copse of grab-and-go Christmas trees, camouflaged by a constant flow of shoppers as they watched Matty make his way across the square. Pressed up against the branches, they played with Ashley's puppy while Aunt Charley paced around a table of red-garlanded wreathes—on her phone with some big-shot client.

Doing busy lawyer stuff.

Traffic on the street behind them was at an angry standstill, with cars honking as skateboarders ollied through the gridlock on their weathered decks. Diners at a nearby café sipped their coffee in the sunlight, so deep in their conversations that they didn't seem to notice the skateboarders filming each other's tricks or the commotion in their wake. It was too much to see all at once, and Matty was glad for a chance to catch his breath while he tried to take it all in—but Aunt Charley had started moving again as soon as she saw him and was gesturing for him to follow her lead. Ashley and Elizabeth were already trailing behind her, walking backward to make sure they didn't abandon Matty to the tumult of Union Square.

"C'mon!" Elizabeth shouted, so loudly that the sidewalk seemed to clear.

Matty didn't even bother to rezip his suitcase before he started after her.

There wasn't time.

He squeezed it to his chest instead, tight enough

that only one loose sock fell out as he tunneled through the crowds. Matty didn't stop to pick it up. He couldn't, not if it meant losing sight of Ashley and Elizabeth again. It wasn't until they reached a long red light that he dared to kneel on the dirty concrete, zipping his suitcase closed so quickly that it jammed halfway. He was still tugging at its tiny plastic pull tab when the walk signal started flashing, and Matty grit his teeth as Elizabeth took off without so much as a backward glance in his direction: too lost in conversation to even check if he was keeping up. Matty shook his head as he jogged behind her, his half-zipped suitcase clattering at his heels. He and his sister had been promising to look out for each other in New York City for *months*— ever since they'd booked their flights—but after one minute with their cousin it was like he was completely invisible.

"Hey," he gasped, catching up at another busy intersection.

"Can you even believe we're here?" Elizabeth asked.

Matty bit his lip.

He was too exasperated to answer and she was breathless with excitement anyway, so he stared up at white limestone buildings that were lining the streets instead—following his sister's awestruck gaze. They were all so tall and stately, their windows winking brightly with reflected sunshine. Aunt Charley was still talking on her phone as she walked, quick enough that they were all rushing to keep up. But as annoyed as Matty was, he had to admit that it felt good to be outside in the world again—to be somewhere fresh and new, with the sun warm on his cheeks. The sidewalks cleared as they headed south, away from the subway, the suited workday crowds giving way to college kids with backpacks slung over their shoulders. The students smiled and waved as they passed, laughing at Ashley's puppy, who was still being carried but scrambled her legs in the air as if she was running alongside them. One of them, a girl with chunky blue hair and dirty white sneakers, broke away from her own group of friends to match their pace.

Matty fell farther behind as the girl gravitated toward his cousin.

Too nervous to join in the conversation.

"Cute dog," she said. "Okay if I pet her?"

"Her name's Fang," Ashley said, playing it cool while she and Elizabeth scratched behind the puppy's ears. Fang barked and squirmed, happy for the attention, and Aunt Charley looked up from her phone call. She'd stopped walking halfway down the block, her phone sandwiched between her ear and her shoulder as she dug in her purse with both hands. "It's short for *White Fang*—I was reading that book when we got her."

The girl with the blue hair laughed.

"But she's so tiny!"

Ashley shrugged and smiled.

"She's tougher than she looks," she joked, rocking Fang like a baby.

Aunt Charley was still searching for her keys when they caught up to her.

She looked like she was on the verge of emptying her oversized purse onto the sidewalk when the heavy metal door of their apartment building pushed unexpectedly outward. Aunt Charley held it open with her shoulder as her neighbor wheeled his bicycle down the front steps and onto the street. *"Thank you,"* she mouthed, sighing with exaggerated relief as he fastened his helmet. "No problem. I'll see you soon," she said, turning back to her phone—then slouched against the front door as she hung up, motioning everyone into the foyer. "I'm so sorry," she sighed. "I have to run to the office for an hour. In and out. You'll be okay at home until I get back, right?"

"Just an hour?" Ashley asked, raising an eyebrow.

Her mom tousled her hair.

"Order in if you're hungry," she said, blowing kisses as she jogged back down the stairs. "Ashley knows how. I'll be back soon, okay?" The door closed heavily behind her, its green paint peeling from years of use. It was so dark inside that Matty saw spots. He rubbed his eyes with his palms as Fang's claws scratched against the waxed wooden floor, her tail beating against their legs while she ran in figure eights.

"Is she . . . okay?" Elizabeth asked, but she was too late.

A puddle had started to form on the floor at her feet.

Ashley groaned, the foyer filling with light as she picked Fang up and raced out of the front door with her arms outstretched, like she was carrying a live grenade. Elizabeth followed her onto the stoop, propping the door open with her foot while Matty stood next to the suitcases and watched motes of dust swirl and settle behind them. He could hear them joking around in the sunshine and wanted to run after them, to join in on the fun, but something about the siren wailing in the distance told him to stay put.

They weren't supposed to go outside.

They were supposed to stay home.

With his hands finally free, Matty reached for the silver dollar in his pocket and rubbed the worn ridge of it with the pad of his thumb. The siren was just a fire truck or a police cruiser threading its way through congested city streets. It was probably nothing, but there was always *something* happening in a city this big . . . and even though his sister didn't seem to remember, he'd promised their mom they'd look out for each other. The last thing he needed was to be locked out of Ashley's apartment building, alone and a thousand miles from home with his phone packed safely in his parka on the other side of a thick metal door.

Outside, Fang barked as Elizabeth shrieked with laughter.

Matty winced just thinking about it.

ETERNITY FJORD, GREENLAND

December 19, 1:45 p.m.

The arctic fox crept gingerly across the windswept ridges of Evighedsfjorden, her ears pricked for the slightest sound of scratching beneath the snow. She had winter stores back in her den—a treasure trove of goose eggs, chilled and waiting for the long nights of winter—but the voles and lemmings were stirring beneath the ice, warmed into action by the winter sun. It would set soon, cloaking the fjord in polar darkness, and the young fox knew she didn't have much time before she, too, would be forced to slink back underground. She tilted her head, hardly daring to move—every muscle of her body tensed as she listened to her prey shift and stretch in their burrows, her lean haunches quivering with the thrill of the hunt.

Spring had come early to the rocky cliffs the arctic fox called home.

Too early, by far.

The still glacial waters of the bay dazzled beneath the ice-rimmed peaks of the surrounding mountains, their scarred white slopes glistening—on the verge of melting. The arctic fox pressed her small black nose into the snow. The seasons had barely turned, but she could already sense the roots of bilberries and dandelions spreading through the frozen soil beneath the frost. Anticipating spring. When the days lengthened, the crags and crevices of her fjord would transform, filling with greenery so lush that a den of mewling kits could wean without hunger. For now, though, food was scarce and the crunch of snow was loud beneath the arctic fox's paws—so loud that she could hear it startling the lemmings, scaring them farther into the humid depths of their straw-lined tunnels.

Her cover blown, the arctic fox leapt skyward.

Twisting in midair, she dove into the snow, a missile of fur and muscle forcing her snout into her best guess at the burrow beneath her feet . . . and missing. Hunting by ear was a gamble at best and the odds were never in her favor, so the arctic fox wasn't discouraged by a mouthful of ice. One lemming beneath a frozen tundra was a target too small for even the most experienced trackers. But still: she persevered, digging past the snow into a crust of dormant lichens—too preoccupied to notice the towering clouds, dark and ominous, gathering on the horizon. Uncovering the ragged edge of an entrance, she leapt again, slamming down into the burrow and searching with her jaws until they met with soft and round resistance.

There was no celebration and no victory howl.

Just relief, and a thankfulness to the fjord for its unlikely bounty.

The lemming was too big for the slender fox to swallow, so she cradled it in her jaws, careful not to crush it while she ambled homeward—her trot quickening as storm clouds raced to meet her beneath the waning sun. They roiled across the glacial peaks as she ran, the blue sky bruising as a sudden northern squall churned the bay. The arctic fox's fur rippled, too, windblown like the white-capped waves. Her coat was dense and warm despite the bitter cold, but the weather turned quickly on Eternity Fjord, and she felt the pressure dropping like a warning in her bones. Whimpering through her teeth, the startled fox dropped her struggling prey as she hopped from rock to rock, the thick pads of her paws gripping the ice as the last of the sunshine shattered in a burst of frigid hail.

UNION SQUARE, NEW YORK CITY

December 19, 3:15 p.m.

Ashley jumped up from the couch, blocking the television.

She didn't have a plan, exactly.

She just couldn't stand to think about hanging around their new apartment for one more second, watching the entire day slip away in front of her eyes. Elizabeth looked up with an expectant smile . . . but Matty was so distracted by his phone that he didn't seem to notice. Ashley waved her hands to get his attention, then made faces when that didn't work: sticking her tongue out and wrinkling her nose, her lips curled in a movie-monster grimace. No matter what she tried, she couldn't seem to break his concentration. His sister rolled her eyes as he reached into a family-sized bag of cheese puffs and pulled out a handful, never once looking up. Not even when he wiped his orange fingers on his jeans.

Ashley sighed.

It had been over three hours since her mom had left.

Which made her two hours later than she'd promised.

It wasn't fair, but it wasn't a surprise either. Her mom had been working twice as much ever since they'd moved out of their old apartment a few months before. So much that they hadn't even had a chance to get a tree yet. She kept saying she'd make time for it—that they'd make a day out of shopping for all new decorations and that this was going to be their "best Christmas ever." Ashley knew better than to believe her . . . but now that her cousins were in town, she thought she'd be having a *little* more fun. She'd even come up with a long list of things she thought they could do together, so they could hit the ground running.

She had it all mapped out and everything.

Not that it mattered.

Matty actually seemed happy to be stuck inside all afternoon, and Ashley wasn't even sure how much she had in common with Elizabeth anymore. It had been a couple of years since she'd seen her in person, but they used to spend entire summers chasing each other down carpeted hotel hallways on family vacations and cracking each other up after bedtime. Now that they were older, she'd been looking forward to picking up where they left off—but everything just felt weird now, like they were already running out of things to talk about. It wouldn't have felt so awkward if they were running around the city, like Ashley wanted.

She was sure of it.

And the heat didn't help.

It was the kind of hot that made you feel like you were half-asleep, like the bearded dragon in her homeroom. Napping through the mornings on a heated rock, it barely moved except to eat a mealworm—oblivious to the prying eyes just beyond its smudged glass cage. Ashley closed her eyes and held her breath, doing her best impression of a lizard . . . but the last thing she wanted was to nod off between her cousins. Not when she'd been looking forward to winter break every single day since the last day of summer, which felt like a million years ago—time-wise, anyway. In terms of sweating through her shirt, not much had changed since August.

Even Fang was passed out and drooling on the cool kitchen tile.

Too hot for her usual spot on Ashley's lap.

She had to do *something*.

"Does anyone want an ice water or anything?" Ashley asked, pulling the cord on the ceiling fan until it churned into its highest setting. She was hoping to feel energized, but the dusty blades only stirred the stale air around the living room. The password-protected thermostat in the new apartment was still a mystery, so—thinking on her feet—Ashley parted the curtains and opened the windows instead, letting in the sounds of the city along with the sunshine. A little fresh air couldn't hurt, Ashley thought, then pretended to gag for her cousins' benefit as a blast of dry heat immediately proved her wrong. She dropped to her knees, groaning theatrically while she rolled on the floor, knocking against the legs of the couch for extra effect.

Outside, a taxi slammed on its brakes and honked. A woman on the crosswalk shouted at the driver, her curses mixing with the smell of sweet honey-roasted peanuts and sunbaked garbage as it wafted up into the room. Ashley squinted through her eyelashes to see if she'd shaken Matty out of his stupor, but he was still just staring into his phone while Elizabeth smiled quietly at her performance. Ashley didn't know how they managed to sit so still for so long, not talking or roughhousing or doing anything, really. She felt so stir-crazy, being trapped inside while the world swirled all around them, but everyone else seemed happy to camp out in front of the TV all day while they waited for her mom to get home from work. It was about as far as you could get from the break she'd been daydreaming about all semester, counting down the minutes until she had her life back again.

So far, eighth grade had been a nightmare.

There was so much homework to do and so little time.

After soccer practice and endless problem sets and pretending not to listen to her parents argue on the phone, it felt like she had less than half a minute to herself every night. And it was only going to get worse, not better. That's what her teachers kept saying whenever anyone complained: "If you think this is hard," they'd say, "just wait until you get to high school." They made a big show out of it, like they were doing everyone a favor when they sent them home for the holidays with a folder full of practice tests . . . but what Ashley needed more than anything was a vacation. It didn't even have to be a real one—like the kind you saw in movies, where kids learn how to surf or ride bikes around London. She would have been happy doing almost anything other than sweating her face off in her mom's tiny apartment.

Ashley rolled onto her back and sighed.

The holidays were never as good as she wanted them to be, anyway.

Even when her parents had been together, it was just a lot of pressure to act like everything was perfect . . . even when it wasn't. *Especially* when it wasn't, Ashley thought, remembering their last Christmas together as a family. In their big, old uptown apartment, before her entire life fell to pieces. Ashley could work her way through the thick folder of practice tests that she was supposed to finish and act like she was excited about a sweater she didn't ask for—and that didn't even fit—but it was harder to force herself to smile when they'd walked out on her dad and acted like nothing was going to change. Even when he'd brought Fang home with a red bow around her neck, like that was supposed to automatically fix everything.

Like he could just switch himself out for a puppy and call it even.

Christmas was complicated for Matty and Elizabeth, too.

Ashley *knew* that.

She wasn't a monster.

"It must be hot like this all the time in Florida," she said, staring up at the ceiling fan while Spider-Man swung from building to building on the television screen behind her. "You're just used to it, right—like, being this hot just feels normal for you?"

Her little cousin Matty shrugged and picked at his braces.

"I guess so," he said. "It's so much better here, though."

Ashley sat up so quickly the blood rushed to her head.

"Seriously?" she asked.

It was hard to believe that anyone could be having a good time in the sweltering boredom of their new apartment, with most of their stuff still taped up in cardboard boxes. Ashley squinted at her cousin, searching for the smallest shred of proof that he was having fun as he ate his way through another handful of cheese puffs. Matty just looked up from his phone and smiled, like he was just noticing Ashley for the first time all afternoon—and Elizabeth sat beaming next to him, bright-eyed and brimming with excitement for the days to come.

"You're so lucky," she said. "To get to live here all the time."

Ashley blinked in disbelief.

The last thing she felt was lucky.

Looking past the scuffed toes of her black army boots into the mess of the living room, Ashley tried to see her life through Elizabeth's eyes, like she was in *Eloise at the Plaza* or something. But less rich, and a million times more awkward. Another taxi honked outside. Ashley and her cousin were almost the same age, but Elizabeth seemed a lot younger than Ashley. Like her mom still bought clothes for her when she was out running errands. Most of Ashley's clothes were from one of her favorite places in the city: a vintage store down the block that played cool music and didn't charge too much for faded band shirts or a pea-green corduroy jacket. Ashley didn't think her cousins had anything like that in Florida.

Especially not now.

From what she'd heard, it sounded like fun stuff

was the last thing anyone was thinking about in Tampa Bay. She'd seen the footage when the flooding started and she still couldn't believe that she actually *knew* people in the swirling darkness. That Matty and Elizabeth's house was down there somewhere—on the other side of the television screen. And that it was still down there, getting a new roof nailed on it or something. The storm had been all anyone talked about for a few weeks, and then it wasn't. The world moved on to other things, and so did Ashley. There was always something happening, and it was easy to forget that everything wasn't just . . . *magically* better because it wasn't in the news anymore. Even though she felt like she was having a panic attack literally every morning, it made sense that Elizabeth thought she was lucky— and that they were happy just hanging out on the couch, doing nothing.

They hadn't been able to go home for the last six months.

Ashley was living the dream, in comparison.

Which reminded her . . .

"I have to go to a museum with my dad in the next few days," she said, not mentioning *why* he was taking her. One of his photographs was hanging in the Metropolitan Museum of Art, in an exhibition that was closing after Christmas. Now that school was out, Ashley had finally run out of excuses not to go see it with him. She used to love to visit art museums with her dad, but everything was different now. It was like he'd forgotten how to talk to her and she couldn't stand the tortured silences, so she'd been avoiding his calls ever since they moved. It was just too hard. And even worse, their big reunion at the museum was supposed to be a special bonding thing. It was so painfully obvious, especially when her mom kept saying how "important" it was for her to go.

Everything her mom said just made Ashley dread it more.

If she closed her eyes and thought about it, she could see the entire day playing out like a terrible movie: her dad was going to ask her how she and her mom were doing and Ashley was going to give him a thin-lipped smile and say that everyone was fine. She didn't think she could bear to tell him the truth. Besides . . . it was Christmas. Her dad was going to tousle her hair and say "Just fine?"—as if everything was normal and he could tease her, like the old days—and she was going to scream forever and never stop until a team of security guards asked them to leave the museum and never come back. The curators might even take down his picture.

Just because.

Ashley grinned at the thought, her first genuine smile in days.

"Can we come, too?" Elizabeth asked, perking up in her seat.

Ashley nodded as she replayed the movie in her head, making sure to cast her cousins in supporting roles. She hadn't added the museum to her list of things to do because she didn't want to go ... but with her winter break slowly circling the drain, it felt more and more likely that she didn't have a choice either way. And if she had to go, it would be better if Matty and Elizabeth went with her. There'd be fewer awkward silences with them around, and no hard talks about feelings. Nothing that would get Ashley kicked out of a museum, anyway.

Outside, it started to rain.

Gently at first and then louder—pounding against the open windows and spattering onto the floor as distant thunder echoed through the skyscraper canyons of Manhattan, reverberating against walls of steel and double-paned glass. Fang's nails skittered against the tile as she ran into Ashley's bedroom, barking furiously at the sudden storm as the curtains filled with wind and billowed out into the living room, knocking an empty soda can to the floor. Ashley rolled to her feet and sighed, wiping the sweat from her forehead as she followed Fang to the bedroom.

"It's only rain, dummy," she said, peering under her bed.

But there was something about the sound of it that made Ashley walk back into the living room and stare at the growing puddle beneath the window, eyes widening as someone yelped on the street below. A taxi honked once, and then twice—the driver holding down the horn in one long blast as he skidded to a halting stop. In the eerie half-second of quiet before the street erupted in shouts, she heard it: the sound of hard pellets of ice pinging against the glass, then bouncing off awnings and onto the asphalt where they melted with what she could only imagine was a cartoon sizzle. Fang growled distrustfully from deep beneath Ashley's bed, then whined, high-pitched and keening, but Ashley couldn't stop staring, openmouthed, into the gathering clouds.

"Is this for real?" Elizabeth whispered.

She and Matty had sidled up beside Ashley, their sweating shoulders pressed against her own as they watched pedestrians jogging for shelter from the improbable hail. "It's like, a hundred degrees," Matty said, laughing nervously. "How is this even happening?" He was still staring into his phone, Ashley noticed, but for once he wasn't distracted. She watched him zoom in on the roof of a delivery van parked across the street, focusing his camera on the ice as it ricocheted off the hot metal roof and onto the street.

UNION SQUARE, NEW YORK CITY

December 19, 3:45 p.m.

"Do you think it hurts?" Elizabeth asked, trying to hide the worry from her voice as she settled down next to her brother and Ashley at the living room window. The hail was starting to collect on the sill and her cousin had opened the screen to inspect it, sweeping a small pile into an outstretched hand and watching it slowly melt in the warmth of her palm. Ashley just shrugged, distracted by the tendril of water that was dripping down her wrist and into a cluster of neon-green friendship bracelets. "When it hits you, I mean," Elizabeth said.

Shivering at the sight of it.

She'd never seen hail before.

Not in person, anyway, but it seemed like it would have to hurt at least a little. It *was* ice, after all. It even sounded dangerous, the way it was skipping against air conditioners and parked cars—like someone was throwing tiny handfuls of gravel from a rooftop garden. The rain had sounded the same way, during the worst of the hurricane. Elizabeth could tell from the way Matty stiffened beside her that he was remembering it, too: how they hid with their parents in their windowless bathroom as the wind buffeted the walls, the rain hammering so relentlessly that it pounded its way into both of their nightmares. Elizabeth blinked the image from her mind as she squeezed her brother's shoulder, reassuring herself as much as him . . . then swallowed her fears and forced herself to smile.

They weren't in Florida anymore.

And this wasn't a hurricane—it was a Christmas vacation.

Outside, the streets were slowly clearing as grumbling New Yorkers crowded in doorways and fruit vendors stretched bright-blue tarps over their bananas and mangoes, laughing at their bad luck. Ashley laughed, too, pointing down at the confusion on the sidewalk while Elizabeth watched a lone delivery scooter take advantage of the empty crosswalks to speed through an intersection. As its taillights faded into the distance, she worked up her courage enough to stretch her hand out the window and into the unknown.

It was still kind of hot outside, which surprised her.

She'd braced herself for the cold of the unexpected hailstorm, but she hardly felt anything. Just surprise at the gentle patter of tiny pellets against her arm. They weren't sharp or hard like she thought they'd be, either. It was like a summer drizzle, only less wet and . . . bouncier. There was no other way she could think to describe it. Elizabeth cupped her hand to better catch the hail that was popcorning through her outstretched fingers, her nervous smile widening as the strangeness of the day started to sink in. She was still sweating in a tank top and the one pair of shorts she'd remembered to pack (as an afterthought, "to sleep in") and here, out of nowhere, was a handful of ice. "You've gotta see this," she said, pretending to toss it at her little brother, who grimaced as he ducked behind the lens of his phone.

"Ha," Matty deadpanned. "Funny."

"Seriously," she laughed. "Feel it."

Elizabeth squeezed her fist around the hail, squashing it into a melting clump of ice before dropping it into Matty's outstretched hand. He stared at it—focusing his camera on its glistening angles and filming as it thawed. "This is weird, though, right?" he said, drying his hand on the back of his jeans after the ice had softened. He squinted out of the window, past the hailstorm and into the growing masses of white, puffy clouds lined in golden sunshine. The day was somehow sunny despite the low rumble of rolling thunder, the sky a brilliant, crystalline blue. "Because it seems *super* weird."

Elizabeth nodded.

It did feel weird, but she turned to her cousin for confirmation.

For all Elizabeth knew, New York was always like this: stormy in the sunshine and impossible to predict. Like Ashley. It hadn't been easy, trying to break through to her all afternoon. As soon as Aunt Charley left them alone in the foyer, it was like she and her cousin were strangers on the first day of school. For Elizabeth, that was so much weirder than the hail. It had only been a few years since they'd laughed so hard that root beer shot out their noses . . . and all of a sudden it was like they'd never even met. There were only so many times Elizabeth could marvel at how fun it must be to live in such a big city, and it wasn't long before she'd run out of things to talk about—or at least, *good* things to talk about. As curious as she was, she knew not to ask about what it was like to have to choose between her mom and her dad.

Especially at Christmas.

It was easier to pretend that everything was normal, even if "normal" felt so boring that Elizabeth was actually grateful for the storm. She wished she could say the same for her brother—and for her cousin's little dog, who hated the hail with each and every ounce of her seven-pound frame. She almost felt guilty for laughing as Fang scampered beneath the couch, whimpering and wailing like the entire world was about to end. Matty looked like he might want to join her, but Ashley was so excited she was bouncing on her toes.

"We should go outside," she whispered.

More to herself than anyone else.

Elizabeth raised an eyebrow as her cousin draped an arm around her shoulders, her hand cold and wet on Elizabeth's arm as a new plan for the day started to take shape. "Just for a couple of minutes," Ashley promised, gesturing with ice-numbed fingers at the neighborhood beyond the living room window. "So you can see what it's like."

Small pockets of hail had started to collect on windowsills and awnings, but the streets and sidewalks were still too hot for it to stick. They mostly just looked wet, like the dripping folds of the fruit vendors' tarps. Elizabeth frowned as a man in a suit jogged down the street holding a newspaper over his head and Ashley—sensing a lack of enthusiasm—pulled her into a conspiratorial hug. "We have to pick up some food while we're out there, anyway," she said, so brightly that Elizabeth felt her frown melting like the hail, despite her better instincts. "There's nothing good to eat in this house and my mom left us money for pizza and everything."

Elizabeth's stomach growled just thinking about it.

She chewed her lip as she watched the man with the newspaper slow to a walk, then squint skyward. His hair was glossy and gray and slicked back with pomade, and small pellets of hail bounced off of it, falling harmlessly to the ground. Satisfied that he'd been running for no reason, the man tucked his newspaper beneath his arm and strode across the street, ignoring the calls of a fruit vendor who had started selling five-, ten-, and fifteen-dollar umbrellas that he'd stored beneath his crates—stashed away, Elizabeth guessed, for just this type of rainy day.

Only it wasn't even raining.

Not really.

"I guess that sounds fun," Elizabeth said.

Ashley nodded approvingly, squeezing Elizabeth even tighter.

Elizabeth leaned into the hug, finally letting go of a sigh she'd been holding all morning. It came out louder and longer than she expected: a wavering moan with a squeak at the end, like a mouse getting caught in a trap. She winced at the sound of it, her cheeks flushing pink with embarrassment as her cousin shook with silent laughter. Elizabeth shook along with her, pinned in the hug and laughing despite herself . . . which made Ashley laugh even harder—and just like that, the weirdly tense boredom that had been building like storm clouds all morning dissolved. Like hail on a hot summer sidewalk, Elizabeth thought, wiping an unexpected tear from the corner of her eye and squeezing her cousin back for good measure. It would have been perfect—just like old times—if it wasn't for Matty poking her side.

A brother-shaped pin to pop her good mood.

"Matthew," Elizabeth hissed.

But a half-second glance told her everything she needed to know—and what she should have known already, she reminded herself, her shoulders slumping beneath her cousin's arm. It wasn't rocket science, not for her little brother. He'd always been a little nervous—the kind of kid that was happier drawing treasure maps in their bedroom than chasing down actual treasure—and the hail hadn't made him feel any braver. The pleading, panicked look in his dark brown eyes was almost enough to melt her annoyance into concern.

Almost.

She squinted at Matty, weighing her options.

It was obvious, now that she thought about it, that he wouldn't want to leave the apartment. Not by themselves, not without permission, and *definitely* not after all of the hours he'd logged tracking storm clouds on his phone and worrying himself sick about the weather. He wouldn't admit it—not out loud—but Elizabeth was supposed to be looking out for him, and as much as she hated the idea of spending the rest of the afternoon slowly sinking into Ashley's oversized couch, it was up to her to make sure they didn't have any problems on their big trip to New York. Even if it meant wasting an entire day of their big trip to New York.

"Maybe . . ." She paused, then sighed.

She could feel both Matty and Ashley staring as they waited for her to finish her thought, and she tried not to groan with frustration as she considered her options. It was just so hard, knowing that whatever she said, she'd be letting *someone* down. Elizabeth took a deep breath and peered out at the hail, not wanting to face Ashley and her inevitable disappointment. "We should probably keep hanging out here until Aunt Charley comes back?" she ventured, nodding at her brother to show she understood. He barely met her eyes as he pushed his glasses up the bridge of his nose, but Elizabeth knew him well enough to know he was relieved. She turned back to Ashley and shrugged, hoping her cousin could tell that she didn't have a choice.

"One sec," Ashley said.

She held up a finger, then smiled as she pinned her own phone to her ear. It was hard not to eavesdrop when they were all clumped together at the window, so Elizabeth tugged Matty to the couch—to give her cousin privacy—but Ashley just put her phone on speaker, as if to prove a point. Fang trotted out into the living room at the sound of Aunt Charley's voice, her ears perked as Ashley grinned and bowed, performing for her audience.

"Have you seen the hail?" her cousin asked.

She was practically shouting so her mom would hear her over the clattering ice and the hum of the ceiling fan. Despite the sudden change in weather, the sky outside was so bright that Ashley was silhouetted against the clouds . . . and Elizabeth squinted, trying to read her cousin's face while Matty scrolled through the pictures he'd taken of the glistening lump of ice, pretending not to care. Aunt Charley hadn't looked up from her computer since she got to the office, she said—her voice echoing out from Ashley's phone—and she still had a few more hours to go until she could clock out for the holidays.

"I'm so, so sorry I'm late," she said. "Is everyone having fun?"

Elizabeth looked down at the toes of her socks, her lips twisting into a smirk as Ashley covered her mouth and whispered into the receiver. It was impossible to hear what she was saying as she paced into her bedroom and back, but she gave Elizabeth a big thumbs-up as she walked back into the room and slipped her phone into her pocket. Elizabeth couldn't help but smile, even as Matty sank farther and farther into the crack of the couch.

"Tonight," she sang. "We feast!"

UNION SQUARE, NEW YORK CITY

December 19, 4:15 p.m.

Matty stood by the front door, watching the hail shimmering outside the window—halfway between ice and rain—as his sister and Ashley struggled to zip Fang into her little bomber jacket. Fang yipped and squirmed, her nails catching on her fleece-lined hood, while his cousin fussed with a paw-shaped toggle. Under any other circumstances, he would've joined them, but Matty wasn't feeling up to it. Not when he'd been sweating by the door for the past fifteen minutes with his own parka zipped all the way up to his chin, ready and waiting for a worst-case scenario while his sister shrieked with laughter, dodging the puppy's lolling tongue and razor-sharp teeth.

Fang had four waterproof booties, too.

They hadn't even started on those.

Anticipating a sudden shift into winter weather, the floor-mounted radiator in the foyer sputtered to life, filling with hot water from the boiler in the basement as Matty absentmindedly thumbed through the forecasts on his phone for the hundredth time. He scrolled past the hourly predictions, scanning all the way down to a map of the Eastern Seaboard overlaid with pixelated pinks and blues—cold fronts, Matty guessed. He wasn't an expert, but checking the radar was something he'd started doing every time it rained: tracking the slowly creeping colors of approaching storms and hoping for the best. The maps ran on real-time data from actual satellites that he liked to picture spinning two hundred miles over his head, looking out for him from above, like the Millennium Falcon.

Only, the radar wasn't making any sense.

It was *supposed* to be hot out.

The forecasts still said it was eighty-two degrees outside and inching up into the nineties. There was even a picture of a sweating cartoon sun wearing wraparound glasses . . . but every time Matty refreshed his screen, the radar map beneath the smiling sun showed a tie-dyed swirl of ice and snow. It was massive, so big, that he thought it had to be a glitch as he refreshed the forecasts again and again, anxious to see how far the temperatures might drop. Even though the heaters in his cousin's building had started running full-blast— preparing for a freeze—it *was* still strangely warm outside, and the looming storm would likely turn to rain if the maps were somehow wrong.

And if they're right . . . , Matty thought.

He blinked down at the icy-blue cold front and refreshed the forecast one last time. If the radar maps were right, a little bit of hail was the least of their worries. Either way, the last thing Matty wanted was to leave the house, but it wasn't any use trying to catch his sister's eye. Elizabeth was just as excited as Ashley to go outside, and neither of them seemed to care if they ended up soaked in a thunderstorm or frozen half to death. Or both, Matty thought, frowning as he stretched his feet in his new wool socks. His snow boots were still so tight in the toes that he'd thought about offering to hold down the fort with Fang instead of joining them . . . but it didn't feel right to watch his sister walk out into the storm without him.

Even if they both knew better than to go.

"One more and we're done," his cousin whispered, hugging the little Pomeranian to her chest while Elizabeth fastened the last neoprene bootie onto her kicking paws. Fully dressed, Fang barked and squirmed her way up onto Ashley's shoulders. Basking in the attention. Matty just rested his face in the palms of his hands while she scrambled to the floor, her butterscotch tuft of a tail whipping back and forth with nervous excitement. Every minute they'd wasted getting ready to go outside just made them another minute closer to getting caught in a downpour . . . or worse.

But it wasn't any use trying to explain that to anyone.

Not when they'd already made up their minds.

"Almost ready?" Matty asked.

He tried to keep his voice low and even, but he couldn't help the impatience he felt bubbling up behind it. He was hoping no one heard it—that it sounded louder in his own head—even though he knew he was right to try to speed things up. Or at least, that he wasn't *totally* wrong . . . He couldn't be, not with all the forecasts and satellites and common sense on his side: the sooner they were able to go outside and get back to the apartment, the better.

That was just science.

Nine minutes and thirty-six seconds later, they trudged down the stairs and into the sunshine. What was left of it, anyway. Matty shielded his eyes, looking up into the cloud banks that were towering overhead as rice-sized grains of hail bounced from his gloves to his jacket. They melted into little wet polka dots in a warm and lazy breeze that made the whole day feel even stranger. Like it was snowing at the beach back home. Which—as impossible as it seemed—had actually happened. *Once.* Before Matty was born. His dad still talked about it like he expected it to happen again every winter: a cold, white Christmas in Tampa Bay.

You never know, he'd say.

Weirder stuff happened every day.

Still, for all the time they'd taken getting dressed, Matty was the only one who was even close to ready for the weather. He'd tried to warn them, but Ashley had only laughed about his parka and snow boots when she just stuck her hand out the window, feeling the residual heat of the day. As if that proved *anything*. She'd decided to wear ripped jeans and a flimsy canvas jacket instead of something warmer, and—after raiding her cousin's closet—his sister had copied her look as best she could, leaving her new winter clothes tucked away in the bottom of her suitcase. It made Matty feel like a dork in his shiny red parka and squeaky-clean boots, but there was no way he would've walked outside in an old black hoodie like Elizabeth . . . not when there was literal ice falling from the sky.

"See," Ashley said. "This isn't so bad, right?"

Her arm stretched as Fang snapped at the hail, straining on her leash as if she hadn't spent the last thirty minutes whimpering at the sound of it. Trailing absentmindedly behind Ashley and Elizabeth, Matty bit the finger on one of his gloves and pulled it off with his teeth, freeing his hand to tap his phone to life. Even outside on the streets of New York with the weather happening all around him, he couldn't stop himself from checking the forecasts. It was like muscle memory or a comfort blanket, and stray droplets of hail turned wet on his screen as a row of smiling cartoon suns stared up at him from the hourly estimates.

Matty shook his head as he scrolled down to the radar.

It didn't make sense.

"Hurry up!" his sister yelled.

Fang had surged ahead on the sidewalk, chasing a flock of pigeons that were seeking shelter beneath a covered scaffold. As small as the Pomeranian was, she'd dragged the girls with her—so quickly that they'd sprinted halfway down the block while Matty zipped his phone back into his jacket pocket. By the time he caught up, Ashley had already disappeared into Paradise Pizza . . . but his sister was still standing beneath its buzzing neon sign, struggling to hold on to Fang while she tapped an invisible watch on her wrist. Like she'd been waiting there for hours. The smell of cheese and baking dough filled the air as she propped the door open with the toe of her shoe, and Matty smiled despite himself as Elizabeth passed him the leash.

"One sec," she said, ducking inside before he could answer.

As usual, it wasn't like Matty had much of a choice either way.

He looped the leash around his wrist while Fang pawed at his leg, streaking his brand-new jeans with a splatter of mud. It was just his luck, Matty thought, peering into the pizza shop's windows and searching for his sister. The glass was so jam-packed with flyers that it was hard to see in, but squinting past a layer of peeling stickers and a sign that said No Dogs Allowed, Matty could just barely make out his sister and Ashley laughing in front of a stainless-steel counter. Outside of the two girls, the restaurant looked empty, and it was hard to tell if that was because of the weather or the grime. Even from the outside looking in, Matty could make out shiny pools of grease congealing on unwashed tables and dirty footprints on the floor. He breathed a circle of fog onto the glass, then sighed as Fang tugged on one of his laces.

"*C'mon*," he said, pulling his foot away from the puppy's teeth.

If Fang understood what he was saying, she didn't show it. She just hung from his boot and snarled with a smile on her drool-wet lips. Matty wriggled his foot, balancing on one leg as Fang's tail wagged, sweeping the sidewalk clean. "Quit it," Matty grumbled.

Then stopped himself mid-wriggle.

The hail was picking up.

He could hear it before he felt it—like static on a radio turned all the way up, or the world's fastest drumroll. A car alarm sounded as Matty flattened himself against the window of the pizzeria, wedging himself beneath its narrow awning just in time. It wasn't that the hail was any bigger than it was before; it was just that there was *so much* of it . . . and it was falling so fast and bouncing so high that it seemed to be jumping up at

Matty from the sidewalk. Fang huddled between his legs, trembling through her fur-lined parka as lightning split the horizon.

"It's okay, girl," Matty whispered, squatting to shelter the little dog.

She growled and whimpered through a mouthful of his shoelace.

The truth was, he wasn't so sure that everything *was* okay.

Not now, with the sickly gray sky swelling with a low and rumbling thunder.

Matty was tempted to check his phone again, to see how much ice a cloud could hold. It didn't seem like there could be an endless supply, not at the rate it was falling, but it wasn't worth risking a cracked screen to find out. Not when the forecast was so clearly wrong. He shivered alongside Fang instead, weighing his options as slivers of hail found their way into the neck of his jacket. They slid beneath his shirt, melting down his back while Fang yelped into the rising wind. Her black nose quivered just inches above the sidewalk, her ruff glistening with tiny flecks of ice. Sign or no sign, it didn't feel right to wait outside anymore.

Besides, he told himself, the restaurant was so dirty already.

And there was only so much damage one puppy could do.

A second bolt of lightning forked between sky-scrapers, casting their mirrored windows and brushed aluminum spires in a sickly pink light. Matty took a deep breath, then wrapped Fang in his arms—ignoring her yips and squeals of protest. Before he had a chance to second-guess himself, he backed into the restau-rant, his glasses clouding up from the heat of the pizza ovens. Fang pawed at his jacket with her neoprene boots, whining as Matty stumbled toward a booth facing a window—as far away as he could get from the unshaved man behind the counter who was tak-ing Ashley's order while his sister read the menu. He slumped low against the vinyl bench, hushing Fang as they hid behind the spicy red pepper flakes and the Parmesan cheese shakers.

One second passed and then another.

It was loud in the restaurant, and it wasn't just kitchen sounds.

There was the slap of mixing dough and the whir-ring of a dishwasher, but the boom box behind the counter was even louder. Its pounding bass mixed with commercials from a television hung crookedly overhead, masking Fang's yelps in a general cacoph-ony. "It's okay," Matty whispered, scratching the soft wisps behind her ears. Suddenly exhausted, she curled up in his arms and tucked her nose beneath her tail. Matty didn't blame her. It felt so good to be dry and warm and watching ice pile up against the glass, the wailing car alarms and sirens muffled like a distant memory while Fang drifted into a soft and gentle sleep beneath his resting hand. It wasn't long before Matty felt his own eyes closing despite the noise, lulled by the smell of pizza in the oven. After the morning he'd had, he was ready for a nap himself.

"Hey," Ashley said. "You made it!"

She plopped next to him in the booth, scratching Fang behind the ears.

Fang grumbled, then twisted in Matty's lap before settling back down. Above their heads, the commercials on the television led inevitably into the afternoon news. He couldn't see the screen, but the tense melodies of its old-fashioned theme song gave it away. Matty craned his neck for a better look, but his best view was of a ghost of the newscaster in the pizza shop's window. Staring into the smudged and stickered glass, he couldn't help but notice his own bedraggled face reflected in the storm: cheeks flushed pink, his hair wet from melted hail.

"Isn't this place so cool?" Elizabeth said, sliding next to Ashley.

Matty shrugged, ignoring her nudge beneath the table.

He didn't feel like talking.

He wanted to listen.

Elizabeth shrugged right back, then turned to the window and wrote her name in the fogging glass. She wrote it backward, in big block letters, so passersby could read it from the outside looking in. Only there were no passersby, and before she'd made it past the letter *z*, the bouncing hail had turned into a wet gray sleet that cleared even the most intrepid New Yorkers from the once-busy streets. Which meant, Matty realized—for all the good it did them—that the forecasts had been right all along. Or mostly right, anyway: there might have been a cold front coming.

But for now, at least, it was *way* too hot for hail.

"Order up," the man behind the counter shouted.

Matty could barely hear him over the thunder.

His heart raced as it echoed through the high-rise canyons, shaking the dirty windows in their frames, but Ashley didn't seem too bothered as she gathered their orders from the counter. "That's our cue," she said, pulling her hoodie up over her hair and stepping out into the weather. She held the door open behind her, filling the pizzeria with the buzz of rain as it power-washed the crusted lid of a nearby trash can. Matty watched it bounce and splash around his cousin's ankles, beading on the waxed canvas of her old black army boots.

"We're not eating here?" he asked.

His voice cracked in disbelief.

He hadn't wanted to come in the first place, but

now that they were safe inside, Matty couldn't believe they were walking right back out into the crash of the storm. He looked at his sister with wide and wild eyes as—half indoors and halfway out—his cousin waved to them from beneath the narrow awning. Loosely taped flyers fluttered in wet gusts of wind while Ashley waited, and Matty wasn't sure if she heard him above the noise, so he asked again—so loudly he woke Fang from her nap. She stretched her bootied paws in Matty's lap, blinking the sleep from her eyes as his sister joined their cousin at the door.

"It's looking pretty bad out there," his sister said.

But she didn't pull their cousin back inside.

"You said this was only getting worse, right?"

Matty felt the blood draining from his face as he nodded.

She'd been listening after all; she just hadn't cared.

"Okay," Ashley said. "Then the faster we run, the sooner it's over!"

Her smile was toothy and bright as rain ran down her cheeks and dripped onto their takeout. Elizabeth—mouthing a silent apology—followed her outside, beneath the awning. It wasn't enough. Matty was so mad that he was tempted to wait by himself in the dirty booth, alone in the city, but his sister was right. Even if she was only right about Matty being right. Cold front or not, the weather was only going to get worse. Fang barked twice and nipped at Matty's wrist, her teeth snagging on his sleeve as he bundled her up in his arms and carried her into the storm.

"We don't really have a choice, y'know," his cousin said.

She tapped the sign on the door.

No Dogs Allowed.

ETERNITY FJORD, GREENLAND

December 20, 9:30 a.m.

The dazzling pink fingers of the late polar sun stretched skyward from an endless blue horizon, but night still clung to the shadows and wavelets of Eternity Fjord. Even at the southernmost reaches of the arctic circle, it would be half dark for another hour at least. So dark that nobody aboard the Swedish icebreaker *Mjölnir* had spotted the flashes of silver winking up at them from between floes of thinning ice: whole schools of Greenland cod, glassy-eyed and bloated. They rolled listlessly against the bow, greeting the day with their sickly white bellies—untouched by the colony of mottled seals barking sharply on the rocky shore.

From the deck of the icebreaker, the seals sounded almost human.

Like a rowdy crowd cheering for their favorite team.

They'd been at it for hours, yelping beneath the ghostly ribbons of the northern lights while ivory gulls shrieked and circled overhead. What the fjord lacked in sunshine, it made up for in noise—and the loudest noise of all was rushing water. Both deafening and hard to place, the hiss of melting ice echoed through the frozen valley as the massive glacier slowly shrank into the rising sea under the watchful eyes of the *Mjölnir*. Thawing from the bottom up, it was hard to say how much longer it would last. How much longer *any* of it would last, from the lichens to the frozen cliffs to the herd of seals that were wrestling in their shadows.

That was what the *Mjölnir* was there to find out.

The big red ship sat heavily in the untouched bay, all twelve tons of it: twenty-four thousand pounds of reinforced steel with a hull as thick as a fist. A Polar-class icebreaker, the *Mjölnir* could spend whole winters in arctic waters that would sink and splinter other ships— punching channels through sheets of ice up to twenty-feet thick. That was how it had gotten its name, after Thor's mythical hammer. But for the past few weeks it had been quietly anchored in the Labrador Sea, home to a global team of scientists in bright-orange survival suits. Designed specifically for glacial expeditions, the bulky "gumby" suits were warm enough to protect against a slip into the half-frozen slurry of the bay and light enough to work in . . . and with every sample the scientists took from the thawing ice of Evigheds-fjorden, the more obvious it became.

Something was seriously wrong in the arctic circle.

The floating fish—felled by a surge of fresh glacial water—were just another piece of a quickly melting puzzle. The scientists shook their heads as they trawled for specimens, maneuvering their inflatable Zodiacs across the choppy surf. Even at its worst, the fjord was beautiful, and an otherworldly wall of blinding white towered overhead as they landed on the rocks. Accustomed to visitors after a busy summer season of Arctic cruises, the seals ignored the scientists and small black boats . . . but they weren't the only living creatures on the fjord. A tiny arctic fox crept alongside their thick-soled boots as they crunched across the ice, drawn by the promise of rotting fish. With the curious cub nearly tripping on her heels, one of the scientists held up an orange-gloved hand, signaling the fox's presence to her team.

With the other, she reached for the tranquilizers on her belt.

"There you go," she whispered, kneeling on the ice.

The little cub nuzzled her outstretched hand, nibbling at the treats in her open palm. It was tentative at first and then insistent, nipping at her glove: demanding more and more of the unexpected snacks. The seals bellowed and clapped as the fox swallowed—quickly, without chewing—and then stumbled, collapsing against a bank of glistening snow as the sedatives took effect. Even with her bulky gloves, it only took a moment for the scientist to secure a tracking collar around the thick white ruff of the little fox's neck. She patted its fur, stroking the soft contours of its head while the rest of her team climbed over boulders and peered into clear tidal pools. They whooped to each other, shouting into the wind about every new find. There was so much to do—a whole lifetime's worth of research—but the little fox was a solid start to another long day on the ice. Its paws twitched as a second Zodiac emptied into the shallows of Eternity Fjord, its scientists splashing through the icy water in their orange gumby suits.

Impervious to the cold.

WASHINGTON, D.C.

December 20, 2:15 p.m.

Joy stirred her soda with a candy cane, then sipped—searching out the taste of peppermint in the fizz. It wasn't her first candy cane of the day or even of the hour. It wasn't even the first one she'd tried mixing into her Cherry Coke. That one had slipped down into the narrow neck of the bottle on her short walk down the hallway from her workstation to the National Climatic Research Center's annual holiday party. She'd unwrapped the second candy cane to have something to do while she stood in the corner, waiting for everyone else to start trickling in—and it was starting to look like she'd have time to open a third. It was already fifteen minutes after the party was supposed to start and the only signs of celebration were the mountains of store-bought cookies and brownies piled high on the glossy conference room table: enough for the entire department to eat their fill with leftovers to spare.

But it was only Joy who'd showed up.

Joy and a handful of stragglers.

If she wasn't so bored she might have laughed.

The NCRC's motto—the guiding principle of their entire operation—was "Forewarned is forearmed." For Joy and her colleagues, being forewarned meant staying one step ahead of every imaginable catastrophe through constant vigilance and meticulous preparation. Lives—literally, thousands of lives every day—depended on them planning for worst-case scenarios . . . but through some ironic twist of fate, it turned out they weren't so great at planning for the good ones. Most of Joy's coworkers had cleared out after their morning briefing, stuffing their laptops into their backpacks and driving home to their friends and families for a much-needed vacation.

Joy didn't blame them.

She was looking forward to her vacation, too.

And she only had a few more hours to go. Once she made it through the awkward small talk of the office Christmas party, she was going to drive to her childhood home outside of Richmond, Virginia. The plan was to camp out on her parents' couch, watching monster movies and playing video games with her nieces until she had to be back in the office again. She wasn't going to read the news or think about the weather once—not even to open the curtains to check if it was snowing: it was going to be 24-7 zombie hordes without any real-life, credible threats to national safety.

Not if she could help it.

Joy took a sip of her Cherry Coke.

She still couldn't taste the candy cane, but the conference room was starting to fill up a little bit. It was mostly assistants and interns standing in for their long-gone supervisors and filling their pockets with red- and green-sprinkled sugar cookies. There were some workaholics, too—the people Joy wasn't sure ever left their desks, even on holidays. Like Joy's own boss: Dr. Abigail Carson, long-term director of the NCRC. Dr. Carson always seemed to be fielding urgent calls on her cell phone and rushing through the hallways from one closed-door meeting to another. If Joy was being honest with herself, it was hard to picture her anywhere but the NCRC's windowless corridors— much less doing anything outside of its walls.

Like playing video games or watching monster movies.

Or even just going to the grocery store.

Joy's lips twitched into a smile as she tried to imagine Dr. Carson watching *Son of Godzilla* next to her at her parents' house, eating oversized bowls of Cap'n Crunch and shouting at the screen. It was impossible. Even in Joy's wildest dreams, Dr. Carson refused to be distracted. Two minutes after she walked into the conference room, she was already talking—inevitably—about the weather. To be fair to Dr. Carson, no one had thought to play Christmas music, so it was more like a meeting than a holiday party, anyway. A meeting with six platters piled high with double-fudge brownies—with one platter for every person who remembered to show up.

Still, there wasn't any getting away from natural disasters.

Not at the NCRC.

Last week it was brush fires in Malibu. This week it was melting ice caps.

It was all anyone could talk about at their morning briefing.

A call from a team of scientists had come in overnight, made via satellite from somewhere off the coast of Greenland. Short and staticky, their message had been too short on details to draw any official conclusions. Especially when the full studies would take years to complete, at the very least . . . but by then it would be too late. Joy had been about to say as much when she'd realized how seriously everyone else was taking the news, and how excited they'd become—scribbling notes in the margins of their agendas and mumbling to each other as Dr. Carson tried and failed to win back their attention.

It shouldn't have been a surprise.

It was simple math.

Melting ice caps meant rising sea levels.

They'd known that for years, but if the ice caps were melting as fast as the scientists said they were, it was going to cause all kinds of unexpected problems for the NCRC—and decades sooner than they'd even dared to predict. It wasn't *just* the flooding, but almost half of the country lived within fifty miles of a coastline: over a hundred million people, spread out across cities like New York and Houston and foggy San Francisco. The densest populations were always on the water, in towns that built up around ports and never stopped growing, and not just in the United States. Eight out of ten of the world's largest cities were on the water.

From Osaka to Jakarta to Mumbai, the list went on and on.

The worst-case scenarios were too big to even comprehend.

Climatology was supposed to be a long-term science by definition, with shifts so slow they were measured in generations. The world was barely ten degrees warmer now than it was twenty *thousand* years ago, during the last Ice Age, and the researchers at the NCRC were tracking yearly temperature changes in fractions of a fraction of a percent. A ten-inch rise in sea levels over an entire century was the kind of thing they usually worried about—ten tiny inches since funny-looking people from black-and-white photographs bounced around in Model-T jalopies. They'd had such a long time to fine-tune their estimates and projections that it was all anyone had been able to talk about all morning, before they drove home for the holidays: how wrong they could possibly be—and how much fresh water had already melted into the sea.

They'd even formed a task force to look into it.

It didn't help set the holiday mood, that was for sure.

As scarce as the data from the fringes of the Arctic had been, it mentioned whole schools of saltwater fish dead at the scene. Thousands of cod sloshing in the waves around windswept Zodiacs, their silver bellies flashing in the sunrise—so bright they were almost blinding. Joy piled a paper plate with cookies while Dr. Carson fielded questions from the room. She didn't even have to listen to know what Dr. Carson would tell them because she'd heard it a hundred times before, in a hundred different meetings: "panicking isn't an action plan," and they didn't have enough data to act on, anyway. Not yet. The most likely scenario was that they were facing a hundred-year problem. Polar ice caps shrank . . . but they grew, too, and even a fast melt could be glacially slow. Despite what you read in the news, not everything was gloom and doom.

Not even at the NCRC.

Except sometimes, it was.

"We're going to have to cut this short," Dr. Carson said, checking her phone.

Joy frowned, studying her boss's face as she walked out into the hallway and held the door open behind her, motioning for Joy to follow. On a good day, Dr. Carson was impossible to read. She wore the same serious expression for every occasion, but her furrowed brows and downturned lips always looked more natural in a crisis. It made Joy wish she'd left early, when she'd had a chance, like everyone else. The party hadn't been worth staying for, not if it meant working through Christmas. The brownies weren't *that* good. But it was too late now. Joy abandoned her plate on the corner of the conference table and left the room full of wide-eyed assistants to wonder if they should just go back to their desks.

"What is it?" Joy asked, keeping her voice low.

Dr. Carson just pointed at her screen.

She had it open to the weather.

While their entire office was busy worrying about coastal flooding models and double-checking their predictions, there was an even more urgent problem forming over the North Atlantic Ocean. The same sweaty heat wave that was thawing the glaciers in Greenland and dashing every kid's hopes for a snowy white Christmas had pushed even farther north than anyone had expected. So far north, in fact, that it had warmed and weakened the wall of strong polar winds that kept all the cold air trapped in the Arctic. Freed to roam wherever it wanted, a massive cold front was rushing south. It was so big on Dr. Carson's phone that Joy had to zoom out three times just to get a sense of the frigid expanse of it.

"So much for the holidays," Dr. Carson said.

Canceling Christmas.

UPPER EAST SIDE, NEW YORK CITY

December 21, 10:00 a.m.

Fang tugged at her leash, straining after Ashley and her cousin.

It was her first walk outside since the weather broke, and she couldn't help herself: she'd spent a full day and a half shivering beneath the couch, hiding from the endless roar of rain and thunder while Matty and Elizabeth moped silently at separate windows, waiting for the clouds to pass. They weren't the only ones. Nobody was happy, trapped at home. The minutes had stretched into hours that slowly curdled into one long and awkward silence. To make things even worse, the temperatures had dipped so low that the soft bud of her nose was starting to chap.

For once in her life, Fang didn't mind her jacket.

Her neoprene booties were another story.

She'd spent the better part of the morning gnawing at their Velcro straps and when that didn't work, she'd tried her best to shake herself free of them . . . but no matter how high she stepped, the shoes stayed fixed to her trembling paws. It was exhausting, wriggling and twisting her way down the street, but it was just as well. The rain had turned into a wet and icy slush that had gathered and frozen solid overnight, and even now—with the air so crisp and the sky so clear—it was snowing. Her booties were warm with rubber soles, and the flakes were delicate and light enough to drift upward in the breeze.

Perfect for chasing.

Still, Fang had to choose her steps carefully.

Sharp chunklets of salt had been scattered across the streets, spread by the truckful to melt the gathering snow into puddles of brine. It crunched awkwardly beneath her paws, impossible to avoid—not without veering off the path and slipping on the ice. She'd tasted it once, before she knew any better: investigating the grit of the sidewalk with the tip of her tongue and sneezing at the sensation. It wasn't just salty—it was bitter and strong, with an unnaturally blue hue that stained the cement where it fell. As close as she was to the sidewalk, the smell of the salt was almost overwhelming and Fang's nostrils flared in protest as she pulled at her leash . . . but she didn't have any choice but to walk where she was led. Every time she tried to buck her collar, Aunt Charley only tightened her grip.

"The kids are *loving* the snow," Aunt Charley said.

She'd been talking with Matty and Elizabeth's parents ever since they'd left the house, her phone pinned to her ear with her one free hand while she watched Ashley and her cousin run ahead. Fang watched, too, her eyes darting between the two girls as they threw snowballs scraped from marble benches. The boy, Matty, was boring in comparison. He just kicked his way through the ice—sulking as he trudged alongside his Aunt Charley, trying his best to listen in on her conversation. Unable to contain her excitement, Fang threaded back and forth between their boots, willing Aunt Charley to drop her leash. But Aunt Charley only laughed as Fang barked into the wind. "And they're going to the museum this morning," she said, spinning around in circles to untangle herself. "But let me know what you hear about your flights, okay?"

Fang growled, unwilling to give up so easily.

There was so much to see outside, in the world, and not just the snowball fight. A flock of pigeons hovered overhead, their feathers ruffling in the frigid updrafts blowing in from Central Park. Every few minutes—as if by clockwork—two or three would touch down in front of a hot pretzel vendor and stay grounded long enough to patrol the sidewalk for crumbs. Fang watched two groups of them circle the pretzel cart, pecking hopefully at bitter salt and the cracks in the cement while a man playing a trumpet with fingerless gloves stopped long enough to rub a balm on his wind-chapped lips. It was getting too cold to play, but not for Fang.

She was just getting started.

Or, she would be if she could somehow manage to break free.

Fang's haunches quivered as Ashley ducked and weaved through the plaza in front of the museum's steps, beneath the towering limestone colonnade, while the pigeons taunted her from above. She wanted to run, to jump and yank her leash from Aunt Charley's fingers, but she wasn't big enough—or strong enough—and there was an inevitable point in every walk where Fang was scooped up and carried like a baby. It happened so often she could almost feel it coming and she didn't mind it, usually. Especially now, with the salt and the cold and the ill-fitting booties slipping beneath her paws. On a normal day, she would have barked and nuzzled herself into Aunt Charley's arms. Only: Fang hadn't expected to like the snow as much as she did. There were so many smells and so many distractions.

Not to mention the pigeons.

Fang sat dejectedly between Matty's and Aunt Charley's legs, hiding from the wind while she considered her limited options. They mostly consisted of bite-based plans to startle Aunt Charley into dropping her leash—but Aunt Charley's galoshes were thick and they were rubber and they went all the way up to her knees. It only took one tentative bite for Fang to realize they were just another problem she couldn't chew her way through, like the puppy gate in the bedroom or the tub of kibble beneath the sink. But watching the snowflakes swirl and eddy around the plaza was too much for the little Pomeranian to handle, and Fang felt a whine rising in her chest as the man with the trumpet squawked his way through a tentative scale.

Hanging her head in defeat, she finally realized what she had to do.

She couldn't believe she hadn't thought of it sooner. . . .

But Fang had never sat still long enough to notice how her collar sagged around her neck. When she wasn't stretching against it with all her might, she had at least a half inch of wiggle room—maybe more. It wasn't much, but it was something. She just needed to stop straining long enough to make her move . . . and she needed to do it while Aunt Charley was staring absentmindedly into the middle distance, distracted by her phone. Fang blinked up at her, barely daring to breathe as Ashley and Elizabeth skipped and slid their way across the frozen sidewalks. Every second she waited was another second she wasn't chasing them, so—ears pricked and on high alert—Fang clawed at her collar with the rubber soles of her shoes.

It was up around her ears before anyone even noticed.

"Hey!" Aunt Charley shrieked.

She dropped the leash to free her hand, but Fang just slipped beyond her grasping fingers and pulled backward through the snow, bucking herself free from the loop of her collar as best she could. It was tighter around her head than she'd expected, and the more she squirmed the tighter it felt. Her face was squished into such a furry squint by the time Matty lifted her up into his arms that she could feel his hands around her chest before she saw them. A flock of pigeons exploded into flight, their gray and purple feathers thrashing through the crisp December morning as he tugged her collar down around her neck and smoothed her tangled ruff.

Fang panted from her effort with a smile on her lips.

She hadn't made it, not this time. . . .

But all she'd needed was another minute.

METROPOLITAN MUSEUM OF ART, NEW YORK CITY

December 21, 10:30 a.m.

Ashley unzipped her jacket—a real down jacket this time, not one of the hoodies she'd been wearing all winter—and fanned the sweat from her neck. Her dad had only met them at the ticket counter a few minutes before and he was already striding so purposefully through the museum's Great Hall that she had to jog just to stay within sight of him. His footsteps echoed loudly from the shiny marble tiles to the high, domed ceilings as she turned around, hissing at her cousins to keep up. It was hard to remember to keep her voice down when Matty's nose was always in his phone— even when the guards in blue blazers were watching her every move.

Like she was planning to knock over a statue or something.

Ashley grinned despite herself.

A guard with a buzzing walkie-talkie returned her smile as they passed into the Egyptian wing, and all at once—out of nowhere—Ashley felt like crying. She grabbed Matty and Elizabeth by the hands instead, guiding them past noseless statues of ancient pharaohs and well-wrapped mummies as her dad disappeared behind yet another corner.

Some of her favorite memories with him were here.

Surrounded by sarcophagi.

They'd skip the line for the big sandstone temple that was always packed with tourists and spend entire afternoons searching for ancient cats in the displays. Hidden in hieroglyphs and blue stone beads or curled up in sculptures and gold filigree, they were almost everywhere you looked—and seeing them now, out of the corner of her eye—Ashley realized how long it had been since she'd gone cat-spotting with her dad. The museum might've been packed with priceless artifacts, but it was full of her own priceless history too. . . .

And these days, it was like none of it had ever happened.

Her own dad was barely even talking to her anymore . . . and he'd been late to meet them, too, even though he'd been bugging Ashley to come for months and months and months. When he did finally show up, he'd furrowed his brows at the sight of her cousins. It was super awkward, but it was going to be awkward no matter what.

With Matty and Elizabeth, at least she had a buffer.

For all the good *that* was doing her.

Her dad was speed-walking twenty steps ahead of them, rushing through every exhibit so quickly that it was like he was trying to lose them. Matty barely looked up from his phone as she dragged him through a bright, sun-washed conservatory and into a hallway filled with statues of knights on horseback in their suits of armor. The horses had armor, too, and they stood in formation—javelins at the ready beneath checkerboard banners and coats of arms, like the kind you'd see at a Renaissance faire, with lions and eagles clawing at their seams.

But it was all real.

Everything in the museum was real, from the mummies to the oil paintings lining the walls. It just didn't *feel* real, chasing her own dad through the Christmas crowds at the museum with her super-slow cousins in tow.

"Wait up," Ashley hissed.

She barely dared to raise her voice above a whisper as she watched her dad slip through another doorway, but the hallway amplified it like a megaphone, anyway. A white-haired couple looked up from their guidebooks—so startled, as if she'd shouted at them—while a guard motioned for her to slow down. Ashley ignored them, pulling her cousins into a courtyard filled with statues so smooth and white they seemed to glow. She didn't see her dad at first—just a circle of artists sketching a massive statue from every angle with stubby charcoal pencils. Elizabeth stopped to watch as they smudged and smeared the charcoal with their thumbs, shading it into twenty different versions of the same mythic warrior brandishing an alabaster sword. Most of the sketches were furry black clouds, blurred beyond recognition, but some were so good they could've hung from the museum walls in oversized frames.

"This looks really serious," Matty said.

He tugged at his sister's sleeve, pointing at his phone while Ashley spun on her toes and scanned the courtyard for her dad's scruffy beard and corduroy jacket. It wasn't any use. They'd fallen too far behind and there were too many people milling around the museum: visitors from all over the world, taking red-cheeked selfies in their winter jackets and scarves. Ashley tied her own jacket around her waist and rubbed the sweat from her arms as she circled the courtyard, her pace and heartbeat quickening in a momentary panic.

"Dad!" she said, not quite shouting.

But the courtyard was so full of laughter and excited conversation that he wouldn't have heard her even if she did shout. Only the high-pitched whine of her cousins arguing over Matty's phone seemed to cut through the noise, and—as she looped the courtyard a second and third time—a pulse-pounding frustration set in. Ashley was practically seeing red by the time she finally spotted him, waiting in a darkened alcove just beyond the water fountains.

She rolled her eyes as she circled back to her cousins.

"You *have* to listen," Matty snapped. "You promised."

His cheeks were flushed, but Ashley didn't have time to babysit—not when her dad was waving at her from the shadows. She tugged on their arms instead, pulling them through rooms and anterooms filled with statues that they barely stopped to notice while Matty fumed beside her. Thousands of years of artistic expression blurred together around them as they chased her dad's footsteps from chambers filled with fancy royal tea sets to abstract canvases that filled entire rooms: big emotional paintings spattered and streaked with flashes of colors that were wild and messy and a little confused.

Like Ashley.

She'd never understood them before, but for the first time in her life she found herself slowing down long enough to lose herself in their splotches and swirls. *This was going to be hard no matter what,* she reminded herself, blinking back the tears she'd been fighting ever since she stepped foot in the Egyptian wing. She'd known as soon as her dad invited her to the museum that it wasn't going to be easy coming here with him. Not at Christmas, with their lives so different than they used to be. It was why she'd put him off for as long as she could. . . .

But everything she did just ended up making her life even harder.

And at the end of the day, she didn't even have a choice.

If she'd had any say at all, they'd still be a family.

"Sorry," Ashley whispered, squeezing between a tour group and their guide and wiping a tear from her cheek while she waited for Elizabeth to tie her shoe. "The last time this portrait sold," the guide lectured, "it went for forty million dollars. Today, that'd be closer to a hundred million." The tour group squinted and nodded at the art in unison. Ashley squinted and nodded along with them, but it all felt so suddenly random that she couldn't help but laugh. She tried to stop herself as Elizabeth caught up, but that only turned it into a sort of strangled snort that echoed from one end of the gallery to the other—from the half-finished Picasso all the way to a big red statue of a stick figure at the far corner of the room.

"Sorry," Ashley mumbled again, sidestepping away from the group.

But it felt good to smile again.

"Where's he taking us, anyway?" Elizabeth asked.

"Home," Matty grumbled. "We need to go home."

Ashley shrugged as they made their way toward the stairwell at the back of the exhibit hall, smiling to herself as she took the steps two and three at a time—making as much noise as she could before they emerged on the second floor, where the unbridled splashes of color gave way to mazes of smaller and smaller rooms. Gray, fabric-covered walls and worn wooden floors replaced the sparkling marble, muffling their footsteps as they tracked her dad through the lesser-traveled hallways of the museum. The selfie-taking tour groups had thinned out on the second floor, replaced by a few nearsighted retirees and the security guards who were watching them inch closer and closer to the art . . . and Ashley's dad, who was leaning proudly against an empty information desk, waving for her to hurry up from the next room down.

Ashley took a deep breath.

"You made it," he said. "Finally!"

His grin was so wide it was glowing as he nodded at a line of framed photographs that were hanging on the wall across from him: completely oblivious—as usual—but happier, now that he'd finally gotten Ashley to his own little corner of the Met. The picture he wanted to show her was going to be taken down soon, she knew. After the holidays. It was part of a temporary exhibit, and if they'd waited any longer she might have missed it. Ashley returned her dad's smile as she walked over to the photos, trying to play it cool, but she was feeling so nervous she could puke. It was her dad's big moment—one of his photographs, on display in the museum he'd been taking her to since before she could walk—and she didn't know how she was supposed to react, or if she'd be able to make the right face and say things he wanted to hear.

She hadn't even thought to ask what picture he was showing.

Everything had been so weird lately.

The last thing she wanted to do was disappoint him again.

"Merry Christmas!" he said. "Whaddya think?"

Ashley swallowed as she inched closer to the wall.

It was a group show, and Ashley slowly walked from picture to picture, trying to see if she'd be able to pick out her dad's reading the placards. There was a flock of pigeons taking flight in front of a corner bodega, and a group of kids playing next to a man who was sleeping on a park bench. The photos were all black and white, and blown up so big that there were film grains speckling every sunbeam and shadow. Her dad watched as she studied each photo in turn. She could almost feel him bouncing on his toes, his expectant smile burning a hole in the back of her neck while she searched for landmarks or clues—for *anything* that would let her know which photograph was his. She wasn't sure why it felt so important for her to be able to pick his picture out of a lineup, except she had the feeling it was important to him, too.

Like it would prove they still had something in common.

The only problem was, Ashley didn't know if they did.

At least, not until Elizabeth screamed in her ear.

"That's you!" she yelled, pinching Ashley's arm so hard she was sure it would leave a bruise. Ashley furrowed her brows. Her cousin was right: it *was* a picture of her. With her face half cast in shadow, she looked so cool that she almost didn't recognize herself as she leaned against the black-iron fence in front of her school, waiting for the bus.

Ashley blinked as she stared at her own face on the wall.

Scanning her memories.

Out of the hundreds of afternoons she'd taken the bus home from school, there was only one that really stood out. Her dad had surprised her with an early dinner, right after the split. They'd ordered spicy pad thai and bubble tea (Ashley's favorite) and walked back to her mom's new apartment together, stopping to take pictures along the way. Looking at the black-and-white smile in her eyes, it seemed like the last good day she'd spent with her dad.

It was hard to know for sure, but it hadn't been an easy year.

For either of them, she realized.

Matty poked his sister in the side and Elizabeth shrugged him off, sparking another whispered argument . . . but Ashley barely heard it as she turned and ran across the room, sprinting past the scowling guard and jumping into her father's arms. He staggered backward, stumbling into the empty desk and knocking a stack of pamphlets to the floor as hot and happy tears ran down her cheeks. They both laughed as he hugged Ashley back, squeezing her as tightly as he could while the walkie-talkie on the guard's hips vibrated to life.

"Love you," he said. "Always. You know that, right?"

Ashley nodded, wiping her eyes with the palms of her hands as an alarm sounded overhead. It whooped twice, like the warning siren on an ambulance, before a loudspeaker buzzed into action. *"Attention,"* it said. *"The Metropolitan Museum of Art will be closing in fifteen minutes due to inclement weather."* Ashley cocked her head, squinting at her dad through her tears. He gave her one last squeeze as he turned to the museum guard.

"That can't be right," her dad said. "Can it?"

ETERNITY FJORD, GREENLAND

December 21, 10:45 a.m.

The little arctic fox crouched behind a rocky out-cropping, her small white ears perked forward as she watched the researchers collect their gear. The echo of running water through the creaking valley had been a constant presence for days, so constant that she'd almost gotten used to it—and it had only gotten louder since the icebreaker had anchored in Evighedsfjorden. The little fox could actually feel the glacier melting, like the entire fjord was trembling beneath her paws. She wasn't the only one. Sensing danger, the lemmings and voles she'd been hunting throughout the fall and barren winter months had tunneled even farther underground.

And out of reach.

It was infuriating.

The little fox could hear them scratching at the loose and sandy soil, huddled deep within their dens—but no matter how hard she dug or how far down into their mossy burrows she wedged her snout, they were always just beyond the snap of her searching jaws. Finally, admitting defeat and driven by a growing hunger, she'd taken to creeping along the edges of the bay—inching closer and closer to the scientists on the beach. The smells she found there were strange and new, but also familiar. The fish especially. The little fox snuck closer to a group of biologists, her nose twitching at a cooler filled with the cod they'd netted from their Zodiac boats, drowned by the sudden influx of fresh water that was melting into the bay and collected for dissection . . . but otherwise safe to eat.

At least, the little fox hoped so.

She mewled at the scientists, pawing the rocks as if she intended to pounce, then settled back down on her quivering haunches. The last time she'd gotten close enough for treats she'd woken up groggy on the rocks with a half memory of being pricked with a needle, then petted. Every fiber of her being told her to run, to put as much distance between herself and the scientists as she could . . . but the growling in her stomach argued otherwise. The glacier rumbled, too, as if urging the little fox to action. She mewled again, even louder this time, and—when that didn't get their attention—she barked. Halfway between a squeak and a scream, the little fox's bark was in a register so high-pitched it was impossible to ignore. A scientist with a big brown beard turned and laughed when he finally saw her, tapping his colleagues' shoulders to get their attention while he reached for his camera.

The wait only made the little fox yowl even louder.

"It's okay," the scientist said, trying to keep a straight face as she growled and stamped her paws, squirming nervously in the spotlight. The scientist reached into his cooler with a bulky black glove and tossed her a raw and slimy filet. It landed in the dirt a few feet in front of the little fox, and she inched forward—her black eyes squinting suspiciously as she sniffed the air . . . then swallowed without chewing. She licked the oil from her lips as the scientist snapped photographs from a distance, then howled for another. It didn't take long for the little fox to develop a taste for the flakey white meat, kept doubly fresh and cold by the breeze off the bay.

She didn't even mind the scales.

The scientist tossed her another chunk of cod, then turned back to his work.

Judging from the mess of unlabeled specimens strewn across his wobbly folding table, he had a lot of work left to do. He wasn't the only one. The entire base camp was in disarray. They hadn't expected to be leaving so soon, but the *Mjölnir* had pulled closer to the shore overnight—close enough that the sailors had been able to lower a long aluminum ramp down to the rocky beach. After the glacier started calving into the bay, they'd lost the option of loading everything back into the icebreaker with their lightweight Zodiac boats. Even if the waves hadn't been too rough for the Zodiacs to handle, it would've taken too many trips— and as fast as the scientists had been working to pack up their camp and go, they were still running behind the captain's schedule . . . and the captain had promised to leave without them, if he had to.

The scientists were *pretty* sure the captain was bluffing.

But they weren't willing to bet their lives on it.

The first ice had sheared free from the splintering cliffs in the small hours of the morning, crashing so heavily into the sea that the big red boat rocked in its wake. It wasn't the last crash of the day, and the researchers had been climbing up and down the long ramp ever since: loading their crates back onto the icebreaker as the glacier crumbled before their eyes. The arctic fox licked her lips with her eraser-pink tongue, her eyes darting back and forth as she watched them bounce between the ship and their samples in their orange gumby suits.

"That's enough," the bearded scientist said, shooing the little fox back home.

She wrinkled her nose in frustration as she retreated into the shadows, then circled back—tracing the scientist's footprints to his cooler of fish. She looked left and right, making sure the coast was clear before she climbed over the ledge and tumbled onto a pile of fresh Greenland cod. Half of the fish were sliced and sampled in labeled Ziploc bags. The rest were stacked and stored whole for later, when the scientists had more free time to run their tests. Settling down into the insulated cooler, the little fox purred as she chewed at the corner of a Ziploc bag, freeing the juicy white meat within. It was only fair to eat her fill, now that the voles and lemmings were gone, and that's exactly what she intended to do. Out of sight and sheltered from the wind, the little fox smiled to herself as she licked the plastic bag clean and started on the next— too distracted to notice the commotion on the *Mjölnir*.

"Hold on for your lives!" someone shouted.

The scientists on the steep metal ramp dropped their plastic tubs, freeing their hands to grip the guardrails as a Volkswagen-sized chunk of glacier calved into the bay. They were right to brace themselves. Even from a distance, the falling ice looked massive—so massive that it smashed into the waves with a deafening crack, like a high-speed car crash in the middle of the Arctic. A strange and quiet stillness seemed to fill the fjord in the seconds after the initial impact. Outside of the scientists and a handful of swooping gulls, the bay had been eerily empty all morning . . . as if the braying seals knew something the scientists didn't.

The stillness didn't last.

Tubs full of specimens and samples tumbled down to the empty beach as the icebreaker rolled in the aftershocks of the crash. Swaying from port all the way to starboard, it scraped the long ramp across the rocky beach as the onboard crane creaked ominously overhead. Stumbling and falling back to shore, the scientists raced to pack the rest of the gear. The shimmering bellies in the surf should have been warning enough, but the groans and murmurs of the fjord had turned into a shout they couldn't afford to ignore. The time to board the *Mjölnir* had come and almost gone—and, not wanting to miss their chance, the scientists in the orange suits shouted as they rushed back up the ramp. Curled up in the cooler and so full of fish that she could barely move, the arctic fox stretched her paws and yawned.

METROPOLITAN MUSEUM OF ART, NEW YORK CITY

December 21, 10:50 a.m.

Matty wasn't surprised that their big day out was ending early.

He'd been expecting the worst all week, and the anxious knot in the pit of his stomach had gotten so tight that he'd almost felt relieved when his phone buzzed him awake at six in the morning—chiming to life with a hundred extreme weather advisories. Proving he'd been right to worry all along. Matty didn't even have to read them to know what they said: one quick look at the thick layer of frost on the living room windows told him everything he needed to know, but when he'd tried to warn his aunt about the arctic blast, she'd only smiled and nodded.

Comforting him like he was just a little scaredy-cat.

"It'd be weirder if it *didn't* snow," his sister said.

Conveniently forgetting all the promises she'd made back home.

Even the big purple blob on his radar maps hadn't convinced them . . . but now that the entire Metropolitan Museum of Art was closing early, they'd have to take him seriously. There weren't any flashing red lights or droning alarms, but after the security guard double-checked the early closure on her buzzing walkie-talkie, she'd speed-walked them down two flights of stairs like the building was on fire—retracing their steps through a maze of cracking oil paintings and ancient sculptures. By the time they made it back beneath the high, domed ceilings where they'd bought their tickets, Matty's pulse was roaring in his ears so loudly that he hardly even noticed the waves of excited conversation echoing across the Great Hall.

He wanted to run, to get back home as quickly as they could.

But nobody else seemed to know what to do.

Not even the people who worked there.

Matty spotted five of them in their blue blazers and red ties: pacing up and down the snaking coat-check line, they looked just as bewildered as all the tourists. He turned on his heels and frowned. The museum had felt almost empty when they were racing through it, but now that everyone had made their way to the lobby, there was barely any room to stand. Like marbles, they'd all collected in one tiny corner of the Met—as if the entire building had been lifted and shaken to the side. Holding his red parka in one hand while he gripped his sister with the other, Matty trailed after Ashley and his Uncle Jack—squeezing past the tour groups that were laughing at their own bad luck while they slowly funneled toward the exit.

Uncle Jack was laughing, too.

"Nothing like a little family togetherness during the holidays," he said, twisting in place so his niece and nephew could see him grimacing at his own bad joke. Matty was too upset to force a smile, but even squished in the crush of the evacuation, his uncle seemed much happier than he had before . . . and so did Ashley. She hadn't said anything about her picture on their dash down to the lobby—there hadn't been time, not while they were jostling each other on the stairs. But she didn't have to say anything: she was smiling so hard that her eyes had turned into crescent moons above her flushed pink cheeks. Matty shook his head, doing his best to ignore a growing sense of dread as they snaked their way through the milling crowds.

"To your left, please!" a guard shouted, waving the tour groups into formation.

Or trying to, anyway.

No matter what the security guards said or how loudly they thanked the museum attendees (desperately and in advance) for forming a single-file line, it was wishful thinking. As big and imposing as the

Great Hall was, it was so packed full of tourists that there wasn't room to move more than a few feet in any direction—which meant that everyone slowly mashed together at the exit, pushing gently toward the open doors. That's where traffic stopped, stymied at the narrow end of the funnel. After a few long seconds staring blankly at the glossy flip of his sister's ponytail, Matty stretched on his toes, but he couldn't see through the open doors.

"Sorry," he mumbled, stumbling against a stranger for support.

If they heard him, they didn't show it.

Everyone was too busy gasping and shrieking as a strong gust of snow filled the room. The flakes were big and airy, and they shimmered as they drifted beneath the darkening skylights while the security guards struggled to keep the knotted lines moving in an orderly fashion. The closer they got to the exit, the more Matty realized how little chance there was of that ever happening. The wind was ripping across the open doors so quickly that it whistled and howled, and Elizabeth squeezed his hand as it caught the brim of someone's bright-orange baseball cap. The cap tumbled back into the museum as they inched forward, step by tiny step.

"Ready?" Ashley's dad asked, tightening his scarf.

Matty nodded, then remembered his parka.

The tour groups swelled behind him as he zipped it up beneath his chin, then tugged his gloves and hat into place. Ashley and Elizabeth rushed to do the same as they pushed closer and closer to the exit—and to the looming cold front that was waiting to greet them there. Even in his fancy winter clothes, Matty could feel the chill creeping in at his ankles, where his wool socks met his pants. With all of his down padding and thermal lining, he'd hoped to be warm no matter what . . . but as his hair whipped in the freezing wind, Matty started to doubt himself. Growing up on the beaches in Florida, he'd never seen snow before—not real snow, like the kind kids had fights with in cartoons and movies. Now, as he stepped out of the museum, he saw so much of it at once that it was almost unbelievable. It wasn't just *snow* blanketing Manhattan. . . .

It was a full-force blizzard, or it would be soon enough.

The museum wouldn't have closed down for anything less.

"Let's keep it moving, please!" a guard called from just inside the door.

Matty blinked the oncoming snow from his eyes as he followed Ashley and her dad on their long and perilous climb down to the plaza. They weren't steep, but the steps leading up to the Metropolitan Museum of Art were as wide as the building itself, and a crew of maintenance workers in navy blue snowsuits were visibly sweating as they shoveled, fighting to dig a path that the wind and snow was filling just as quickly as they could clear it. Matty's glasses, though blocking the worst of the weather, kept fogging up. He tried wiping them clean, but his gloves were too bulky and ended up smearing the lenses—so Matty held on tightly to the well-worn handrails instead, feeling for the crunch of salt beneath his boots as they slowly and carefully made their way to the sidewalk and the eerily quiet street it bordered.

Fifth Avenue.

With four lanes of southbound traffic running almost the full length of the city, it was one of the major arteries of Manhattan. When they'd first arrived at the museum, it had been clogged with double-decker buses and a line of yellow and green cabs that were standing at the ready, waiting for an easy fare. Matty hadn't given the traffic a second thought. It was just another part of New York City, where people took half a million taxi rides every single day of the year—but in the time it had taken them to look at one little picture on the wall, the entirety of Fifth Avenue had been reduced to two slush-filled ruts in the snow where cars could pass. . . .

And even that was disappearing right in front of his bleary eyes.

Matty took his glasses off and blinked.

The blurred form of a bicycle messenger raced down the middle of the empty street, her hair blowing in the wind while she stood in her saddle. Her tires slipped in and out of the icy ruts as she powered down the avenue, and Matty watched her disappear into a whirl of snow as the rest of the museum emptied out onto the sidewalk behind him. The locals rushed to the subways, ducking against the wind with their hats held tightly to their heads, but the tour groups just stood marveling at the weather as they waited for their buses—erupting into a chorus of high-spirited shrieks and whoops every time a particularly hard gust of wind tore through them.

Matty shielded his eyes while Ashley's dad checked his phone.

The pretzel and hot dog vendors that lined the plaza had shuttered their carts, their yellow and red umbrellas collapsed into fluttering spears tied down with bungee cords and random bits of string. The vendors themselves were long gone, and so were the pigeons. Matty checked the balustrades and cornices of the museum, then turned to the mansions across the street—wondering where they could possibly be hiding. The snow was blowing sideways now, so quickly that he couldn't imagine them being strong enough to fly against it. Not when they'd been eating fried dough and stale hot dog buns their entire lives. Matty looped his arm around his sister's as another blast of wind swept down the avenue, threatening to blow them both away.

Or at least knock them back a few feet.

"*Shoot*," Ashley's dad said. "I can't get a car."

He frowned at his phone, then looked up for the first time since they'd left the museum. Ashley was still smiling but her cheeks were red from the cold and Elizabeth was literally shivering in her boots beside her. She'd decided to try to look "cool" and dress like their cousin again, so she wasn't bundled up like Matty—and even Matty was cold. He'd tried to tell her to wear layers, like their mom had made them promise to do, but she'd just smirked and left her sweaters folded in her suitcase. A big tour bus pulled up in front of the museum, as close to the curb as it could get, and a group of older women stumbled past them—their fancy leather shoes slipping and sliding in the slush as they carefully made their way on board.

"Quickly," the bus driver called out. "Before they close the roads!"

"Are you going downtown?" Ashley's dad asked, shouting over the wind.

The bus driver shook her head.

"New Haven," she said. "If we can make it."

Uncle Jack nodded.

"The subway it is, then!" he said, making a big show of looking both ways before he stepped off the curb. Matty's lips were starting to feel chapped from the wind, so he bit them to keep from smiling. As annoyed as he was, he couldn't help but laugh as he watched his uncle kick his way through the snowdrifts of Fifth Avenue with his hand outstretched like a crossing guard. Outside of the idling bus, the street in front of the museum was completely empty. So empty that they could've done cartwheels down the middle of it without having to think twice about traffic. Another blast of wind tore down the street, lifting loose snow from the sidewalk and shooting it upward, into the whirlwind of the blizzard. Matty instinctively reached for his phone to take a picture, then remembered his bulky winter gloves and gave up.

There was no way he was going to take them off now. Not in a blizzard.

He'd save the cartwheels for another day, too.

Even standing totally motionless on the slippery sidewalk felt treacherous, and Matty let go of Elizabeth's arm as he followed his uncle—spreading his hands out in front of him as he sank into the gathering snow, just in case he fell. It crunched wetly underfoot, soaking the hem of his jeans. "We'll take the six train down to Union Square, and then we're home free," Uncle Jack said, walking backward as he talked. "Your mom's not expecting us until three of four, anyway, so I'll just call and let her know that we'll be stopping for some hot chocolate . . . or maybe lunch?"

"Yes!" Ashley shouted. "I'm starving."

Uncle Jack grinned as he answered his phone.

"Hey," he said—then stopped midstep. "What's wrong?"

Matty caught his sister's eye and shared a nervous glance as Ashley jogged through the slush to keep up with her dad. Matty's ankles were wet and his hands were sweating in his gloves, and even though Ashley's wide, happy smile was still plastered across her face, he had a sinking feeling that it wouldn't be for long. He'd been trying to tell everyone all morning, if they'd only listen: the weather was only going to get worse and worse, and it was safer to just stay inside. That wasn't just nerves or being scared of his shadow, it was *science,* and Matty frowned as he watched his uncle slip his phone back in his pocket.

Bad news was easy to spot, even from a distance.

Especially when you were used to it.

"Change of plans." Uncle Jack sighed, pulling Ashley into a two-armed hug so tight she lost her footing. "Fang slipped her leash while your mom was walking home—she ran away." Elizabeth gripped Matty's arm so hard it hurt. On either side of the empty street, redbrick town houses and fancy brownstones looked down on them from behind wrought-iron fences and snowcapped maples. If it wasn't for Ashley's stunned silence in the middle of the street, the scene would have been so picture-perfect and serene it could have been nestled in a snow globe.

"Don't worry," Uncle Jack whispered. "We'll find her."

PART

TWO

NANTUCKET, MASSACHUSETTS

December 21, 11:20 a.m.

The fog was thick over the Atlantic Ocean—so thick that the two ensigns from the United States Coast Guard could barely see ten feet beyond the shore. They stood in silence, shivering as they watched the big gray waves swell up from hidden depths and break against the sand. As far as they could tell, they were the only people left on 'Sconset Beach . . . and neither of them was happy about it. The smaller of the two pulled off her standard-issue gloves and checked her phone, her hands trembling in the cold as she turned to scan the sandy bluffs behind them.

Then tugged her knitted cap around her ears.

Thirty miles off the coast of Cape Cod, Nantucket sat covered in a thin layer of ice and snow—the first of the season. Originally built for whaling, the seaside village was filled with tiny fisherman's cottages refurbished into million-dollar getaways. Most stood empty in the frigid winter months, but life was different in the summer, when reams of climbing roses spilled across their gently sloping roofs. That was the picture on all the postcards, anyway. In the off-season, Nantucket's trademark roses were just a tangle of creeping branches and jagged thorns.

Not that the Coast Guard was there for the view.

But it didn't hurt.

The ensign wished she could say the same for the freezing cold sand beneath her boots. It felt like she was standing barefoot on ice, and her toes curled in her socks as the foam from crashing whitecaps washed around her feet. A morning jogger had called them in when his golden retrievers had pulled him down the shore, where the tides had left a long night's worth of the usual flotsam and jetsam alongside the remains of two frozen sharks.

The ensign almost gagged just looking at them.

It wasn't the smell: that would come later, when they thawed.

She took a bracingly cold breath, forcing herself to study the raw pink frown of their lifeless jaws. To the untrained eye, they still looked dangerous—like great white sharks but smaller, with long, almost whipable tails . . . but these were only threshers, mostly shy and harmless to humans. Their rigid fins carved rough and random lines in the sand as they rolled in and out with the waves, their belated winter migration cut tragically short.

It was almost unthinkable.

No strangers to the rough-and-tumble currents circling the island, it took more than just a little wind to sweep the threshers all the way to shore. Shocked senseless by the bitter arctic front, they'd been trapped in shallow waters and frozen solid overnight. The ensign wouldn't have believed it if she hadn't seen them with her own two eyes. In the tourist season, it would've caused a panic, but there wasn't much chance of a crowd gathering now. Not with the cold wind blowing so hard off the Atlantic that she had to strain her voice just to make herself heard.

"Ready!" she shouted.

Her partner nodded as she tossed him a rope.

Together they stepped into the surf, just deep enough to lasso their neon-yellow ropes around the threshers' fins. Once secured, they looped the ropes around their waists and stepped backward toward the shore. Their boots sank into the sand and snow while they huffed and grunted, shouting encouragements to each other with every step as they dragged the heavy sharks free from the pounding waves. As heavy as they were, the ensigns were lucky the threshers were so small: just two or three hundred pounds apiece, if they had to guess. A full-grown shark would have been too much for both of them combined and the ensign was already sweating through her sweater as she strained against the currents, pulling the frozen sharks to shore.

"Sharksicles," her partner joked, doubling over from the effort.

The ensign shook her head.

Ignoring him.

Once the sharks were on the sand, she circled them twice, double-checking that they were well above the tide line. Her muscles were burning despite the cold, and if the threshers weren't safe and secured by the time the scientists showed up with their nitrile gloves and waterproof notebooks, she wasn't sure she'd be able to fish them out of the waves again. Just doing it the first time had taken the better part of the morning.

And the surf was only getting rougher.

It was nearly noon, but the sun had yet to rise above the fog and—pacing up and down the beach to keep her body warm—the ensign's fingers trembled as she checked her phone for updates. Scrolling through a red and orange cluster of winter advisories and warnings, she slowed and then stopped—then shouted for her partner. The storm was an arctic blast, according the NCRC, and they were supposed to stay inside. To "shelter in place," for all the good that did the ensign. The spray from crashing waves dripped down her cheeks as she wiped the snowflakes from her screen.

As bad as the weather already was, the cold front was only supposed to get worse. But with two frozen sharks washed up beside the driftwood, the ensign wondered...

How much colder could it get?

77TH STREET SUBWAY STATION

December 21, 11:45 a.m.

Elizabeth pretzeled her arms in front of her chest and folded her shoulders inward—into the smallest possible version of herself—as she shuffled sideways down the narrow subway stairs. No matter how small she made herself, though, it wasn't making any difference. It felt like all of Manhattan was crushed together on the slick and muddy steps, as if every single person in the city was trying to catch the downtown six train at exactly the same time . . . and it didn't help that they were all puffed up and double-sized in their bulky winter coats.

Elizabeth shivered in her own tapered parka.

It was slim-cut and had looked cute in the mall back in Tampa, but it wasn't anywhere near as warm as the bright-red nerd alert her brother had picked out for himself. She wouldn't admit it, not out loud and *definitely* not within earshot of Matty, but she wished she'd worn a sweater or something beneath it. The snow was gusting down the stairs and into the fluorescent depths of the subway station, and there was nowhere to move and no way to hide from it. Not without pushing about a thousand New Yorkers down the stairs. It felt like they'd been standing in place forever, trapped by the fidgeting crowds—halfway between the blizzard and a subway that was so exasperatingly close that Elizabeth could hear the trains running. The floor almost shook with the sound of them as they rattled and squealed on their tracks.

Their Uncle Jack had sworn it was just a ten-minute trip.

"Super quick," he'd said. "We'll be home before you know it."

Elizabeth hoped he was right this time.

The walk from the museum to the subway was supposed to have been a short ten-minute hike, but with the unshoveled sidewalks and the check-ins with their Aunt Charley, it had taken almost three times as long to get this far: a full thirty-minute trudge through the snow, in a blizzard, wishing she'd worn some thermals beneath her jeans. Elizabeth sighed, wrapping her arms around her chest as a snow-wet strand of hair dripped onto her cheek. She wasn't going to make that mistake again—and she didn't care what she looked like anymore. If New York was one of the fashion capitals of the world, it definitely didn't look like it. Everyone around her was bundled up in pom-pom hats and hand-knit scarves, and as soon as she got back to her suitcase, she promised herself she was going to double up her socks and pull on as many sweaters as she could squeeze beneath her parka. She'd even borrow some from her brother if she had to.

She'd do anything to feel warm and dry again.

If they ever made it back to their suitcases, that is.

The subway trains were still squealing on their tracks every few minutes, but Elizabeth felt her heart drop as they slowly pushed toward the bottom of the stairs and swiped through the turnstiles. She'd expected the stairwell to open up into the station, like when they'd transferred to the subway from the airport shuttle—and it did, but there wasn't any more room to move around now that they'd finally made it down the stairs. Just more people, as far as Elizabeth could see: thousands of them, packed on the puddling and mud-streaked floors. Waiting for trains that came . . .

But never seemed to stop.

A melting snowflake ran down Elizabeth's neck and into her collar as a ten-car train trundled through the station at quarter speed, slow enough for her to count the rows of empty seats that were streaking past the pressing crowds. So close and yet so far away. Outside of the conductor, there wasn't a single person on any of the cars. It didn't make any sense: the train's horn blared—warning everyone away from the tracks—as a groan swelled across the platform, then broke out into curses and irritated sighs when the taillights on the last car disappeared into the darkened tunnel. She turned to her cousin with a half-formed question on her lips, but she looked so distraught that Elizabeth squeezed her hand instead. As miserable as she might have felt, she couldn't even begin to imagine how bad it was for Ashley.

Being stuck underground while Fang was all alone. Outside and lost in the snow.

If they wanted to help find her, they had to get home first—and *that* didn't seem like it was going to be happening anytime soon. Frowning, Elizabeth braced herself against the crowds that had started shifting unhappily around her. Even though nobody had boarded the passing trains, everyone was pushing ever closer to the platform's edge. Like there was actually a chance they could get on the next train if they could only inch close enough. There was no chance, not as far as Elizabeth could see, but only a handful of commuters had decided they'd had enough. They cursed under their breath, pushing their way against the current of the 77th Street station as the crowds reluctantly parted—then rushed to fill the gaps in their wake. A stranger's backpack pushed against Elizabeth's spine as they settled back into a cramped and cranky formation, pressing so hard that she was sure she could count the pens inside its zippered pockets. She twisted in place, straining to get out of its way, but there was no room to move.

"Is this how it always is?" she asked, gritting her teeth.

"We'll make it on the next one," Uncle Jack said.

But he didn't look so sure.

Not sure enough to convince Elizabeth, anyway.

She was so far back from the tracks that even if the trains started running like clockwork, it felt like it was going to take hours just to get to the front of the line. Elizabeth stood on her toes for a better view, balancing against the stranger's backpack for support. From where she was standing, you didn't have to be a New Yorker to know that the only way the station could be so jam-packed—so *overflowing* with coughing and grumbling commuters in soggy tennis shoes—was if something was seriously wrong. As if on cue, somebody shrieked. It was so loud and bloodcurdling that Elizabeth's first thought was that someone had been accidentally nudged onto the tracks . . . but the shrieking turned to laughter as she scanned the station.

It was just a group of teenagers.

They were roughhousing on the platform's ledge, so close that the train was just inches from their smiling faces as it trundled past them. Too close for comfort. Elizabeth held her breath as she watched them, her heart still pounding in her chest as the squeal of its wheels against the rusty metal tracks swallowed the teenagers' shouts and laughter. They didn't seem to notice or care—but Elizabeth couldn't exhale until the train had passed. Without stopping. *Again*. A detail that wasn't lost on the crowds. They seemed to almost ripple with indignation, and Elizabeth gripped her little brother's hand as another indecipherable announcement crackled from long-suffering speakers. Even if she could somehow understand what they were saying—even if she could go back in time and zip a thick cashmere sweater beneath her parka . . .

It wouldn't have made any difference.

She wasn't having a good time anymore.

All Elizabeth wanted was a fun winter break after the worst year ever, but with Ashley on the verge of tears and her brother working himself up into a full-blown panic, it was looking like Fang had run away with her last hopes for a carefree Christmas. That everyone was pushing and jockeying for position on the slippery floor only made it worse. There weren't any fences or guardrails separating the crowds from the tracks, and even though she was about as far away from the platform's edge as she could possibly get, Elizabeth held on to the hood of Ashley's jacket like she was holding on for dear life. It helped keep them together as they trailed after Uncle Jack, who was still pushing his way through the station—determined to find some mythical opening in the crowd. Elizabeth was sure it didn't exist, but there wasn't anything she could do but follow along. It wasn't like they had a lot of options if they wanted to get back home—not until the streets were clear enough for taxis and buses again.

One way or another, they were going to have to board the subway.

"Excuse me," she said. "Sorry . . . excuse me."

She was stepping on toes more often than she wasn't, but nobody paid her any attention. Almost everyone was staring into a phone or a creased paperback book, and not one person looked up as Elizabeth inched her way after her uncle—ducking and weaving behind backpacks and beneath outstretched arms. Two more trains whooshed past them, one in either direction, as more announcements crackled overhead. Elizabeth pricked her ears, but it was impossible to hear anything over the rush and clatter of the subway trains and the frustrated sighs that inevitably followed them. It didn't help that someone, somewhere, was drumming their heart out on a pair of plastic buckets and screaming "Jingle Bells" for tips between the passing trains.

Uncle Jack tapped his watch as he peered down the tracks.

Weighing their options.

"Okay," he called out, pivoting toward the exit. "New plan!"

Matty tripped over Elizabeth's heels as they turned against the flow of pushing bodies, slowly wedging their way back to the subway stairs while their uncle shouted over their heads. "Comin' through," he hollered, waving them into the reluctantly parting crowds. Elizabeth's cheeks flushed as everyone looked up from their phones and she stared down at her muddy shoes on the slick station floor, too embarrassed to meet their eyes.

It was just the heat that was turning her face red.

That's what she told herself.

With so many people crushed together in their winter coats, the station had gone from cold to almost unbearably hot in the time it had taken to walk down to the subway's crowded platform and not catch a train. Elizabeth sniffed, rubbing her nose with the back of her hand as she led her family to the exit, past the shirtless man on his makeshift drums and the thousands of commuters who shifted to fill the empty space behind them.

Like they were never even there.

It was just as well.

The snow continued to gust and flurry down the stairs and Elizabeth took deep, refreshing breaths as she climbed into it, filling her lungs to bursting with the bracingly cold air. Even walking against the flow, it was easier to leave than she thought it would be . . . and it felt good to be outside again. Surprisingly good, considering how happy she'd been to duck out of the wind just a few minutes earlier. She still wasn't wearing enough layers and the snow was coming down even harder now—but it was better to be outside in a blizzard than trapped underground with half of Manhattan breathing down their necks.

Elizabeth smiled despite herself.

She felt almost like a local as she stepped out onto the windswept street, as if she'd lived in New York City her entire life and not just for a couple of days on winter vacation. The tip of her ponytail whipped against her face as she turned to make sure everyone was still behind her—and that they hadn't been lost to the depths of the 77th Street station. Elizabeth shuddered just thinking about it . . . then shivered as a gust of snow enveloped her in an unexpected updraft. It was bracingly cold, but the sun had emerged from behind a towering bank of clouds while they'd been trapped in the station, and it was hard to see anything but the dazzle of falling snow against the faded blue sky. A car's engine revved in the distance, its tires spinning and squealing for traction on the icy street as Elizabeth blinked the sparkles from her eyes.

UPPER EAST SIDE, MANHATTAN

December 21, 12:15 p.m.

A steady stream of New Yorkers rushed down the subway stairs, like minnows caught in a whitewater current. They huffed and grumbled, racing to get out of the snow as Ashley climbed to join her cousins on the icy sidewalk outside of the 77th Street subway station. Stepping up into the blizzard, the sheer force of the wind took her by surprise. It had only gotten stronger while they were underground, and—bracing herself for the cold—she leaned into it, her brows knitting in frustration as a woman in a fancy camel-hair coat shouldered her way down the stairs.

"*Excuse* you," the woman snapped.

Ashley bit her lips to keep from screaming.

She didn't blame the woman for shoving her way out of the storm, but Ashley was already so upset that she felt like she was literally going to explode. All she wanted was to get back home so she could find her little dog . . . and everything was going wrong at once, from the art museum closing early to the hot and overcrowded subways. And now this: an impassable blizzard in the middle of the hottest winter she'd ever seen. It was like the entire world was conspiring against her, and one quick look at the deepening snowdrifts told Ashley everything she needed to know about their chance of catching a cab. It was less than zero, and shrinking with every passing minute. She swore she could even feel the temperature dropping as she stood at the top of the steps, just like she could feel someone staring a hole into the back of her head.

Ashley spun on her heels.

The line for the subway had backed up all the way to the sidewalk and—standing halfway underground, unhappily wedged in the middle of a group of sunburned men in yellow hard hats—the lady in the camel-hair coat was still glowering up at her. Ashley narrowed her eyes and stared right back at her, scowling at the unfairness of it all. Unless her dad had some magic trick up his sleeve, she was pretty sure they were trapped uptown—at least until the plows could clear the streets . . . and she didn't have that much time to lose.

Ashley squeezed her hands into tight and angry fists. But there was nothing she could do.

She'd give anything to be scouring the streets around her apartment, checking all of Fang's usual haunts—from the dog parks to the dumpsters. But with no way to get back home, she didn't have a choice. The snow was flying so hard and fast that it stung her face, and Ashley felt so suddenly defeated that she didn't even struggle when her cousin pulled her into a tight and warming hug. She hadn't worn a scarf and her cheeks felt cold against her cousin's, so Elizabeth wrapped her own long scarf around both of their heads—pulling it up high, above their ears, so they could feel the warmth of their own breath beneath the knobby wool. It was so thick that Ashley could barely hear her dad until he was right behind her.

Muttering at his phone as he tapped through their options.

As far as Ashley was concerned, they weren't good.

"So what's the plan?" she asked.

Her dad held up one finger instead of answering, buying another minute to think as he paced to the corner and back with his phone pinned up against his ear. The snow on the sidewalk outside of the subway station hadn't been shoveled so much as trampled down into a thick and muddy slush that splashed around his boots. Ashley couldn't make out what he was saying over the wind, but she didn't have to hear the stress in his voice to know they were in trouble. She could see it in the way he chewed his cheek while he talked, oblivious to the ice-encrusted truck that was parked just outside the station and the driver who was noisily revving its frozen engine back to life. She felt a little guilty, knowing he'd been wanting to take her to the museum for such a long time—that it was supposed to be a special day for them, with her picture on the wall and everything . . . and now all of his plans had turned upside down.

Ashley's frown deepened as she watched him pace.

And not just because they were stranded.

The revving truck's tires were spinning so quickly that they'd started to smoke and then squeal, and Ashley flinched as they finally found traction—and surged unexpectedly forward on the slick and trampled snow. She couldn't see the driver behind the glare of his windshield, but even squinting through the storm it was obvious. He'd lost control. The skidding truck veered over the shallow curb and onto the sidewalk as Ashley jumped through the slush, dragging Elizabeth and her scarf with her while Matty stumbled in their wake. He yelped as the truck clipped a NO PARKING sign, bending both the metal pole and a bicycle that was chained to it. The sign creaked and swayed in the wind while the driver stomped on his brakes and spun his steering wheel back toward the snowy drifts of Park Avenue. . . . Only the truck wasn't stopping.

And it was headed straight for her dad.

"Look out!" Ashley shouted.

But the crash didn't happen in slow motion, like in a movie.

Before the words had even left her mouth, the hood of the truck had crumpled against a heavy metal trash can—so close to her dad that he'd tripped backward to escape it, dropping his phone into the snow as he landed in an icy puddle. Sprawled out across the sidewalk, he blinked into the glare of headlights that were staring right back at him, just feet from where he'd been standing seconds before. The crack of quickly filling airbags echoed down the avenue as paper cups and oily napkins from the toppled trash can swept downtown, like tumbleweed. The truck's engine continued to whine, its wheels spinning for traction as its alarm blared—drowning out the murmurs of onlookers that had gathered from the crowded subway stairs.

The whole thing was over almost as soon as it had started.

"Are you kids okay?" her dad asked, looking up at Ashley and her cousins.

Matty stared openmouthed as Elizabeth rubbed her neck.

Ashley had pulled on her scarf so hard that the yarn had stretched out of shape while it was wrapped around their heads—but they were better off than if Ashley *hadn't* yanked them out of the way, scarf and all, so she nodded for the three of them.

Her dad nodded back, then turned to the driver.

"Are you okay, man?" he shouted.

The driver ignored him as he pushed his door open to survey the damage, then ducked back into the safety of his cab. Ashley's entire body tensed as he settled behind the wheel, but the driver didn't try to reverse or drive away. He turned the key in the ignition instead, switching the engine off and reclining his seat back as far as it would go. Like he was exhausted by the entire ordeal. Once the crowds realized there was nothing to see but a dented trash can and the truck that had hit it, it didn't take long for their interest to fade . . . and after the wheels finally stopped spinning and the alarm quieted down, the streets felt even more deserted than before. It *was* New York City, after all—everyone had someplace to be, and nobody wanted to lose their spot in the subway line just to rubberneck outside in a blizzard.

Ashley didn't blame them.

She didn't want to wait outside, either.

It felt wrong, standing in the snow with her heart pounding in her chest and no police sirens speeding toward the scene of the crash. The wind screamed through the skyscraper canyons, whipping powder from the peaks of growing snowdrifts like the crests of breaking waves as Ashley's dad wiped the snow from his jeans and walked toward the truck. He knocked on the window to check on the driver one last time, but the driver just pointed at his phone—miming that he didn't want to be interrupted. Ashley's dad gave him a parting shrug, then shook his head as he joined Ashley and her cousins on the side of the road.

"Are *you* okay?" Ashley asked.

"I will be," he said. "Once we get you home."

Ashley nodded as he pulled her into a hug.

"It's just going to take a little longer than I expected." He sighed, taking Ashley's hand and guiding her to the center of the snow-choked street. They started off walking single file through the ruts left by the last cars unlucky enough to have had to force their way down Park Avenue. A handful of supers were starting to shovel and salt the walks in front of their apartments and storefronts, and the driveway of the hospital halfway down 77th Street was so spotless it was like it had never even snowed . . . but the rest of the sidewalks were so slippery you could slide down them, like ice-skating. As fun as it might have sounded to run and glide all the way back home, Ashley wasn't in the mood—and it was safer to avoid them.

They'd been through too much already to risk a broken leg.

Especially now, with the roads so wide and empty.

Ashley kept her eyes peeled regardless, peering behind her every few seconds for oncoming traffic. It felt strange, walking in the middle of the street, but every step they took was one step closer to Fang and

Ashley was happy to be moving. Park Avenue was six lanes wide, with three lanes in each direction—but you couldn't tell by looking at it. There wasn't any sign of asphalt, just a vast expanse so white and empty that she almost couldn't believe it. The entire city was like a blank sheet of paper with an errant smudge of activity every few blocks: a shadow leaning into the wind or an old woman covering her eyes as she peered down from her second-story apartment window, her pink curlers bobbing overhead. Even the endless lines of cars parked on the side of the street were covered in a blanket of snow.

Erased by the storm.

It gave Ashley goose bumps, seeing the streets so deserted.

There were millions of people living in the city, not to mention all the tourists, and she wondered where they could possibly be hiding. They couldn't all be stuffed underground, endlessly waiting for the subway, and she didn't think they were all peeking out at the snow from their heated living rooms, either. Wherever they were, it figured that Ashley and her cousins were the only kids unlucky enough to be fording their way down the middle of Manhattan like old-fashioned explorers. Even in the ruts, the snow was so deep that they had to kick through it with every step. It was more tiring than Ashley thought it would be—and she didn't want to scare her cousins, but it was a *long* walk down to Union Square.

More than sixty blocks, when she did the math in her head.

And that was without any detours.

It was more of a marathon than an afternoon stroll, even on a clear summer day. *And in the middle of a blizzard* . . . Ashley shook her head. They had to try, but unless her dad had some sort of plan up his sleeve, she wasn't sure they were going to make it. In fact, she was sure they wouldn't—especially if her cousins were going to be fooling around in the snow the whole way home.

"Think fast," Elizabeth shouted.

Matty toppled into a snowbank as she finished packing a handful of snow into a glistening ball and tossed it idly skyward, but the wind ripped the snowball into a thousand tiny flakes as soon as it left her hand. They shimmered and fell just a few feet from where Matty had been standing, and Ashley couldn't help but smile as Elizabeth patted and smoothed another snowball in her bulky gloves. It was her cousin's first time seeing real snow, and even though they'd grown apart, all Elizabeth had ever wanted was to have a little fun. On any other day, it would have been fun for Ashley, too—being the only ones out in the middle of the storm.

Especially when the streets were always so jam-packed with people.

Even before the sun had a chance to rise above the Hudson River every morning, there were ferries zigzagging across its sparkling waters that were full of commuters reading newspapers that had been dropped off in the middle of the night. When Ashley stayed up too late watching movies on her phone, she could hear the delivery trucks trundling beneath her bedroom window, and there was always someone arguing or laughing or rushing to catch a bus or a train . . . so seeing the city so empty felt like a special, once-in-a-lifetime kind of thing.

Like swimming with dolphins.

Or walking on the moon.

More than anything, Ashley wanted to be in the mood to chase her cousins down the middle of Park Avenue. To give them the best snowball fight of their lives. But there was no way she could find her way back into the Christmas spirit, not until Fang was safe and sound and out of the storm. Until then, all she wanted to do was get home . . . and her cousins didn't have a clue how far they still had to go, or how tiring it was going to be to trudge for miles through the snow.

Red-cheeked and sweating through their jeans.

Hot and cold at the same time.

And wet-socked.

Ashley grimaced just thinking about it.

There was no way they were going to make it more than ten blocks, much less all the way back to Union Square, but she didn't have the heart to tell them. She didn't want to admit it to herself, either. Not when Elizabeth was chasing her brother down the middle of the street, her happy shouts lost in the tumult of the blizzard as they tossed snowballs into the wind. It was easier to grit her teeth and pretend that everything was going to be okay.

WASHINGTON, D.C.

December 21, 1:00 p.m.

Joy wasn't sure when the fluorescent light above her desk had started to buzz, but there was an occasional flicker at the end of its glowing white tube and the high-pitched buzz that went along with it was suddenly all she could think about. That and her growing nausea. She'd felt like puking ever since she sat down in front of her computer, and her first thought was to blame the flickering light—until she remembered all the candy canes she'd been stirring into her sodas. She'd lost count of how many she'd eaten since the holiday party. . . .

But it was at least five or six.

Maybe more, if she was being honest.

And even after she made herself chew two chalky pink tablets to settle her stomach, Joy couldn't stop herself from snacking on a tray of leftover brownies. There were still so many of them laid out in the conference room. Not to mention whole plastic tubs full of chocolate-covered pretzels and peppermint bark, unopened and stacked in the middle of the table like a half-hearted centerpiece. It wasn't any big surprise that Dr. Carson didn't have a sweet tooth, but with almost everyone else working from home, that left Joy with an entire Christmas party's worth of snacks all to herself. It would've felt like a dream come true on any other day—but even with all the free brownies she could possibly eat, Joy wished she could be home, too.

It wasn't looking like that was going to happen anytime soon.

The forecasts were that bad.

So bad that she'd stayed up all night just thinking about them.

Even though Joy had been working for the NCRC for half a decade now, she hadn't seen anything like the forecast Dr. Carson had shown her at the holiday party: the forecast that ruined all of her plans in a five-second glance. The smiling suits on the local news were still joking about white Christmases when they shared their warnings about "a little winter weather."

But it was so much more than that.

Joy sighed, rubbing her eyes with the palms of her hands as she looked over the ice-blue projections for the hundredth time. Cold fronts came and went, but this was no normal front: the frozen boundaries of the arctic circle were redrawing themselves as she watched, and it wouldn't be long before the entire Eastern Seaboard looked like windswept Siberian plains. There was no telling how long it would last—and it wasn't even the cold that Joy was worried about, either, even though a drop of almost a hundred degrees in less than twenty-four hours was more than just a little winter weather.

It was the extremes.

Joy had been wearing flip-flops and T-shirts all month, which was already weird for December, and things were only going to get weirder once the cold weather hit. They called it a "cold front" for a reason. It was like a battlefront: a combat line between huge masses of hot and cold air. The bigger the difference between the two temperatures, the more violent the clash. For the NCRC, that meant being prepared for freak thunderstorms and blizzards. Even tornadoes were on the table. It was Bad Weather Central, and with the temperature swinging so hard and so fast in either direction, there was no way for anyone to know what would happen next.

Almost anything was possible.

Even for the NCRC, a snap that dramatic was uncharted territory.

So much so that their fancy modeling programs gave an error message every time Joy tried to run the numbers. She kept trying anyway, ignoring her computer's indignant beeps. Without the projections, there was no telling what they were up against. The sun could rise and melt the Eastern Seaboard back up to a balmy seventy degrees . . . or the temperatures could keep on dropping until they were all popsicles. Even with so much technology at their fingertips, it turned out that all the old jokes about forecasters just guessing the weather weren't so far from the truth. Joy took another sip of Cherry Coke to settle her nerves, then rested her head on her desk.

All she wanted was to drive home and take a nap.

But she had too much work to do.

While the scientists were busy tweaking their forecasts, it was up to Joy to call as many mayors and city councilors and emergency management commissioners as she could. Her job was to brief them with the latest data. And to try to convince anyone who would listen that they were dealing with a weather event the likes of which they may have never seen before. There wasn't much to go on yet—just the massive cold front and a hunch—but by the time they knew more, it could be too late . . . and it was still early enough to make plans for possible evacuations and emergency shelters, in case a storm took out the power.

And the heat.

They weren't easy calls to make.

No mayor on earth was willing to risk a panic while

the sun was still shining over their cities, and even fewer would admit that winter storm preparedness meant more than just gassing up a couple of plows and staying off the roads. It was easier just to hope for the best and take a wait-and-see approach, so Joy was the last person any of them wanted to hear from . . . but the NCRC was dealing with a thousand unknowns, and millions of lives were at stake.

For all anyone knew, it was the start of another ice age.

Joy shuddered as her telephone chimed.

"NCRC," she said, tapping her headset into action.

She could barely hear the captain of the *Mjölnir* over the hum of the big ship's engine, but she'd been expecting his call all morning. It was going to take years for the scientists on board to fully analyze the samples they'd collected on Eternity Fjord, but their preliminary findings were clear enough for him to cancel their multimillion-dollar expedition and chart a last-minute course out of the Labrador Sea—and as soon as Joy had seen the projections on Dr. Carson's phone, she'd reached out to the captain with a last-minute thought of her own.

The thousands of rotting fish in his wake were just a symptom.

Even without a degree in marine biology, that much was obvious.

They'd been old news for hours, anyway, replaced

with the frozen sharks on Nantucket. An ensign from the Coast Guard had called them in just before lunch, and it was all the NCRC scientists had been texting about for the past thirty minutes. That was always a bad sign, even though it didn't prove anything. Not on its own. But all of the bad signs were starting to add up into a worst-case scenario. Joy's stomach twisted just thinking about it, roiling with Cherry Coke and half-stale brownies. If her instincts were right—if something was *seriously* wrong in the Arctic—it was going to mean trouble for everyone.

They just didn't know it yet.

Joy hoped she was wrong.

But hoping for the best wasn't planning for the worst, and that was Joy's entire job description. Dr. Carson didn't like it when her team took chances—the "real work" of the NCRC was supposed to happen at their desks—but Joy wouldn't be any help to anyone if she was iced into her basement office, without power and cut off from the people she was trying to save. If the entire world was going to freeze around her, she couldn't think of a better place to be than on board a Polar icebreaker. As far as contingency plans went, it was one of her best: the *Mjölnir* was built for the worst, and—give or take a few hundred miles—it was sailing right into her lap.

"Are we still on?" she asked.

The connection crackled in and out of service while

the captain talked hurriedly in his clipped Swedish accent—relaying coordinates that Joy could barely hear. She cupped her hand over her earpiece to block out the hum of the flickering bulb above her desk, but it still buzzed with the sounds of crashing waves and white noise from the deck of the *Mjölnir*—so loudly that she had to raise her voice to make herself heard over the hiss and roar of it.

"I'll meet you in New York, okay?" she yelled, alone in her empty office.

Surrounded by crumbs and blinking Christmas lights.

She couldn't be sure if the captain heard her.

Either way, she just kept shouting.

THE LABRADOR SEA

December 21, 3:15 p.m.

The little arctic fox uncurled herself and yawned, arching her back and stretching her paws until her entire body shivered awake. The air was cold and thick with the smell of fish, and her belly was so full of their fatty white meat that it was stretched taut, like a drum. Even nestled on top of the slippery pile of freshly caught cod—an early-winter jackpot, if there ever was one—she could hardly bring herself to eat more. She gave a tentative sniff anyway, licking her chops at the thought of the greasy scales lining her makeshift bed.

But she was still too full from breakfast.

She blinked her eyes open instead.

The dim arctic sun was nowhere to be found, and neither were the familiar spangles of distant stars in the sky. There was no rush of wind in her fur and the crash of waves were gone, too, along with the barks and claps of raucous seals. Trapped in an unexpected and suffocating darkness, a sudden panic filled the little fox's heart. A panic . . . and the rush of adrenaline that came with it. She jumped to attention, her head knocking against the lid of the cooler as her paws slid for purchase on the slippery bed of fish.

With no exit in sight, she started to dig.

Her sharp brown claws caught on soft and slimy bellies as she scratched around the edges of the cooler, frantically searching for fresh air and freedom. It wasn't any use. Her claws scraped helplessly against the smooth, hard plastic and she yelped in despair, unable to dig her way through it. Short and mournful, her yelp echoed loudly in the cooler—giving the little fox a sense of her newfound cage. Shivering on her haunches, her fur wet from the innards of the unlucky fish she was trapped with, the little fox howled.

But she wasn't ready to give up.

Not yet.

The cooler was designed to hold an entire day's worth of samples but was still small enough that her hours were numbered. There was no telling how long the little fox had been trapped . . . and without air holes, she only had so much time left to make her escape. The little fox's whiskers trembled as they traced the plastic contours of the cooler, searching for an invisible weakness. Between her own ragged breath and the oily stink of the fish beneath her paws, she very nearly missed it: a barely perceptible draft where the lid met the double-walled body of the cooler. She pushed up against the lid with the soft black nub of her nose, then barked with frustration as it pushed back against her.

Unwilling to budge.

The resistance only made the little fox push even harder.

She growled, energized by the promise of progress—however small—then wedged her snout against the lid. Whether it was weighted down or tied in place, the little fox didn't know, but it creaked slowly open regardless: millimeter by straining millimeter. At the first crack of light, she doubled her efforts. Forcing herself against the bright, razor-thin line with all of her might, her body coiled like a loaded spring as she scrambled with her slipping paws. Designed for lifeless soda cans and picnic lunches, the flimsy lid bent open when it finally yielded, and it wasn't long before the arctic fox had nudged it to the floor. Freed at last, she filled her lungs before stepping out of the cooler and into the sickly white light.

Disoriented and alone.

The ground was smooth and warm beneath her paws, and it rocked gently—from side to side—as she crept along the walls of a long and narrow room. Her legs twitched and wobbled with every step and she fought for balance with her thick white tail, swishing it back and forth in anticipation of the imperceptibly rolling floor. She wasn't on her rocky fjord any longer and—scared and annoyed—she wanted to howl. To bark and whine and gnash her teeth. But the little fox mewled quietly instead, cowed by a natural fear of the unknown.

It was the lack of sky that worried her most.

Even on the darkest winter nights, she'd keep one eye on passing clouds from the moss-lined entrance of her burrow. Without the stars and the salty arctic winds to guide her, the little fox felt lost in time and space. No matter where she looked, there was nothing to help guide her back home: just a tangle of wires and dripping pipes where the moon should have been, and the clang and hum of an engine muffling the roar of distant waves. The little fox scrunched her nose as she bobbed with the roll of the boat, scanning the room for familiar smells.

For *something* to help her get her bearings.

There were so many smells that she couldn't help but sneeze.

Some she recognized, like fish and salty algae—and the grassy stink of melting permafrost. The coolers were no match for the stench of the specimens they held . . . but for every smell the little fox knew, there were a hundred others—and none of them were very nice. Wide-eyed and scared, her nose quivered at the unfamiliar tang of diesel. And burned from a trace of half-diluted bleach that was mopped across the floors. It smelled like home and far-from-home, all at the same time, and the little fox pricked her ears as she crept into the shadows—darting beneath a desk that had been screwed in place with heavy bolts.

Everything in sight was bolted down.

And if it wasn't bolted, it was tied.

Even so, the walls were lined with heavy metal shelves. Some cradled laptops and microscopes and thick manila folders, but most were brimming with scientific samples—and everything was strapped into place to keep it from shifting. Like the cooler she'd escaped from. It was one of hundreds. More than half had been duct-taped closed, with indecipherable names and dates scrawled in marker on the silver tape. The rest were secured with faded yellow bungee cords— a last-ditch replacement for when the tape ran out.

The little fox was lucky.

Her own cooler had been packed in a hurry, with a frayed and sun-bleached rope.

She watched it roll limply on the floor beside the dented lid, no match for the little fox. Not anymore. If she'd been packed up earlier in the day and taped in tightly, like the others—when the rolls of silver tape were thick and plentiful—she might not have made it out alive. A loose bottle of water rolled across the room, following the subtle pitch of the boat. Its wrapper crinkled against the scuffed linoleum floor and the little fox jumped backward, against the wall. Making herself as small as possible. The sharp metal corner of a stowed filing cabinet pressed insistently against the ridge of her spine as the bottle rolled in front of her fish-stained paws, then backtracked across the empty room—tracing the flow of the waves beneath the boat.

Hurried footsteps weren't far behind.

The little fox shivered as they stopped just inches from her hiding place, barely daring to breathe as a woman kneeled to collect the rolling bottle. Her face was so close that the little fox could count every freckle on her wind-burnt cheeks. "You saw the latest forecasts, right?" the woman asked, twisting the cap open and absentmindedly taking a sip. Her companion mumbled, out of view except for the muddy tread of his boots. The little fox's heart pounded as he ambled toward the lid of the cooler and then stopped, considering it from above.

"Because they're no joke . . . ," the woman said.

She joined her friend by the wall of samples.

"It's starting to feel like we should've just stayed home, because we're bringing bad luck everywhere we go." She took another long sip of water, then crushed the empty bottle in her hand as she gestured at the stacks of labeled coolers. "It's sad, you know? These are probably the last healthy samples anyone's going to get from there. And if this thing ends up being half as strong as everybody's saying, we'll be setting up our next camp on Coney Island instead."

Her friend grumbled in assent as he picked up the dented lid.

"This must have fallen," he said. "In the rush."

The woman kneeled again, squinting at the smudges on the floor where the little fox had made her escape. She ran a finger through a shallow puddle of melted ice and peered across the room, into the corners and crevices beneath the shelves—then shook her head and smiled at the vivid depths of her own imagination, her nose wrinkling at the thick and salty smell of fish. The little fox backed up even farther into the shadows and squeezed her eyes shut, not daring to look or even breathe as the woman helped her friend tie the loosened lid back into place and then reshelved the little fox's cooler alongside the rest of their samples.

THE PARIS THEATER, MANHATTAN

December 21, 3:20 p.m.

"Matty, *stop!*" Elizabeth shouted.

"It's okay," Ashley said. "Nobody's around to care."

Elizabeth glowered at Matty, shivering beneath bangs that were plastered to her forehead with melting snow. She was too busy trying to impress their cousin to admit it, but after three whole hours hiking in the snow, the novelty of the blizzard had worn off. His sister looked so wet and miserable that Matty almost felt sorry for her, but if she'd bothered to listen to him for half a second before they'd left the house, she might've dressed for the weather instead of trying to look cool in front of Ashley. It was too late for that now, and it wasn't *his* fault that their never-ending nightmare of a day was starting to get the better of her.

He hadn't even wanted to go outside in the first place.

But wrong or right, it didn't matter anymore.

And it was *way* too cold to fight.

Matty sighed as he dropped his snowball to the ground, his warm breath fogging up his glasses for the thousandth time as he tramped behind their Uncle Jack. It wasn't that fun, anyway, tossing overhanders at stop signs on the empty street. Even with gloves on, his fingers were chilled to the bone—and the narrow limestone channel of Park Avenue was the perfect wind tunnel. Every plodding step he took was a battle against the storm, and Matty's hood billowed like a bright-red sail: filled by frozen gales blowing in from Central Park.

It was just their luck to have to walk into the wind.

If the blizzard had been at their backs instead, they would've flown down Manhattan with effortless leaps: carried by the wind instead of fighting it. As it was, all four of them were doubled over in the middle of the street, their noses pink and running as they pushed their way forward—into the blinding ice and snow, toward the promise of dry socks and warm snacks back in Ashley's apartment. Wherever that was. With the flurries so thick he could barely see, Matty had lost all sense of where he was in time and space . . . and he would've given a hundred dollars just to check and double-check their location on his phone, but his thick thermal gloves were too wet and unwieldy to unzip his inner pockets and bare hands weren't an option.

Not when his fingers were already ice cubes.

Matty lowered his head against the wind.

With one heavy step after another, he traced his uncle's windswept tracks down what was once the dashed center line of Park Avenue, staring at the toes of his boots as they kicked their way through the glowing white snow. Seconds turned into minutes and minutes stretched into hours as the roar and shredded whistle of the blizzard filled his ears. It was better to be walking, is what he kept telling himself: to be outside and on his own two feet and not trapped underground with the rest of New York, waiting for long and empty subways that never seemed to stop. Or skidding across the ice in an out-of-control taxi.

Matty shivered just thinking about it.

But the walking kept him warm, at least at first, and it wasn't long before he'd worked up a thin layer of sweat. Matty could feel it, hot and slick at the back of his neck. Just like back home in Florida. Blizzard or no blizzard, he was tempted to unzip his parka and tie it around his waist. To forge ahead in his T-shirt and bulky gloves, like a big-fisted winter warrior. That is, until the sweat started to chill in his thick woolen socks. Matty's toes curled at the sensation, and he flexed and rolled them in his boots to keep them warm—but there was no middle ground: he was either sweltering hot or so cold he was freezing.

Matty frowned as he checked the street signs.

It felt like they'd been walking forever. . . .

But the frosted signs told another story.

They'd started out at 77th Street, that much Matty knew. It was the name of the subway stop by the museum, spelled out in green and white tiles on the grimy station wall. And most of the streets in Manhattan were like a ladder, with every asphalt rung counting down to Ashley's house: from 77th Street to 76th and 75th . . . all the way down to 14th Street, next to Union Square and his cousin's favorite pizzeria. Just thinking about it made Matty's stomach rumble. Marching home was one of the hardest things he'd ever done, and his thoughts bounced back and forth between the map on his phone and a steaming slice of pizza. He didn't care about the unwashed tables or the dusty ceiling fans. All he wanted was to eat his way through the entire grease-stained menu at Paradise Pizza. But so far they'd only made it to 60th Street—less than twenty blocks from where they started and about a million miles away from home.

Or just about, at the rate they were going.

It didn't seem possible, to have worked so hard and made so little progress, but they weren't the only ones who were taking forever. Matty squinted over his shoulder, searching for the telltale signs of a snow-plow on the horizon. All of the streets in New York were big streets to Matty, but the plows were working their way through the biggest streets first—clearing routes for police cars and fire engines and ambulances, to give them a fighting chance of making it through the blizzard and to whoever needed their help. There were hundreds of plows working overtime to clear the streets, or that's what Uncle Jack said.

And it wasn't that Matty didn't believe him.

It just didn't feel like nearly enough.

Manhattan was over thirteen miles long and two miles wide, and there were a *lot* of blocks to clear. Thousands of them, was Matty's guess. He reached for his phone to look up the number . . . then dropped his hands to his side, remembering his heavy gloves and the tiny zippers on his parka. His fingers were too cold to swipe his screen to life, anyway—and even if he'd been able to stop and triple-check their location at every street corner, it didn't really matter. He was tired and he was cold and the storm was only getting worse. With almost fifty blocks left to hike, the snow was getting so deep that Matty wasn't sure they'd make it home.

Even the plows were having trouble.

Not that he couldn't hear them trying.

The screech of their blades against the frozen streets cut through the howling wind, and he'd even seen them pushing their way through the snow—en route to Fifth Avenue and the West Side Highway. They rolled together, in tiny caravans, with an all-purpose dump truck lagging behind three bright-orange plows. The beds of the dump trucks were piled high with salt and the plows themselves were hulking, like garbage trucks—but with enormous orange blades suspended from their metal grilles with hydraulic lifts. They trundled through the city with their blades lowered, scraping the asphalt clean . . . and the streets *were* clearer in their wake.

But the plows were only shifting the snow.

It had nowhere to go after they passed.

There were no city workers in shiny yellow vests shoveling the snowbanks into waiting trucks for removal, or melting it down into the sewers. In the middle of an active blizzard, there wasn't time for that. Not with so many streets left to clear. The plows pushed the snow to the side of the road instead, piling it so high that it covered both the curbs and the cars that were parked alongside them: hiding them from the world and their drivers, who would have to dig them out after the worst of the storm was over . . .

If they could even find them.

So far, Matty had only trudged across two streets that had been cleared, and the plows seemed to be working so slowly that most of the snow would melt on its own, the old-fashioned way, before they had a chance to clear it all. He'd wanted so badly to follow the wide trails of slush the plows had left behind—to walk normally, without having to worry about snowdrifts or half-frozen puddles of slush—but it would have only taken them farther out of their way, and they were already so far from home. Just thinking about it made Matty trudge a little slower, and the heavy tread of his boots dragged through the snow as he leaned into the wind and sighed.

"Careful!" his sister yelled.

But she was too late.

One second Matty was trudging after his uncle and the next he was on the ground, struggling to catch his breath as he fumbled for his glasses. As soft and pristine as the snow had looked on the surface, the entire jagged island of Manhattan was buried beneath it. Matty learned that the hard way, when the rubberized toe of one of his boots connected with a hidden curb and sent him sprawling—his arms outstretched to protect his face.

The wind knocked clear out of him.

"I'm . . . I'm okay," he stammered, rolling onto his back.

It didn't sound convincing, even to Matty, but nobody could hear him over the storm. Nestled in his parka, he was surprisingly warm as he sank and settled in the snow. It felt good to rest—even if he was doing it in the middle of Park Avenue, laid out on his back and staring up into the streetlights. They were already glowing, Matty noticed, even though it was just a little after lunchtime. Blurred by his perpetually fogged lenses, the snowflakes looked almost like fireflies as they passed beneath the lights, ducking and weaving and surfing the currents and updrafts. Effortlessly racing in the direction of the wind. Matty took a deep breath and sighed, then watched as the warm cloud of his breath rose to meet them overhead.

"You're not hurt, are you?" his sister asked.

Matty squinted up at her, then smudged his glasses clean—or what was left of them, anyway. Their thin metal arms were bent at the hinges and the right lens rattled in its frame as he smeared Elizabeth's face into focus with the thumb of his glove. Wide-eyed, she stared down at him alongside their cousin, their expressions halfway between amusement and concern. Matty blinked up at them as he tapped the pockets of his parka, feeling for his phone.

"He fell *so* hard," Ashley said, announcing it to the empty streets.

"I know," Matty said. "I was there."

But it all happened so fast that he couldn't really remember it.

"I don't think I've ever seen anyone fall that hard before," she said.

Matty bit the finger of one of his gloves and pulled it off with his teeth. As cold as his hands were inside of his gloves, they were even colder outside of them—but cold or no cold, Matty had to find out if he'd crushed his phone when he'd face-planted into the snowbank. Just thinking about the spiderwebs in the jagged screens of all of his friends' phones, it felt like the wind was getting knocked out of his chest all over again. That was the last thing Matty wanted. His uncle joined his cousin and his sister, staring down at Matty as he unzipped his parka and inspected his phone's mirrored face—turning it over in his cold-numb hands and rubbing his thumb across its edges. Feeling for chips in the glass as the snow swirled around his head.

"I think you're bleeding," Uncle Jack said.

Matty shook his head.

"I'm good," he mumbled.

But suddenly, he wasn't so sure.

"He's right," Elizabeth said, pointing at Matty's ungloved hand.

Matty shrugged away from his sister's pointing finger—more out of instinct than anything else—but she was right. Like a big orange plow, he'd scraped against the cement as he'd slammed into the snow. To prove it, there was a trio of light pink scratches on the meat of his palm. Just above his wrist. It could have been worse, but his gloves and his glasses and his parka had borne the brunt of it. The gloves were fine—their pads were tough and reinforced for scrapes and tumbles—and he could bend his glasses back into shape. The slick nylon sleeve of Matty's parka was another story, and his heart dropped just looking at it.

It was just a little rip, barely an inch long.

That's what he told himself, anyway.

It's not anything to cry about.

But fingering the tiny down feathers gathering at its edges, Matty felt an unmistakable pressure building up behind his eyes. The tiny feathers shivered in the wind, on the precipice of freedom, and he clamped his hand over his arm, trapping them in his snow-wet sleeve before they had a chance to fly. It hurt him more than the raw skin on his palms, knowing that his brand-new parka was more or less ruined, and he tried not to show it as he rolled to his feet. Luckily for Matty, he had plenty of distractions. He hadn't been resting for more than a minute, but it was long enough for his ankles to stiffen in the cold. They throbbed in his boots as he found his footing, and Matty groaned as the endless wind buffeted his face.

"You sure you're all right?" Ashley asked.

Matty bit the inside of his cheek and nodded.

Elizabeth raised an eyebrow as their uncle scanned the street.

"That's it," Uncle Jack said, blinking into the wind. "I'm calling it."

The sidewalk exploded in little clouds of snow as he kicked a soggy path to the corner and called for them to follow. Matty dragged his heels at first, staring down at the toes of his boots. The soft, white blanket covering the streets didn't feel so safe anymore. Not now that he knew firsthand how treacherous it could be. The last thing Matty wanted to do was fall again, so he took his time as Ashley ran ahead, feeling the ice crunch and settle beneath his feet with every step. By the time he caught up, his sister was rolling her eyes at him from beneath the sparkling marquee of a fancy-looking theater. Matty rubbed his runny nose with the back of his glove and craned his neck skyward. The sign above the marquee said PARIS in yellow cursive, with a happy little star dotting the *i*.

"Is this Broadway?" Elizabeth asked.

Matty shrugged as he cupped his hurt hand to the door.

Everything was a little blurry through the smudged lenses of his glasses, but the amber glow of a snack bar—and the display cases that lined it, filled to the brim with buttery popcorn—was unmistakable. It felt like they'd stumbled into a golden oasis in the middle of the storm, and Matty smiled so widely that his lips nearly cracked as he stomped the ice from his boots and crossed into the lobby. The black-and-white tiled floor was waxed to a sparkling shine and the heat was cranked up so high that his cheeks flushed on impact. Warming up on the dry side of the glass, it was easy to forget how bad it had been on the outside.

In the never-ending roar of the blizzard.

Especially when the doors closed behind them.

Matty hadn't realized how deafening the wind had been until he was out of it, and now that he was inside—in the hush of the theater—his own labored breathing echoed in his head, much too loud for the gold-trimmed lobby. Old-style jazz played softly from a speaker as his Uncle Jack bought tickets and popcorn from an usher in a shiny black vest with Ashley sulking at his elbow. Matty didn't blame her. His hands were still stinging from his fall and he didn't think he could walk another step if his life depended on it . . . but Fang was still out there, all alone in the blizzard. It wasn't fair, but until they made their way back to Ashley's apartment, there wasn't anything they could do about it. Matty's wet boots squeaked on the waxed and buffed tiles as he turned on his toes, scanning the framed posters on the wall.

Taking stock of their temporary shelter.

The Paris wasn't like the multiplexes back home in Florida.

There weren't any claw machines or photo booths, and the floors weren't carpeted with stainproof swirls of purple and red. There was just a single door to a solitary theater, propped open behind the concession stand, and a flight of stairs to the balcony. Matty's uncle waved them along as he waited for the usher to fill their sodas at the fountain.

"We'll meet you in there," he said.

Ashley slouched against the counter as he pocketed his change, refusing to look Matty in the eye. Matty could tell she was mad—that she wanted to keep moving, to get home so she could look for Fang—and he hoped she didn't blame *him* for stopping. Matty never wanted to go outside in the first place and he would've told her that, too, if Elizabeth hadn't dragged him up the balcony stairs. His hold on the rip in his sleeve loosened as he jogged after her—and then walked, blinking, into the darkness. The theater was mostly empty thanks to the blizzard and none of the artsy moviegoers who had braved the storm wanted to climb the extra flight of stairs to the balcony. None except for Matty and his sister. He felt his way to the center of the very front row and sat heavily in a soft velvet seat beside her, then leaned forward—resting his head on the cool metal railing as he scanned the rows of the level beneath him.

The movie had already started, not that it mattered.

Matty had never been to a theater with a balcony before and he stared down at an old man who was trying to bite the plastic wrapper off a packet of Milk Duds in the soft white light of the screen. The movie itself was in something like French, with subtitles, and Matty could tell that his sister expected him to whine about having to read and watch at the same time. She kept glancing over at him every time any of the actors on the screen said anything—which would have been annoying on any other day, but Matty was happy just to sit down and dry out for as long as he could. He leaned back into his chair, propping his knees up against the railing. It was even hotter in the theater than it was in the lobby, and he sniffled as his nose started to run.

"Everything okay?" his sister whispered.

Matty nodded as he tucked his legs into his chest to make room for his uncle and Ashley. Their arms were brimming with sodas and an oversized bucket of popcorn as they shuffled down the aisle, and he helped himself to a handful as the music swelled, the screen filling with a woman's scowling face in grainy black and white. They'd walked in late, that much he knew, but Matty wondered how much of the movie they'd already missed. Not because he wanted to keep up with the plot—he was too tired to read the subtitles even if he'd wanted to—but because he wanted to know how long he was going to be able to sit down and rest.

It was so exhausting, trudging into the wind.

Through the ice and the slush and the snow.

If it wasn't for Fang, he never would have wanted to leave the Paris Theater—but even though he'd only just sat down, Matty knew they'd have to go back outside sometime . . . and he was already dreading it. Sitting in the darkness, eating fistfuls of warm and salty popcorn, was a like a dream he never knew he had. It was so much like a dream, in fact, that it wasn't long before his eyelids were heavy with sleep. Every time he blinked, they stayed closed for a few seconds longer—until, soon enough, he wasn't opening them at all. He convinced himself that he was following along as actors argued and sang and ordered *"un café, s'il vous plaît"* in a language he didn't understand. But Matty didn't stand a chance. Not against an early afternoon showing of an old black-and-white movie in an overheated theater.

The credits were rolling by the time he stretched awake.

Yawning—and out of habit—Matty checked his phone.

The first message he saw was from their mom.

Just saw the weather, she'd typed. *Call when you can* ☺

Matty's thumb hovered over her number . . . but he didn't have a chance to answer. Not with five unread messages from his Aunt Charley and more coming in every second. Wide-awake, he sat straight up in his chair, oblivious to the theater's brightening lights and the usher waiting to sweep the candy wrappers from the aisles. The fresh scrape on his hand twinged as he scrolled through his texts, his phone buzzing with new, rapid-fire messages while his sister curled up in her seat beside him. She'd fallen asleep, too, and she frowned and twitched at the muffled ring of her own phone, which Matty could see glowing and buzzing in her jacket pocket. It was their Aunt Charley, Matty was sure of it—as sure as he was that something was wrong. The overhead lights flickered as Matty nudged his sister awake, but he was too late.

As soon as Elizabeth's phone stopped ringing, Matty's buzzed to life.

"Hey," Matty whispered. "Wake up!"

Elizabeth grumbled, wiping the sleep from her eyes.

"Just *answer* it, Matty," she groaned—then shrieked as the theater lights flickered on one last time and then died. With the screen completely blank and the projector whirring down, the Paris Theater was even darker than before. Matty blinked the fireworks from his eyes while his uncle jerked awake in his seat, woken by the tumult of the few remaining patrons stumbling toward the twinkling exit lights. The only other sounds were the click and hum of the heating system cycling off and Matty's ringing phone. It echoed in the darkness as he passed it to his older sister, too nervous to answer himself.

"I think we're in trouble," he said.

ROCKEFELLER CENTER, NEW YORK CITY

December 21, 6:30 p.m.

It looked like it was two in the morning when Ashley finally pushed her way out of the overheated lobby of the Paris Theater—and after warming up on their soft velvet seats, the cold, wet blast of the storm hit her like a freight train. She zipped her jacket up beneath her neck and double-wrapped her scarf, shivering as she peered up and down Fifth Avenue. It wasn't just the Paris that had lost its power. Every streetlamp and traffic light in sight had clicked off, and—without the reassuring glimmer of its windows lighting up the night—even the Empire State Building was just a speck of shadow on the horizon. Its steadfast antenna was lost in low-hanging clouds, shrouded in a sky that was both dark and strangely bright, and Ashley bit her lips to keep from cursing as her cousins joined her on the sidewalk.

All she wanted was to get home.

But every step of the way just felt harder and harder.

The streets were supposed to have been plowed while they were inside, for starters. That's what her dad had *promised* her: that they'd wait out the snow in the theater, then catch a cab. That they'd be home "even sooner" than if they tried to walk the whole way down. And he wasn't wrong. Ashley had to grudgingly hand it to him—the roads *had* been cleared . . . but with the blizzard still raging, they'd only filled up with snow again while Matty and Elizabeth napped through three long dance numbers and the closing credits.

Ashley was so mad she could scream.

She kicked her way to the center of the street instead, her long brown hair whipping across her face as she squinted into the storm. It was hard to see more than ten feet in front of her, but Ashley didn't have to see very far to know that there weren't any taxis making their way down the wastelands of Fifth Avenue. Not when the snow was halfway up to her knees—and if the subways were having trouble running on time when the blizzard was just getting started, there was no *way* they were going anywhere in the middle of a blackout.

Which meant they were stuck.

For the second time that day.

"*C'mon!*" Ashley shouted, fighting her way down the middle of the street while her dad mumbled into his phone beneath the darkened marquee. As miserable as it felt to be outside again, she was happy to finally to be moving. To be doing *something*. She'd felt like she was going to lose her mind sitting in the stuffy old theater and worrying about Fang, and as badly as every single muscle in her legs was burning, she wasn't going to stop until she found her.

They'd wasted enough time already.

"Hold on!" her dad yelled.

But Ashley was already running ahead, into the darkness.

She would have slowed down if she hadn't heard them racing to join her—the last thing she wanted was to be even *more* lost and alone in the storm—but knowing that they were at her heels, Ashley didn't even bother to look back. She didn't want to blame them after everything they'd been through. It wasn't their fault that the subways stopped running or that Fang had pulled free from her collar, but not blaming them was harder than it sounded.

Especially with Elizabeth whining in her wake.

"Wait up!" she yelled, already winded.

But Ashley kept jogging.

If she and Matty hadn't been such babies, they could have been home by now—and Ashley wasn't going to make the same mistake twice. She'd tried to do things her dad's way: she'd ignored all of her instincts and gone to the movies when she should've been home, looking for her little dog—and now they were right where they started: one never-ending, seven-hour mile from the Metropolitan Museum of Art. She hadn't even wanted to go in the first place, and as much as she loved him, her dad had already ruined her entire life once.

If Ashley let him, he was only going to do it again.

Now it was up to her to get everybody home.

"Hurry *up*," she shouted.

The light was so scattered by random gusts of snow that her eyes refused to adjust in the eerie glow of the storm, but she could just barely make out a faintly pulsing light in the distance—bright enough that it gave her something to point toward as she dragged her family behind her. Her first hope was that it was a team of plows, and her heart pounded in her chest as she ran, anticipating bright-white floodlights and freshly cleared streets packed with yellow taxis. Taxis that could get them down to Union Square in fifteen minutes flat. Looking back over her shoulder, she waved for her cousins to hurry as they traced her foot-steps through the snow . . . but as she finally neared the source of the pulsing lights, Ashley's excitement inevitably faded.

It wasn't a team of plows, not even close.

The music was the giveaway.

"Jingle Bells."

The happy, old Frank Sinatra version.

It was one of her mom's favorite carols, but muffled by the snow, it sounded so out of place and ghostly that she slowed to a crawl as she crunched across the ice. Inching toward the warbling speakers and into a windswept plaza. The music echoed between the limestone buildings, joined by a high-pitched wail that cut through the night. Offbeat and out of tune, it stopped Ashley in her tracks—and it wasn't long before she sensed her cousins crunching up behind her, casting long shadows in the light of the world-famous Christmas tree in Rockefeller Center.

The tree had been on her list of things to show Matty and Elizabeth.

Before everything went wrong.

Towering over them at eighty feet tall, the twelve-ton spruce was anchored to its base by a network of steel cables. The cables—once taut and stabilizing—were wildly thrumming like guitar strings in the wind, and the tree itself had shifted from the pressure. Its star-topped boughs tilted precariously over the ice-skating rink at its feet while its colored lights twinkled, powered by a backup generator that had clicked on to keep the spirit of the season shining. Ashley couldn't help but stare as the massive tree groaned against its moorings, its heavy branches shedding broken ornaments into the gathering snow while Sinatra sang.

Oblivious to the gale-force winds.

"There you are!" Ashley's dad said.

He panted as he doubled over, catching his breath with his hands on his knees. It wasn't until he finally looked up that he jumped into action, his face twisting in horror at the sight of fifty thousand flashing lights. The Rockefeller Center Christmas Tree was over eight stories tall, and he pulled Matty and Elizabeth back by their collars—shouting for Ashley to follow as it swayed in front of their eyes. It was too far gone to stay upright much longer, and her cousins slipped and tumbled backward through the snow, shielding their faces as the whistling cables creaked and strained against the weight of the falling tree.

But Ashley didn't move.

Transfixed at the sight of her own bad luck in action, she stood motionless, watching as the thick cables stretched and then snapped. They whipped free from their stays with a deafening crack, and—untethered—the big tree groaned as it toppled from its perch above the rink. Crashing into a thick cushion of snow, it erupted in a sparkling cloud of ice that swept upward in the swirling winds, joining the blizzard that continued to rage. Yanked free from their wiring, the thousands of red and green lights wrapped loosely around its core flickered and died.

Plunging Ashley, once again, into darkness.

"Ashley!" her dad yelled.

The crash was so loud that even with her dad shouting her name and the storm howling through the plaza, it was still ringing in her ears as the music on the speakers in Rockefeller Center switched over from "Jingle Bells" to "Joy to the World." Ashley couldn't help but smile at the irony, but her face was streaked with tears as her dad wrapped her in a tight-armed hug.

"It's not *fair*," she whispered.

"I know," he said. "It's not."

Her cousins pretended not to notice as she buried her head against her dad's shoulder, so upset that she was shaking. It wasn't just Fang or the divorce, or the blackout and the blizzard. She literally saw her entire Christmas come smashing down in front of her eyes . . . but it wasn't that either: it was everything at once. *Nothing* was going right anymore, and all Ashley wanted was for things to be normal again—like they used to be—but it was too much to hope for.

Even on Christmas.

The plowed streets—already too packed with snow for taxis—were barely passable, but the weather was no match for the fire department. Drawn by the resounding echoes of the crash, their heavy fire engines pushed through the slush with their sirens blazing. Their flashing red lights were on the scene sooner than anyone would have expected and, startled by the sudden rush of activity, Ashley rubbed her tears dry before they turned to ice on her cheeks.

It was embarrassing enough that her *dad* had seen her crying.

She wasn't ready for a bigger audience.

"It's okay . . . ," her dad said. "For things not to be okay for a while."

Ashley nodded, wiping the frozen snot from her nose with the back of her glove as Matty and Elizabeth pointed a team of firefighters toward the wreckage of Rockefeller Center. Their faces flashed under the strobing red lights as they rushed to Ashley's side, wrapping her and her dad in a silver mylar blanket— like they needed rescuing from the bitter cold. "You're not s'posed to be out here," one of them said, his voice gruff as he led them back to their waiting engine. It was parked haphazardly across the intersection, its wheels so crusted with snow that Ashley could hardly see their thick rubber treads beneath the ice.

"Where are we takin' you?" he asked.

"Just trying to get home," Ashley's dad said, wrapping his emergency blanket around Ashley's shoulders like a cape. She looked at Matty and then Elizabeth. It was hard to tell under the flashing lights of the firetruck, but the rims of their eyes seemed a little red, too. Like Ashley wasn't the only one who'd been crying in the storm. Matty looked nervous, like a cornered mouse, and the arms of his bent and twisted glasses were angled funny on his ears. Elizabeth's jeans were soaking wet, and the way she was looking at Ashley made her feel a pang of guilt for having gotten so mad at them. Their Christmas was just as bad as hers.

And as annoying as they were . . .

They were all in it together.

"I'm starving," Ashley said, climbing up the metal stairs and into the back seat of the fire engine's cabin as the firefighter waved her inside. The seats were so high and she was so tired that she wasn't sure if she could even pull herself up, but once she was out of the snow, she reached out her hand to pull her cousins up after her. She could still feel tears welling up behind her eyes, hot and urgent—but there was no way she'd be able to find Fang in the blackout and in a blizzard. Her legs were so sore that she could barely move, and if the Rockefeller Center Christmas Tree couldn't even fight the winds, Ashley didn't think she stood a chance.

It was better to eat and to rest, and to start fresh in the morning.

Ashley took a deep breath and faced her dad.

"Think we can find a slice of pizza?"

UNION SQUARE, NEW YORK CITY

December 21, 8:00 p.m.

The hot and humid depths of the tunnels beneath Manhattan were even darker than usual, and they'd been that way for hours: ever since the subways had screeched to a shuddering halt, leaving hundreds of trains stranded over six hundred miles of lifeless track. Trapped between stations, the cars were all packed to capacity with sweating commuters in oversized coats, their faces lit up in the sickly blue glow of their phones as they waited for the power to flicker back on—wishing they'd taken their chances in the snow instead of catching the subway.

Not realizing how lucky they were to be *inside* the trains.

Outside, the tunnels were teeming with rats.

Emboldened in the blackout, they scurried around

rail ties and over the steel-toed boots of electricians in yellow hard hats who were hunting for rotting wires and smoking transformers in the steaming depths of the city. Darting past the blinding-white beams of their headlamps, the rats climbed—paw by paw—onto abandoned platforms, their eraser-pink noses quivering with excitement at the stench of overflowing trash cans and discarded bags of chips.

It was so easy to forage, with the stations all to themselves.

Not having to worry about heavy boots and high-heeled shoes, a six-month-old *Rattus norvegicus* hoisted himself up the very center of the subway stairs, his whiskers working overtime as he ventured into the cold. The wind was practically slavering as it howled across the exit, spitting snow and ice down into the darkened stairwell, and the young rat's hairless pink paws shivered as he inched forward and sneezed.

Nothing was ever easy.

Not for a rat in the city.

Rubbing his nose warm with his paws, he blinked into the blizzard and—without a second thought or hesitation—bolted into the unlit plaza of Union Square. The salt had melted icy paths through the storm but they'd turned to slush in the hours since the blackout, so the young rat scurried across the ridges of more solid drifts instead. His tail drew a rough line in the

snow as he ran while heavy gusts of wind ripped overhead, whistling and wailing as they swept through the
darkened city. Blowing snow into the young rat's eyes.

He squinted, momentarily blinded.

Somewhere overhead, the loosening halyards of a
flagpole snapped so wildly in the endless squalls that
they threatened to rip the entire pole from its moorings, and the rat flattened his ears. His fur was already
matted and wet, and his paws were so cold he could
barely feel them. But he'd gone so far already. It didn't
make sense to turn back empty-handed, after so much
effort . . . so he hugged the ground instead, his belly so
low that it was practically sliding on ice as he ducked
and weaved through the snow—following his nose as
he struggled toward the lone source of light on the
street: a restaurant, surrounded by a group of milling
bystanders. The young rat peered at them from behind
the rusted lip of a nearby drainpipe.

Not fearfully, but with a quiet expectation.

The windows of the restaurant were fogged from
the stream of people walking through the door, drawn
like moths to a flame. They ate oversized slices of
pizza from paper plates, bathed in a warm yellow glow
that was powered by the chug of a cheap diesel generator that was revving like a secondhand motorcycle.
The young rat took one tentative step into the light
and then another. Skittering across the cold cement,

his whiskers twitched as he hopped over patches of melting slush and loosened boot laces—his little paws scrambling as a girl dropped her pizza and screamed. As small as he was, and as fast as he ran, a healthy brown rat running across the frosted-white sidewalks in a snowstorm was easy to spot.

He didn't stand a chance.

"Matty," the girl shrieked. "Look!"

Startled, the young rat stopped in his tracks—first staring up at the screaming girl and then down at the bounty she'd dropped: a wide, steaming slice of cheese attached to a crisp and chewy crust. The girl jumped and stumbled backward, tumbling in the snow as she wordlessly pointed. Drawn by the commotion, a small crowd gathered on the otherwise empty street. The young rat spared a nervous glance at them, tearing his eyes from his own good luck. . . .

Then made another snap decision.

He couldn't help himself.

A camera flashed as he crawled onto the oily slice, his paws warming in the gooey cheese—and then it flashed again, blinding the young rat in a startling burst of bright-white light. It was enough to send most rats back down into the safety of their sewers and sub-way tunnels, but most rats wouldn't have ventured out into the ice and snow. Shivering with delight, the rat ignored it. He filled his cheeks with red sauce and hot bread instead, lifting one gooey paw to his mouth and then the other as fat flakes fell and melted on his fur. The boy with the camera ventured even closer as he ate, grimacing behind his phone while the hungry rat settled down on the fallen slice—so happy he could purr.

UNION SQUARE, NEW YORK CITY

December 22, 10:45 a.m.

The power was still out by the time Elizabeth stretched awake, yawning on the foldout couch as sunlight streamed in through the cracks in the curtains. She kicked her legs free from the tangled sheets, so hot that she couldn't bear to sleep a minute longer. It was hard to tell that anything was wrong at first. The accordion-shaped radiators were rattling and steaming beneath ice-frosted windows and Aunt Charley was flipping pancakes at the gas-powered stove. Elizabeth sat up and rubbed the sleep from her eyes, taking stock. Only she and her Aunt Charley seemed to be awake. Matty was curled up beside her, his face sticky with sweat, and the gap beneath the stickered door to Ashley's room was dark.

"Morning," she croaked.

"Oh no," Aunt Charley whispered. "I hope I didn't wake you."

Elizabeth shook her head, glancing at the microwave clock to see how long she'd slept—but the display on the microwave was blank and so was the television. They were lucky the apartment was old enough that nothing important was electric: the boiler in the basement was running full blast to keep the cold at bay, and the burners on the stove were flickering with little yellow flames. The entire room smelled like butter, and Elizabeth wasn't complaining. She'd been expecting cold Pop-Tarts or leftover pizza for breakfast, and hot pancakes were better than those any day of the week. Elizabeth ran her fingers through her hair. . . .

It was full of knots, which meant she'd slept hard.

Hard enough not to remember tossing and turning all night, anyway.

After the day they'd had, Elizabeth wasn't surprised. From the crash at the subway station to their breathless ride home in the back of the fire engine, it felt like an entire week packed into one interminable Wednesday. And that wasn't even counting the Christmas tree that had tried its very best to squash them, or passing out in that old-fashioned movie theater. She could almost convince herself that they'd had fun, thinking back on it from the warmth of her cousin's apartment—bathed in sunlight, with coffee percolating on the stovetop.

Almost.

Elizabeth's legs were so sore from kicking through the heavy snow that she whimpered as she knelt beside her suitcase to search for her brush. Her brother groaned and pulled the covers over his head, hiding from the morning sun as Aunt Charley poured more batter into the pan. It sizzled and popped in the heat, and Elizabeth's stomach growled just hearing it. It felt wrong to feel so comfortable when her cousin's dog was still lost in the storm, but there was something about waking up in a ray of sunshine that made anything seem possible.

Like it could actually turn out to be a good day after all.

Elizabeth smiled as she reached for her phone.

Hoping for the best.

Even with the power out, she'd plugged it in before she'd fallen asleep: out of habit and just in case. She wasn't sure what she'd been expecting, exactly, but it hadn't miraculously charged overnight. There was only a thin, red sliver of battery remaining, so narrow that she didn't even bother to check her texts—and there was no telling when she'd be able to charge it again. Elizabeth took a deep breath and told herself not to worry. Aunt Charley was humming Christmas carols in the kitchen, so it couldn't be *that* bad. As annoyed as Elizabeth was, there wasn't anything she could do about it except take her frustration out on her tangles.

She held her thick hair in ponytails as she brushed the knots free.

Wincing with every stroke.

"I'd offer you some orange juice . . . ," Aunt Charley said, trailing off while she tested a half-cooked pancake with the edge of her spatula. It wasn't quite done, so she flipped it again as Elizabeth joined her at the stove. The stack of pancakes smelled so good Elizabeth could hardly stand it, and she waited until her aunt's back was turned before picking a burnt brown crisp from the belly of the pan and popping it into her mouth. It was hot enough to burn her tongue, but she tried not to show it as her aunt spun back around, flipping the pancake onto a fresh white plate and handing it to Elizabeth. "With the power out, I don't want to open and close the fridge too many times. We don't want to let all the cold air out, you know?"

Elizabeth nodded as she carried her plate to the window.

But it was a funny thing to worry about in the middle of a blizzard.

Panes of wavy glass shuddered in the howling wind, their old metal frames rattling as she opened the heavy curtains and flooded the living room with even more bouncing white light. She'd gone to bed hoping everything would be back to normal by the time she woke up, but New York was almost unrecognizable after a full night of snowfall. Elizabeth ripped a chunk from the steaming pancake and absentmindedly blew on it as she watched the flakes piling onto the brick ledges outside the windows—framing the city in a delicate filigree of ice and frost. The fruit vendors and their red-and-white striped umbrellas were long gone, and so was the traffic.

And not because the streets hadn't been plowed.

She'd heard the scrape of the trucks in the middle of the night and the shouts of the crews that were running them. They'd worked their way up and down Manhattan every few hours, fighting an unwinnable battle to keep the city's streets clear. It was a heroic effort, but the storm didn't care one way or the other. The plows would uncover a black ribbon of asphalt, pushing the excess snow onto the cars that were parked on the side of the street . . . but the second they moved on, a thin layer of flakes would settle down onto the empty street—and then another and another, until everyone was back where they started.

Even then, the snow kept falling.

Elizabeth chewed her pancake, zoning out as her cousin's neighbors shoveled the sidewalks in front of their apartment buildings and dug out their cars. It was almost hypnotic, watching the snow fill in behind them as they worked and knowing that everything would only be buried again when the plows worked their way back down through Union Square. It was a never-ending chore, and as irritating as it was that her phone was dead—and that their big city vacation was practically ruined—the one and only silver lining to the storm was that *she* didn't have to go outside and join them . . . which was lucky for her.

Elizabeth had already seen as much snow as she could handle.

She felt a chill in her hands just thinking about it.

"Breakfast!" Aunt Charley shouted.

Uncle Jack shambled into the living room at the same time as Ashley, wearing a wrinkled button-up shirt and the same the jeans he'd had on the day before. Elizabeth wondered if it was weird for her cousin having her parents together again . . . or if the storm that had forced him to sleep over was like some kind of Christmas miracle. Her eyes darted between Ashley and her Aunt Charley, searching for a sign either way—but her aunt was busy plating pancakes and Ashley was squinting through her fingers, blinded by the unexpected brightness of the living room.

"So what's the plan?" Uncle Jack asked.

Elizabeth shrugged.

But she *really* didn't want to go outside.

The northerly winds that were shaking every window in the apartment sounded eerily like ice-cold knuckles rapping against the glass, and just hearing it made her toes feel numb again. Like they'd been the night before, frozen solid in her boots. She shivered in her pajamas as Aunt Charley served another round of pancakes, pointedly ignoring Uncle Jack, who'd joined Elizabeth at the table. Ashley snatched her pancake from her plate instead of sitting down, and she didn't even bother to use her fork as she paced around the living room.

Considering her options.

Elizabeth followed her cousin's eyes as they darted from the darkened television to the microwave clock and the wood grain of the ceiling fan that was finally stilled, wordlessly confirming that the power hadn't come back on while she swallowed a mouthful of pancake and padded to the kitchen sink. She flipped her hair over her shoulder as she twisted the faucet and drank, then wiped her mouth with the crook of her arm—ducking as her mom swatted her out of the way. Elizabeth sighed, her cheeks ballooning as Ashley collapsed onto the unmade sofa bed.

Even in sweatpants and mismatched socks, her cousin was so cool.

And she wasn't even *trying*.

"I'm going out," Ashley said. "To look for Fang."

That was all it took to get Matty's attention. Kicking himself free from the covers like his life depended on it, he reached for his glasses, fidgeting with their two bent arms before he wiped their lenses clean on the hem of his shirt. If Elizabeth didn't want to go outside again, Matty was dead set against it. He shot her a warning look across the dining room table, and

Ashley tried her best not to roll her eyes in acknowl-edgment. Elizabeth had promised to listen to him, but technically—as his older sister—she was in charge.

At least, she should've been.

If Matty actually listened to *her* for once in his life, he never would have tripped or ripped his jacket. Elizabeth pulled her hair into a tight ponytail while her cousin paced to the window and stared out into the snow, then sighed as she reached for her phone. She pretended not to notice her brother glaring a hole through her face as she tapped it to life . . . just in time to watch it die, along with all of the important travel stuff she'd stored on it: emergency phone numbers and flight times and Aunt Charley's address. Her mom had even scanned their birth certificates for some reason ("just in case you need them") but Elizabeth couldn't get to any of it anymore. Staring into her own reflec-tion in the lifeless screen, she suddenly felt lost and far from home.

She didn't even know her own number by heart.

Much less her parents' phone numbers.

She'd pinky-promised to check in with them every day, to let them know that she and Matty were doing well. She'd meant to call them when she had a chance— she really had—but that chance never seemed to come. Not when they were trudging through so many miles in the snow, in the blizzard and the blackout, with their fingers freezing in bulky gloves that didn't work with their phones. It sounded like such a lame excuse in the warm morning light, but she couldn't help it: Elizabeth had been so exhausted that she'd almost fallen asleep while she was struggling up the last flight of stairs to her cousin's apartment. Her pulse quickened as the ghosts of unanswered texts and voice mails taunted her from her darkened phone.

It was still warm in her hand, but it was totally useless.

And their mom was probably worried sick.

"Matthew," she hissed.

She wanted to sound calm and collected in front of her cousin—like nothing was wrong—but even if she'd been able to hide the flutter in her voice, there wasn't anything she could do about her flushing cheeks. Elizabeth could feel them pulsing, like flashing beacons on an ambulance, and she wanted to hide them beneath the covers as Ashley arched a brow beneath her perfectly sunlit bangs. She tugged her brother's sleeve instead, trying not to make a scene while her cousin stared goose bumps into the back of her neck.

"Lemme see your phone, okay?"

Her voice sounded flat and soft in her own ears.

So soft that she wasn't sure Matty had even heard her until he held his phone up so she could "see" it and quietly scrolled through forecasts. He acted like he was some kind of genius, but he could be so dumb, wasting batteries while the power was out. Back home in Tampa, she would have just pulled the phone from his hands—commandeering it until her parents made her give it back—but they weren't back home in Tampa, and for some reason it felt wrong to act like they were. Elizabeth took a deep breath instead, biting her lips to keep from shouting.

The last thing she wanted to do was fight in front of her cousin.

"We have to call home," she said.

She even managed to force a smile as she plucked the phone from her brother's hands and thumbed her way through his contacts. It didn't take long: there were only five of them, including Elizabeth. Outside, she could hear the scrape of plows making another pass at the asphalt while neighbors endlessly shoveled their invisible walks. The snow fell so thickly that it looked like a second curtain, hung on the wrong side of the shuddering glass—but watching it from the breakfast table with the smell of fresh coffee and pancakes filling the room, she could still almost convince herself everything was going to be okay.

That Ashley was going to find her little dog.

And that their vacation was going to be fun again.

"Sorry we didn't check in last night . . ," Elizabeth said, racing to fill her mom in as soon as she picked up. "We were outside all day and the power went out and it's a whole long story, but we're having a lot of fun here!" She was determined to sound cheerful—to make all of her Christmas dreams come true by sheer force of will—but her tight-lipped smiled faded along with her hopes for the day when her parents put her on speakerphone to break their bad news.

Their flights to New York had been canceled because of the storm.

Elizabeth swatted her brother's hand as he reached for the phone.

But all of a sudden, her heart wasn't in it.

34TH STREET—HERALD SQUARE, NEW YORK CITY

December 22, 2:00 p.m.

Fang's golden fur was black despite the snow after a long and greasy night spent ratting in the humid depths beneath the city. The subway tunnels were finally starting to chill as the cold air sank beneath the frozen streets, but Fang was sheltered from the wind and her purple tongue lolled contentedly from the side of her mouth as she bounded down the center of the lifeless tracks—so dirty that a pair of overworked electricians searching for faults in the power lines almost thought she was a rat when she jumped up their legs, barking for attention. The shorter one in a yellow vest was so startled that he even dropped his heavy flashlight.

"How'd *you* get down here?" the other one asked.

Fang scrambled as he lifted her up onto the subway platform. Finally free from the mud of the tunnels, she didn't wait around to thank him. There was too much to smell and so much to do, and her snout quivered with excitement as she raced up the empty stairs of the 34th Street subway station. Except for the clangs and grumbles of the electricians she'd left in her wake, the station was eerily deserted . . . and so dark that she had to follow her nose just to find her way out of it. The tunnels were so stale—their air heavy with a century's worth of mold and accumulated soot—that Fang sneezed as she ran, leaving a trail of dirty paw prints behind her.

She'd expected to breathe freely when she made it outside. . . .

But the stairs didn't lead her up to the streets of New York.

They spit her out into the atrium of a fancy indoor mall instead.

Her booties slipped on polished marble floors as Fang trotted beneath four vacant levels of shops, considering her options. The smaller stores were all locked up for the blackout and there was no one left in sight: not a manager stocking shelves and not even a lowly subway rat. With nobody around to scold her, she paced between two marble columns and into the showroom of a giant department store. Muffled in the distance, she could hear the storm. The swell and scream of it was unmistakable, and Fang's footsteps echoed behind her as she raced through racks of hundred-dollar dresses, jostling delicate displays and knocking perfume samples to the floor as she made her way to the front of the store—and a wall of big picture windows overlooking Sixth Avenue.

The windows were full of fake snow and wrapped gifts.

But Fang didn't pay them any mind.

Disregarding the intricate displays, she pushed her way between three elfish mannequins and clawed her way onto a life-size model of Santa's busy workbench. The glitter-dazzled windows fogged in front of her hot and sour breath as Fang stared out into the snow, whimpering until she finally caught the attention of a man who was slowly and laboriously shoveling the walk. He seemed shocked to see her on the other side of the frosted glass, foul from the subway and covered in grime—furiously barking on top of a table stacked high with clean wooden toys and European chocolates. He fumbled with the keys on his belt as he stared right back at her . . . and it was only a matter of seconds before he'd unlocked a wide, revolving door and unceremoniously shooed Fang out of the mall and onto the sidewalk.

The air was so fresh and so cold that she shivered on impact.

It was what she'd wanted in the first place.

To explore outside again, in the snow and the city.

But after what felt like a lifetime in the stifling

tunnels beneath the city, the roaring arctic wind was even stronger than she remembered. Especially in the shadow of the Empire State Building. Just one short block away, it towered a hundred and two stories over her head and channeled blasts of frigid air down Sixth Avenue and 34th Street. Fang could feel the downdrafts *lifting* her booties from the frozen ground, and—panicked at the thought of blowing away—she flattened her belly onto the shoveled pavement as she inched her way into deeper and deeper drifts. Even with the gale-force winds, it was tempting to try to walk where the sidewalks had been scraped down to their shimmering concrete, especially with legs as short as Fang's—but she felt more anchored in the ice and snow, so she took the hard way instead: jumping and tunneling her way past an entire block of darkened Christmas displays.

Her wet tail shook between her legs as her nose trembled in the wind.

Sniffing out the warmth and safety of another subway station.

And all of the rats inside it.

JUST OUTSIDE OF PHILADELPHIA, PENNSYLVANIA

December 22, 3:35 p.m.

"Hang on as long as you can," Joy said, double-checking the display on the truck's massive dashboard with one eye on the road. She'd been driving for two and a half hours already and had been fielding calls on her headset the entire time. It was almost funny, shouting to be heard above the hum of the highway in the empty cab of the borrowed truck with the heaters turned up as high as they would go. And barely tall enough to see over the steering wheel. A grinning bobblehead of Albert Einstein nodded from his perch above the glove compartment, taunting her with his pink nub of a tongue as she stepped on the gas.

"I'll be there in two hours . . . three hours, max."

If the weather holds up, she thought.

But Joy kept that to herself.

Except for a few roadside accidents, she hadn't run into any traffic since she'd climbed into the driver's seat, and the last thing she wanted to do was jinx herself. She popped a handful of M&M's into her mouth instead, chewing nervously as she eyed the horizon. There wasn't any definition to the clouds or any telltale smudges of rain and snow. Just a formless swath of gray and the odd droplet racing up her windshield. Joy turned on the wipers, but she didn't slow down. She couldn't afford to, not when every minute mattered. With the steel mini-plow mounted in front of its menacing grille, the truck was so heavy that she'd had to fill up the tank two times already . . . and she was going to have to floor it if she wanted to make it past New Jersey before nightfall, while she still had a chance of pushing through to New York.

If she ever even had a chance in the first place.

Joy leaned forward in her seat, peering past the winding black ribbon of Interstate 95 and into the middle distance. It was easy to feel invincible in the big white truck with the National Climatic Research Center's logo splashed across its doors, but at a certain point the borrowed truck and its plow wouldn't do her any good. Even if she stopped to add chains to the tires, big trucks like Joy's got stuck all the time—trapped in snowbanks with their wide-set wheels screaming for traction while their drivers cursed and waited for a tow.

Or for the snow to melt.

Whichever came first.

Joy didn't have time to wait—not after her phone call with the captain of the *Mjölnir*. She shook her head clear and turned on the radio, twisting the dial until she landed on a weather report. It wasn't hard to find: all of the stations were taking regular breaks to breathlessly report on the unexpected cold front that had descended on the Eastern Seaboard. She flipped through them as she drove, changing the channel every time a deejay called it a snowpocalypse or joked about a Snowmageddon. They were the same recycled nicknames Joy heard every single year, and the endless puns made her eyes twitch. If they had any idea what was coming, they wouldn't be laughing . . . but she couldn't really blame them. Not when the subtleties of global weather systems were too intricate for Joy to wrap her head around half the time.

And she *worked* at the NCRC.

Joy rolled her fingers on the steering wheel.

It was easier to crack jokes than it was to think about melting glaciers, anyway—especially in landlocked Pennsylvania, a sixteen-hour flight from the nearest fjord in Greenland. The ice sheets felt too far away from the rolling foothills of Appalachia to matter, even when they were flooding the oceans with enough cold, unsalted water to flip the planet's entire circulatory system upside down and backward. It was already happening, right in front of their eyes: the vortex of strong winds that circled the poles and trapped cold air in the Arctic was weakening while ice floes dripped and disappeared beneath the waves.

Freeing the freezing cold air to roam wherever it wanted.

It was Mother Nature at her most ironic: the more the North Pole melted, the colder everybody got. Or that was the theory, anyway. As far as Joy could tell, there wasn't a precedent for the arctic blast that was currently working its way down the Eastern Seaboard: past Bangor, Maine, and Boston, Massachusetts, and all the way to New York City, which meant there wasn't any telling how far down it would go—or how cold it would get.

Even for the scientists at the NCRC.

Their simulations were like complex machines full of well-oiled pistons and glistening spinnerets, and the ice melt in the Arctic was like tossing a wrench into the gearbox. There was just no predicting how the planet would react . . . but Joy had been trained to think in terms of worst-case scenarios, and everything she'd seen and heard told her to expect the worst. The last little ice age had ended in the 1800s, not so long ago that she couldn't imagine another one—but after months of unseasonable warmth, nobody was preparing for more than a few feet of snow, not even the emergency management commissioners she'd been calling all day.

They all thought it was just a passing squall.

And it was their *job* to be prepared.

Joy took a deep breath.

The wipers had started squeaking, struggling to clear the rain as it turned to tiny pellets of hail and then snow. They left white streaks of ice in the clouded half-moons of the windshield while Joy fumbled to activate the defroster, heating the glass from the inside. Not that it did any good. Even with the wipers running smoothly again, the oncoming snow was so thick that it was all Joy could see. She leaned forward in her seat, crouching over the wheel as her headlights reflected off the enveloping whiteout. A million individual flakes of snow shined back at her, blinding her as they rushed across the steaming hood of her F-250.

Beyond them, the highway had turned to mush.

She could feel it more than she could see it.

Joy clenched her fists on the steering wheel as her tires crunched and splashed across the frozen blacktop. It had happened so quickly—the sudden turn into winter—that it had taken her by surprise, even though she'd been expecting it the entire drive. It was why she'd taken the truck with the plow in the first place: you didn't head straight into a blizzard without expecting a little snow. Not when you were driving a modified NCRC plow truck, anyway. But the plow didn't do Joy any good if she couldn't see, and she'd lost all sight of the road except the two red taillights of the semitruck in front of her. She kept her eyes trained on them as she slowed to a crawl, letting them guide her as her wheels settled into the shallow grooves of its icy tracks.

"You can do this," she said, barely daring to breathe. *You can do this.*

Her phone vibrated on the seat beside her and Joy ignored the call, focusing on what little she could see of the road ahead as her ringer blasted through the speakers in the tiny cabin. She felt for the volume knob and twisted it down, so all she could hear was the squeak of the wipers and the buzzing of her phone on the empty seat beside her. As soon as it stopped ringing, it started again. Out of habit and annoyance, Joy glanced down—checking her phone's display for half a second to see who was trying to reach her.

Half a second was all it took.

That and a slick patch of ice, buried in the snow.

Almost as soon as she took her eyes off the road, Joy knew she'd made a mistake. She could feel the steering wheel pulling away from her as the heavy truck slid out of her control and she stomped her foot on the brakes, pressing the pedal into the floorboards with all of her might . . . but it didn't make any difference. The family-sized bag of M&M's that she'd propped on her lap shifted and spilled as Joy slid out of her lane, the little chocolate candies showering her feet while the big truck spun slowly but inevitably to the side of the highway. It wasn't until it finally stopped—a quarter-twist away from a nearby gully—that she realized she'd been screaming. And that she was still screaming, alone in her truck . . .

Her ears ringing along with her phone.

Joy twisted the keys in the ignition, quieting the truck's engine while she stared blankly into the dark cluster of trees that were lining the highway. She was shaking so hard that the keys jangled in her hand, but even after it nearly killed her, the snow was somehow calming now that she wasn't racing into it anymore. Joy stared as it drifted and gathered on the heavy boughs of the windswept pines, like it was a real-life Christmas card. Right outside her fogging window. For the thousandth time, she wondered what she was even doing with her life: running toward danger when she could've been at home, with her family and her roommate's cat.

All of her friends were home with *their* families.

For all she knew, they were making homemade peppermint bark and drinking hot chocolate while she headed straight for the heart of the biggest winter storm in recorded history. If she could even stay on the road long enough to get there. Joy swallowed, her breath catching in her throat as her adrenaline surged. It didn't seem fair. . . .

But she didn't have a choice.

Joy's phone buzzed to life on the passenger seat,

and—recognizing the number that was flashing across its display—she tapped her headset before it had a chance to ring, startling her colleague on the other end of the line. "Do me a favor and patch me through to the *Mjölnir*," she said, trying to sound collected and professional—like she hadn't just been one bad second away from flipping her massive truck clear off the asphalt and into a snow-filled drainage ditch. The dashboard lit up as she turned the key in the ignition and pulled slowly back onto the highway, her heart pounding in her chest. Visibility was so low that she could hardly see anything except for heavy flakes speeding into the squeaking wipers—but it wasn't going to get any better the longer she waited. Joy reached for a joystick mounted beneath the rearview mirror and caught the look of determination in her own eyes as she lowered the plow into position.

Just in case.

PART

THREE

THE LITTLE RED LIGHTHOUSE

HUDSON RIVER, NEW YORK

December 23, 5:45 a.m.

A solitary doe broke away from her herd, her white tail flagging behind her as she leapt down an impossibly steep embankment and onto the frozen expanse of the Hudson River. Her legs splayed—briefly, at her knobbed and wobbling knees—while she slid across the ice, but she managed to keep her balance until the soft inner pads of her elegant black hooves found traction in the windswept snow. It was thinner on the river than in the wooded cliffs of the Palisades, where it had piled so deeply that even the deer were running out of food.

The doe's nostrils flared as she sniffed the wind.

With the underbrush buried beneath three full days' worth of never-ending snow, half of her modest herd had taken to fighting the sparrows and robins for the bright-red holly berries that dotted the hillside while the rest stripped the soft, green bark from sapling pines. They would've preferred to forage for acorns—or fill their bellies with the dried corn that hunters sometimes left as bait to lure them out of the shrubs and into the sights of their carbon-fiber crossbows—but they didn't have a choice. They needed to eat, to maintain their weight through the lean winter months, and a handful of berries wasn't nearly enough.

Not for a three-hundred-pound deer.

The tendons in the doe's long neck tensed as she waited, poised and attentive—like a ballet dancer in coal-black slippers—while the rest of her herd pushed and jumped their way through the snow and past the steel pilings at the base of the George Washington Bridge. They'd lived near the busy river their entire lives and visited its muddy banks at least once a day, but they'd never thought to cross it. Their haunches quivered as they stepped tentatively onto the ice. It was the farthest any of the whitetails had ever ventured, and the big gray bridge that towered overhead felt both strange and familiar as its thick cables sang ominously in the wind.

An older buck stamped his hooves.

Testing the ice.

It vibrated like the head of an otherworldly drum beneath his heavy frame, but the frozen water seemed to hold his weight. It held *all* of their weight, and the weight of the snow that continued to fall—hiding any sign of the wide river that marked the westernmost border of the whitetail's roaming. The herd cocked their ears, listening for the creak of telltale cracks in the ice . . . but the only sound they heard was a hawk screaming through the haze, its rust-dipped feathers rippling as it circled in the updraft above the steel lattice bridge.

The buck looked to the waiting doe.

She twitched her tail, anxious to keep moving.

It was cold on the water, but not any colder than it had been on the wooded cliffs of the Palisades—and their thick winter coats were built to handle the weather. It was food she needed. They were already starting to lose their summer fat to the blizzard, and their entire herd couldn't depend on bitter bark for long. The wide river hardening for the first time in over two hundred years was a sign they couldn't afford to ignore. It unrolled before them like a red carpet to greener pastures, and with their home behind them, the big buck shook the snow from his antlers and launched himself across the Hudson. The doe and the rest of their herd followed his lead: racing beneath the shadow of the bridge, toward the darkened skyline of Manhattan.

And into the unknown.

They leapt after the big buck in single file, letting

him clear a path with the broad wedge of his chest as the snow-muffled river echoed distantly beneath their hooves. Without any trees to block the wind, the storm didn't swirl and eddy so much as blast across the makeshift plains, painting the herd in matching white with rough and frigid strokes. The visibility was so low on the open ice that it wasn't long before the doe had lost sight of the buck and his proud ten-point antlers. She focused on the flickering tail of the fawn directly in front of her instead, trying not to think about the sickly crunch of the Hudson beneath her hooves or the rumbling in her gut. There wasn't anything she could do about either—except to trust her own instincts.

Kicking one tired leg in front of the other.

And trying not to fall through the ice.

The wind howled even louder as they reached the midpoint of the George Washington Bridge, drowning out the shrieks of the hungry hawk and the doe's own labored breathing. Not falling on the ice was easier said than done, and her hooves slipped with every step. The doe snorted in annoyance, blinking the snow from her eyes. Through the flurries, on the far side of the river, a single light winked brightly through the pre-dawn gloom: a little red lighthouse—a relic from older times, dwarfed and forgotten beneath the darkened bridge. Its gas-powered lamp shone brightly from behind frosted glass panes, guiding the ragged herd of deer with a wavering beam that was barely strong enough to cut through the storm.

Despite the slippery ice, the herd surged forward.

The doe quickened her pace, glancing skyward while they shifted—as a unit—toward the flashing white light. Without course-correcting, they might have followed the gentle curves of the river all the way down to the thinner ice of New York Harbor, through the Narrows and out to the white-capped waves of the ocean beyond. But lost on the ice in the middle of a blizzard, it was doubtful they would have made it that far. The doe was panting by the time she climbed the rocky bank, her coat glistening with snow at the foot of the lighthouse—and then darkening again as the herd pressed forward, into the murky fog of the city.

And out of the worst of the wind.

MADISON SQUARE PARK, MANHATTAN

December 23, 9:45 a.m.

Ashley chewed her wind-chapped lips beneath the long, warm scarf she'd double-wrapped around her nose and mouth. A gritty layer of salt had melted the roughly plowed roads into a patchwork of slush overnight, but the arctic blast was so bitterly cold that it had only frozen over again, icing the six-block stretch between Union Square and the small dog run in Madison Square Park. Not counting every smelly trash can on every single street corner, it was Fang's favorite spot in the city—and after checking all the stoops and sheltered doorways from the East River to the Hudson, Ashley didn't know where else to look. Her throat might have been raw from screaming Fang's name into the wind for the second straight day in a row. . . .

But she hadn't given up hope.

Even if everyone else had.

"C'mere, girl!" Ashley shouted.

Wishing she'd thought to bring a cough drop.

She'd barely had time to tie her laces before she'd rushed out of the apartment, though, jumping and tripping down the stairs before her mom could change her mind. Her mom had said the storm was "too dangerous" now—as if being outside was any *less* dangerous for Fang—and it didn't help that Matty kept whining about polar vortexes and deadly superstorms to anyone who was bored enough to listen. Ashley didn't blame him for being scared after the big tree at Rockefeller Center had toppled in front of their eyes . . . but she almost regretted that it hadn't squished him when it had the chance after he convinced her mom to put their search on hold until the weather cleared.

She would've done it, too, if Ashley's dad hadn't been there.

Promising to make sure that nobody would get hurt.

He was doing a *great* job of that now, Ashley thought, smirking as she watched him running and gliding down the center of Broadway with his arms outstretched. With her aunt and uncle stranded down in Florida for the holidays, he was doing his very best to make a bad Christmas better for her cousins—and so far, it almost seemed to be working. Elizabeth was shrieking and laughing like a toddler on ice skates while her brother sulked behind them. On any other day, Ashley would have tackled Matty onto the snowbanks and tickled him into a reluctant smile, but it felt wrong to fool around while her mom was riffling through kitchen drawers, searching for extra candles and fresh batteries for their emergency radio.

And when Fang was still lost in the snow.

It was one thing to try to cheer her cousins up . . .

But her mom wasn't *wrong*—the storm had gotten so bad that the mayor had even called a state of emergency. They'd all heard the announcement on the same crackling broadcast the night before, and Ashley was pretty sure it was illegal just to be out on the streets. If it wasn't, it should've been. Her socks were soaking wet and bunching at her toes, and her scarf was so coated with windswept ice and snow that she felt like a popsicle. In all of her years in New York, she couldn't remember ever having felt so miserably cold . . . and hearing her dad and Elizabeth laughing on the frozen streets only made her feel worse. If Fang had been safe at home, she would've been happy just to hide in her room until Christmas was over.

To stay inside and shelter in place, like the radio said.

She just had to find her dog first.

Ashley scanned the snowdrifts for the waving flag of Fang's tail, but she couldn't help but watch Elizabeth slide past an entire block of eerily empty storefronts with mountains of snow piled up against their double-locked doors. There were almost two million people on the thirteen-mile-long island of Manhattan and eight million in the city as a whole, not counting tourists. With less than forty-eight hours before Christmas, the streets should have been packed with last-minute shoppers and sightseers from all over the world ... but they'd been walking for twenty-five minutes so far and except for a few lonely supers shoveling the short strips of sidewalk in front of their buildings, Ashley hadn't seen anyone else on the streets. There weren't any coffee carts parked outside of subway stations or Salvation Army Santas ringing their bells.

Even the pigeons were gone.

Ashley shivered as goose bumps tickled the back of her neck.

She'd argued with her mom all morning for the privilege, but fighting the wind as she trudged through the ghost town of her own neighborhood was even worse than she'd expected. It had only taken a couple of days of heavy snow to shut the entire city down, and even if her aunt and uncle still somehow managed to board a flight—if they got all the way to New York without turning back, or making an emergency landing in Charlotte or Pittsburgh—there was no way they'd be able to make the short trip from the airport to Manhattan. The subways hadn't been running for days and the roads that were plowed were still too slick to drive on. They were almost too slick to *walk* on, and every traffic light from Brighton Beach in Brooklyn all the way up to the Cloisters was lifeless and swinging in the storm.

The entire island was an accident waiting to happen.

Still, it was better to be outside than trapped in her tiny apartment.

Ashley felt like she'd been slowly suffocating in the crowded living room, with ancient radiators steaming beneath every window and her two cousins brooding on the couch while her parents pretended that everything was going to be okay (when it very clearly wasn't). The airport wasn't going to magically start rescheduling flights, and Fang wasn't going to trot through the front door like some kind of Christmas miracle. Everything *wasn't* going to be okay, and as much as Ashley might have wanted to spend the holidays together—as a family—she couldn't imagine a worse winter break than watching her mom and dad exchange painful smiles over the cluttered breakfast nook, stuck in the same room for the first time in months.

It was enough to make her want to scream.

She'd spent the better part of the morning digging through closets instead. With the power out, there wasn't anything better to do, and state of emergency or not: nothing was going to stop Ashley from leaving the house. Even if it meant borrowing an old pair of tie-dyed ski pants she'd found in a tub beneath her mom's bed. She kind of liked them, actually. Not that she'd admit it, but it didn't matter either way: no one was around to see her—and everyone looked a little funny, anyway. Matty was wearing bright-red sweatpants beneath his jeans, and Elizabeth had stuffed herself into so many layers that she could barely move her arms.

It was worth it, though, to be outside in the fresh air.

And not freezing to death in the storm.

The wind blew waves into her thick brown bangs as they worked their way up to Fang's favorite park, a fenced-in patch of dirt in Madison Square next to a fancy burger place that sold Milk-Bones on the side. It was a short walk from their apartment off 14th Street, and it usually only took about ten minutes to get there. That was on a good day, but with the blizzard shrouding every street sign and landmark in a thick layer of snow, Ashley wasn't even sure where they were . . . much less how far they still had to go. She strained her neck to peer down cross streets, but it wasn't until they reached the unmistakable intersection of Fifth and Broadway that she was finally able to gather her bearings. With Elizabeth shrieking on the ice, it was hard to say for certain, but she even thought she heard a muffled growl in the distance.

"Did anyone hear that?" Ashley shouted.

Matty spun on his heels so fast he tripped over his heavy boots.

Elizabeth laughed as he tried to regain his footing, his legs slowly spreading into an uncertain split—then lost her own balance. Skidding across the ice, she lurched toward a half-buried mailbox and hugged it with both arms, clutching it like her life depended on it. Her cousins were bundled up in so many extra sweaters and sweatpants that Ashley didn't think she would've even felt it if she'd fallen, but seeing Elizabeth struggle to stand on her own two feet made Ashley much more nervous than she was ever used to feeling . . .

Like she was suddenly Elizabeth's babysitter or something.

Like she was *everyone's* babysitter.

Her dad was just as wobbly as her cousins on the ice, and Ashley didn't even want to think about him falling. The last thing they needed was for someone to break an arm or a leg. Even if she had a fully charged phone to call an ambulance, there wasn't any way it could get to them, and—watching Matty crab-crawl across Fifth Avenue—Ashley surprised herself by wondering if she'd made a mistake. If they should have just stayed home, sweating on the couch and playing awkward games of Scrabble instead of sliding through the storm.

The streets of New York weren't a playground.

Especially not in the middle of a historic blizzard.

"Over here!" Ashley shouted, trying and failing to keep the sharp edge of annoyance out of her voice. The building she'd stopped beneath was triangular and pointing uptown, the narrow point of its limestone facade cutting through the wind like the prow of a giant ship. Ashley backed into the divot of its revolving door, hiding from the downdraft as best she could—but there was no escaping the freezing winds. They were so strong that they were whipping settled snow up into a vortex over the intersection of Fifth Avenue and Broadway.

Ashley shivered as she squinted into the seething storm.

Even shielding her face, the snow was so thick that it was like staring into a cold glass of milk—but she swore she could see something moving. It was hardly a smudge on the ice, no more than a shadow of a shadow in the wind-scoured slush. But Ashley's heart pounded in her chest as she pricked up her ears, listening for a sharp and friendly bark in the wind. Red-faced and panting, her cousins were still stumbling toward the half shelter of the revolving door when she finally heard it: a yelp in the distance, muted by the winds and the icy sludge.

And headed straight for Madison Square Park.

Which meant she was actually right.

That Fang was still alive.

"Is that her?" Matty asked, his eyes widening behind his fogged and twisted glasses. Ashley didn't bother to answer as she pushed past him. Her throat was so ragged from the cold that it hurt to scream her dog's name as she sprinted into the middle of the street, but Ashley didn't care. The ice crunched reassuringly beneath her boots as she slipped and tumbled toward the blur. *Toward Fang.* Ashley was so focused on her little Pomeranian that she didn't even notice her dad rushing out to join her until she heard him laughing at her side.

"You actually found her!" he said.

Ashley could hear the smile in his voice as her own tight smile spread across her cheeks, but she didn't dare celebrate or look away. Not now that she finally had Fang in her sights. Creeping through the wet and heavy snow, she held up one gloved hand for silence— not wanting to startle Fang into a gallop as she shifted her approach. As it was, the little Pomeranian was still just a mirage in the middle distance: completely motionless except for the black nub of her nose, which trembled at the end of her snout as she pointed toward the wind.

Like a wolf on the hunt.

"C'mere, girl!" Ashley whispered.

Then surprised herself by laughing.

Even with her freezing wet feet, it wasn't *not* funny to see such a small puppy looking so very serious— and she was suddenly bursting with so much relief that she was either going to laugh or start crying. But Ashley stopped smiling when Fang lunged suddenly forward. Not wasting a second, both Ashley and her dad sprinted wildly across the ice—their boots gliding like skates over Fifth Avenue while Matty stomped reluctantly behind them, kicking his way through the snowdrifts with his head lowered against the storm.

"Wait up!" Elizabeth hollered.

But something wasn't right.

Ashley slowed as they approached the curiously glacial square of the park, then stopped completely—in the middle of the street—as her dad gripped her shoulder and silently pointed toward a mass of shadows in the distance. Matty caught up in time to shudder at the sight of them, his face slack with wonder as he turned to his uncle for confirmation.

It didn't seem real to Ashley either.

But Fang must've known they were there all along.

A herd of deer, happily swishing their tails as they grazed on the low-lying hedges that bordered the wrought-iron fence around Madison Square Park. In the middle of a blizzard, in the middle of Manhattan. When they finally stepped into focus and out of the milky-white haze, Fang howled so wildly that the deer stopped in their tracks. Ashley could feel her cousin tensing beside her as their eyes locked with a doe and an enormous stag—its wide rack of antlers black against the snow—but she couldn't bring herself to move.

And even if she could, she didn't think she could run.

She'd only slip and fall on the ice.

Or scare them into a panicked stampede.

Matty's fingers dug into Ashley's arm, through two layers of sweaters and a winter coat, as three brown fawns with white-speckled backs joined the stag and the doe, their noses twitching in the wind. The seconds seemed to stretch into minutes as Ashley stared back at the stag, so swept up in the strangeness of the moment that she felt like she was watching it unspool in slow motion. And then speed up, suddenly and without warning, as Fang charged straight into the herd of deer—barking so sharply that they flattened their ears.

Ashley screamed, her voice cracking in the wind.

She wanted to chase after her.

To catch her before she got trampled.

But with Matty clutching one arm and her dad gripping the other, Ashley could only stare in horror as the stag stomped and snorted at the fuzzy cannonball that was bounding across the ice. It wasn't until she was in biting distance that he leapt out of the way, his rippling haunches springing into action as the entire herd bolted across the park and toward the banks and jewelry stores of Madison Avenue. Fang wasn't slowed by her short legs or the thick layer of snow. She took off after them, her frantic barks echoing into the swirling maelstrom as she disappeared without a single backward glance. With hot tears streaming down her face,

Ashley sprinted after her—tumbling through the slush as she shouted Fang's name into the wind.

"Come back!" she screamed.

But it was too late.

Her little dog was already gone.

MADISON AVENUE AND 26TH STREET, MANHATTAN

December 23, 10:00 a.m.

Matty stomped hard with every step, pausing to make sure that the thick rubber treads of his new winter boots wouldn't slip before he pushed forward. It was slow going, but there was a slick layer of ice hidden beneath the snow. He could feel it crackling beneath his heels, where the sidewalk should have been. The plastic tag that had come attached to the bright-red laces on his boots had said their soles were "high traction" and "expedition-proof," but that didn't stop his ankles from wobbling in the slush—one wrong move away from a twisted ankle.

Or even worse.

Matty shivered just thinking about it.

He'd already fallen more times than he could count.

Falling was inevitable when they were sliding on

the ice, and over time he'd learned to lean into his falls, controlling how and where and—most importantly—*when* he landed. It was half art and half science, and mastering the technique as he staggered up the frozen streets to Fang's little dog park might have even been fun under other circumstances. But having the world slip out from under him, completely unexpected, was something else entirely. Tripping against the cold concrete on their way to the movie theater, he'd hit the ground so hard he'd lost his breath, and the sickening thud of his own body against the ice echoed like a warning in Matty's ears.

It was better not to trip, if he could help it.

"Ashley!" he shouted. "Wait up!"

The blizzard was screaming down the wide and empty streets so fast that Matty had to fight to stay upright, and he was sure that nobody could hear his voice above the fray. But he had to try. Without his cousin and his Uncle Jack, he and his sister would be as lost as Fang on the windswept tundra of New York. Matty tried to focus on the swirl of Ashley's tie-dyed ski pants instead of worrying himself into a full-blown panic attack. His cousin's pants were a neon explosion in the white canvas of the storm, and Matty told himself to just keep walking. That he'd be fine as long as he could see their Day-Glo pinks and greens through the snow.

He tapped his pocket as he hiked.

Absentmindedly feeling for his phone.

Its constant alerts and satellite connections weren't doing him any good now that it'd lost its charge, but he couldn't help himself. It was a nervous habit, and Matty was a hundred times more nervous than he'd ever felt before. Even during the yearly hurricanes back home, he and Elizabeth had always had their parents by their side to reassure them . . . and to drive them to safety at the very first sign of a storm. Matty tapped his phone one last time, for good luck, then took a deep breath. His heart was pounding so loudly—so *insistently*—that he could actually hear it beating alongside his own labored breathing, the pulsing soundtrack to a brand-new nightmare he hadn't even thought to have: being lost in New York City.

During a blizzard.

In the middle of a state of emergency.

Matty glanced over his shoulder to check on his sister, then turned all the way around, standing with his back to Ashley and their uncle for as long as he dared. They were already so far behind that Uncle Jack was barely a speck in the wind—but Matty couldn't help it. With his face shielded from the wind, he could feel his cheeks begin to thaw . . . and the snow looked almost peaceful as it danced around Elizabeth's shoulders.

Not that you would know it from looking at her.

Her nose was bright red and sniffling above her oversized scarf as she followed the shaggy outlines of his footprints, grimacing with her entire body pitched forward against the storm. It almost hurt just to watch her struggle—but Matty had *tried* his best to warn her. He'd tried to warn all of them, and it was his own sister who decided not to listen. *After everything they'd been through.* He was still so mad at her that he could slam a hundred doors . . . but not mad enough that he would've let her walk out into the snow without him.

That was their family's number one rule.

Stick together, no matter what.

Matty didn't have the energy to waste on being upset, anyway. Just walking up Madison Avenue was like crawling their way through a wind tunnel—as if the entirety of the superstorm was funneling down into Midtown Manhattan just to sweep them off their feet. Gliding up from their cousin's apartment to the dog park had been so easy in comparison. Sheltered from the weather, the tall limestone buildings on either side of the street had borne the brunt of the blizzard while his sister and Uncle Jack had skated through their shadows.

Above the park, though, everything had changed.

Steeling himself, Matty turned to face the arctic blast.

The snow was flying so fast and hard that it felt like a thousand frozen pinpricks on his chapped and tender cheeks, and he gritted his teeth—grimacing, like his sister—as he peered down the skyscraper canyon:

searching the blindingly white snowdrifts for an unmistakable smudge of neon. They didn't have time to
stop and think, much less overthink . . . not with Ashley widening the distance between them with every
passing second. Matty shouted his cousin's name
again, straining to hear his own voice over the roar of
the wind.

But it wasn't any use.

All they could do was press on.

Matty stared down at his boots as he stomped and
paused, over and over again, focusing every ounce of
his attention on not falling on the ice. *And not falling
too far behind.* It was a balancing act, and so much
harder than it sounded. His glasses were so perpetually fogged that he could barely see the thin line of a
path that had been salted into the sidewalk and then
frozen into slush again. He rubbed a clear spot into the
lenses with his bulky gloves for the hundredth time,
wishing the deer had chosen a better street to dash
down. Wherever the snow was thin enough to walk
through, the streets were so slick that you couldn't—
and every block they'd walked was like walking a mile.
Matty wanted so badly to duck onto a side street . . .

To get out of the wind, even if it was just for a
second.

But not if it meant losing sight of Ashley.

"Look!" Elizabeth shouted.

Startled, Matty jumped—then slipped . . . then

finally steadied himself, grasping on to the soft shoulder of his sister's overstuffed jacket for support. Every spot was a blind spot in the blizzard, at least for Matty, and he hadn't expected to hear her voice so clearly through his triple-insulated hood. She'd crept up on him while he was stomping, like a ninja: her crunching footfalls masked by the endlessly howling wind. Matty took another deep breath, filling his lungs with super-chilled air, and smudged the fog from his glasses.

"What is it?" he asked, not waiting for an answer.

His glasses slipped down the snow-wet bridge of his nose as he squatted, clearing the crumbling ice away with both hands—then digging down into the drifts so he could see the cloven prints clearly. Even without looking them up on his phone, Matty knew what they were. Deer tracks. There was nothing else they could be, and he'd been so focused on Ashley's pants that he hadn't even thought to follow them. Biting the thumb of his glove, he pulled his hand free so he could trace their outlines with the tip of his finger. They were smaller than Matty expected, and it wouldn't be long before they were covered with a fresh layer of snow.

Like they were never even there.

"We must be close," Elizabeth said.

Matty nodded as she held on to his shoulder with one hand—for balance—and shielded her eyes with the other, peering into the middle distance while she shouted Ashley's name into the wind. Even if she was out of earshot, they should have been able to spot her. The snow was so thick on the ground that it made the scaffolding-lined corridor of Madison Avenue seem almost narrow, and everything in sight was so brilliantly white that she would have stood out like a beacon. Even the birds were white. Matty squinted at a flock of gulls with short black legs and beady eyes. They looked so strange and out of place as they lazily pecked at the snow where pigeons should have been, their alabaster feathers ruffling in the wind.

And behind them, a flicker of movement.

Too small to be a deer . . . *but maybe a puppy.*

"Fang!" Matty shouted, taking off across the ice.

The gulls scattered and screeched, wheeling overhead as he barreled down the street—his careful stomp-and-pause routine momentarily forgotten as he chased shadows in the snow, like the little Pomeranian before him. It was exhilarating, to feel the ground sliding beneath his feet with every footfall as he kicked through the delicate tracks, running so fast that he could barely hear his sister calling his name over the wet slap of his boots against the snow. He wasn't sure if it was a hard-earned momentum or just one long fall that he was trying to outrun, but Matty felt like he was flying as he sprinted into the wind—his calves burning from the effort.

But it wasn't Fang stalking strange migratory birds in the snow.

It was his cousin, Ashley.

And she wasn't hunting anything.

She was sitting cross-legged in the snowdrift where she'd fallen, a blur of frosted winter clothes against a chunky mountain of ice that was left over from an earlier plow. Her woolen scarf was unwound around her neck as she cradled her head in her hands, oblivious to the world around her. By the time Matty registered the flash of her pants in the snow, there was nothing he could do. He braced himself for impact as he charged across the street, halfway between sliding and tripping—shouting his cousin's name as his ankles slipped out from beneath him.

But it was too late.

By the time she looked up, they were already midcrash.

Caught off guard by their sudden collision, Ashley screamed as they rolled onto their backs in an awkward tangle of boots and elbows. It all happened so fast that Matty's head spun while he stared up into the looming gray clouds, feeling first for his glasses and then for his phone. With everything accounted for, his first instinct was to laugh as he rolled to his knees, sweating despite the cold as warm waves of relief washed over him.

They were still in a blizzard on the streets of New York.

And the weather was only going to get worse.

But at least they weren't alone anymore.

"Yes!" he yelled, punching his fist against the wind— and then stopping himself as he noticed Ashley shivering on the snow beside him. She was crying, and Matty crouched beside her, his excitement curdling back into a sickening worry as he checked her arms and legs for unexpected angles. Their thick winter clothes could save them from skinned knees, but they couldn't stop a bone from breaking, and Matty eyed the bend of his cousin's wrists as she wiped the tears from her cheeks with the rough pads of her gloves.

"Are you hurt?" he asked. "Did I hurt you?"

Staring past him, Ashley shook her head.

"I couldn't keep up," she said.

She blinked Matty into focus.

"I couldn't stop her."

The snow had turned to hail again in the time it took Matty to stand up and dust the ice from his knees. It was so sharp against his face that it hurt to look uptown, but that didn't stop Matty from trying to spot his Uncle Jack. He was still chasing Fang and the herd of deer up the middle of Madison Avenue, doing his very best to save Christmas. But Ashley *wasn't* okay. Matty could tell by the way she was cradling her arm against her chest, so he shouted into the winds and waved his arms over his head, his adrenaline pumping so hotly in his chest that he didn't even think twice before he took off sprinting after his uncle.

"Wait up!" he yelled.

Matty stomped as he ran so he wouldn't slip again, his new boots landing hard enough to crack the ice with every heavy step he took. His Uncle Jack was still too far away to hear him over the storm, but with Ashley crying on the ice, Matty was determined to catch up . . . and he surprised himself by gaining ground with every frozen corner he passed. It felt good, fighting his way into the storm and winning—for once in his life. He couldn't wait to tell his friends back in Florida that he'd chased a herd of deer through the city, up strangely frozen streets he'd never seen before. He only wished he'd been able to charge his phone before they left so he could take a picture. None of them were going to believe him without some kind of proof. Matty grinned into the depths of the blizzard as he spared a half glance behind him, just long enough to see that his cousin and sister were so far behind him that *they* were the specks on the horizon. . . .

And then—before he knew it—Matty wasn't running anymore.

He was tumbling down a set of metal stairs.

Into the belly of a fully stocked storeroom.

MADISON AVENUE AND 34TH STREET, MANHATTAN

December 23, 1:30 p.m.

"Matty!" Elizabeth yelled. "Come *on!*"

She had no idea how long she and Ashley had been looking for her brother and their Uncle Jack, but the sky was darkening so quickly that it was already starting to look like night—and the darker it got, the colder she felt. Elizabeth shivered beneath two borrowed sweaters and her winter jacket as she hiked back up the empty street, retracing their steps for what felt like the thousandth time. And wondering where her brother could have possibly gone. The middle of the street was crisscrossed with countless footsteps through the heavy snow, and as far as Elizabeth could tell, half of them belonged to her and the rest of them were Ashley's.

She still didn't understand what had happened.

One minute, Matty was squatting next to Ashley on the ice and the minute after that, it was like he'd disappeared into thin air. Even Ashley couldn't tell her where he'd gone and she'd been *right* there, watching him sprint through the snow after Uncle Jack. It wasn't brain surgery, it was Madison Avenue, and Elizabeth had been shouting his name up and down the same stretch of it for hours . . . but she still didn't have a clue where he'd gone.

"This isn't funny anymore!" she screamed.

The colony of strange white gulls that had flown in with the cold air seemed to scream along with her, mocking Elizabeth from the same arctic winds that were making her life so miserable she could barely stand it. She *knew* Matty wasn't hiding on purpose, even though he'd been sulking all day about her "breaking her promise" and making him go outside in the snow. At first, she'd hoped he was just trying to make her worry. And if he was, it had worked. She'd been worried, and then she'd been mad at her brother for making her worry.

In fact, she'd been *furious.*

But now—after scouring the same street for hours, when her legs were so tired that she was more stumbling and falling than walking—Elizabeth felt as cold and empty as Manhattan itself. Everything that could go wrong was going wrong, and she would have given anything for Matty to pop out of some hidden storefront. To tell her it was all some big prank. Elizabeth closed her eyes, letting the frigid waves of panic and hopelessness wash over her. As much as she hated to admit it, her brother hadn't been wrong about the storm. It was fun to try to act tough in front of her cousin and pretend that a little snow was no big deal, but she wished she'd listened to Matty after their first long day on the ice, when the power went out.

Or when their parents' flights were canceled.

It was too late for that now.

The clouds were racing so quickly above their heads that Elizabeth couldn't even look up without feeling dizzy. Like the entire world was spinning so fast that she might fall off of it. It didn't help that the squalls were only getting stronger. Elizabeth pushed through them, tumbling forward into the snow and shouting Matty's name while the storm churned overhead—so suddenly dark that it swallowed whatever was left of the day. Ashley shouted at Elizabeth to slow down, yanking at the hem of her parka as flashes of lightning crackled in the depths of the ominous sky, like lightbulbs exploding behind a cotton candy veil.

The thunder was quick on its heels.

And so loud it was deafening.

"Over here!" Ashley shouted.

She tugged Elizabeth beneath the narrow lip of a sheltered doorway as the blizzard turned into a full-fledged superstorm. Right in front of their eyes, like Matty said it would. Elizabeth wanted to sit down in the hail and cry. Wherever he was, she hoped her brother was safe and warm inside. But it wasn't like there were a bunch of open stores he could be hiding in. Every building they passed was locked and bolted for the blizzard, and the cheerful Christmas wreathes and garlands that had been hung from their doors with elaborate bows and ribbons were all grounded by the wind and waterlogged beneath two feet of frozen snow.

"I'm sure he's with my dad," Ashley said.

She was so cold that her teeth were actually chattering.

"They might have even gone home, to w-w-wait for us. . . ."

"I'm not leaving without him," Elizabeth snapped, so forcefully that her cousin bit her lip to keep from arguing. Her anger had numbed into a trembling shock and desperation as they searched through the snow, but Elizabeth could feel it starting to warm her up from the inside out all over again. And she was just getting started: she was mad at Ashley for dragging her out into the blizzard . . . but she was even madder at herself. None of this would have happened if they'd all listened to Matty—and now, when she needed it most, she didn't even have a phone to call him with.

To check if he was okay.

She tried to think like her brother, to put herself in his shoes.

But Matty wouldn't willingly be out in the storm in the first place; he'd be home. And he couldn't have gone far, anyway. He'd been running for two minutes max, and then he was gone. It didn't make sense. Elizabeth tried to focus as the hail bounced down from the stone lintel above their heads and landed in the snow, to think her way into finding her brother and their Uncle Jack. The pellets themselves weren't any bigger than a pencil's pink eraser, but with all of them falling at once, they were so loud that they sounded like a freight train. Ashley leaned against Elizabeth for warmth and Elizabeth leaned right back, wrapping her arm around her cousin's shoulders as they stared out into the hail—wondering what they should do.

It isn't fair, Elizabeth thought.

All she'd wanted was a normal vacation.

Instead, she'd tried to help look for Fang in a blizzard and now her brother was missing. Hiding from the wind, Ashley pulled her scarf up to cover her entire face. It was still just after lunchtime, but it felt like midnight—and the streets were only getting colder the longer they waited. Her cousin was still cradling her arm from when she'd fallen, and with the temperature dropping and the hail punching angry little holes in the snow, Elizabeth wasn't sure how much more of the storm either of them could take. Hot tears streamed down her face and into the pom-pom on Ashley's hat, their trails blown dry by the wind before they had a chance to freeze.

"It's all my fault," she whispered. "I'm the worst sister in the world."

"Not true," Ashley mumbled. "I wish I had a sister like you."

Elizabeth just shook her head as she cried.

She'd actually *lost* her brother.

But before she had a chance to explain how wrong her cousin was, Madison Avenue came alive with the familiar wail of passing sirens. Ashley was still tangled in her arms, but Elizabeth jumped onto the sidewalk so quickly that her cousin tumbled into the snow-drifts behind her . . . and Elizabeth's heart seized up in her chest when she saw it: a bright-white box of an ambulance, tracing their footsteps up the middle of the street so slowly that it was barely moving. Time seemed to stop in the strobe of its flashing red lights as it pushed its way through the snow, and Elizabeth didn't even bother to shield her face from the hail as she chased it.

"Matty!" she screamed.

She felt so suddenly sick to her stomach that she wanted to puke, but she jumped into action instead. Sharp little pellets of hail bounced off her cheeks and her shoulders as she sprinted in the flattened grooves that the heavy tires of the ambulance were leaving in the snow, powered by a hot rush of adrenaline and fear. She could hear her cousin pounding in her footsteps, and she didn't even stop to look back as she followed its tracks all the way up to 34th Street, where the ambulance veered into a lane of recently plowed asphalt and sped off into the storm. Its sirens blared and echoed behind it—lighting up the street as Elizabeth fell to her knees, breathing so heavily that she was worried she might actually pass out in the snow.

"I thought . . . ," she huffed.

Ashley rubbed her back.

"It's okay," she said. "They're okay."

If Matty had ended up in an ambulance, Elizabeth never would have forgiven herself. But now they were right back where they started. Only a little more tired and a longer walk from home. Elizabeth brushed off her pants as she stood in the middle of the street, staring up at the towering silhouette of the Empire State Building and wondering how she—of all people—had ended up in this situation. Her cousin was probably right. Matty was probably with Uncle Jack, hanging out in the warmth of Ashley's apartment and waiting for them to come home. Elizabeth was just about to follow the trail of the ambulance back down to Madison Square Park for one last loop when she heard it: a muffled voice in the hail.

"Is someone out there?" the voice yelled.

Elizabeth stopped in her tracks.

There was a warm square of light emanating from the sidewalk.

She wouldn't have noticed it in the sparkling brilliance of day, but with the city cloaked in its strange arctic shadows, the open cellar door beamed up out of the ground like a portal into another dimension. A portal that was powered by the chug of a hidden generator. With Ashley at her side, Elizabeth crunched over to its snowy ledge—where the two rusted metal sheets of the flimsy cellar door were bent inward, forced free from their hinges by a heavy, stomping boot. At the bottom of the stairs, trapped beneath a pile of metal shelves and covered in snack-sized bags of plantain chips and dusty cans of soda, was Matty.

"Little help?" he squeaked.

TIMES SQUARE, MANHATTAN

December 24, 1:25 a.m.

Times Square was unrecognizable in the dark.

Without the flashing lights and the billboards—and the long ticket lines for fancy Broadway shows—it was just another intersection covered in snow. Fang had scrambled past more than thirty of them already, following her nose from Herald Square to Bryant Park and beyond. She'd even taken a short detour after losing sight of the deer, contentedly gnawing on a frozen ball of falafel in a toppled garbage can for a full fifteen minutes before carrying it out of the wind and down the stairs to Grand Central Station . . . where she'd quickly lost interest. There were too many distractions underground, and after tailing a waddling brown rat back into the storm, she'd finally made her way to "the Crossroads of the World."

It had been a short trip by normal standards, barely over a mile.

But Fang had even shorter legs.

With her belly so low to the ground, it hadn't been easy to fight her way through the snow. She'd had to jump and dig across heavy drifts that the stag had barely noticed . . . but there were advantages to being short. Especially in a blizzard. Her low center of gravity kept her stable on the ice while the strongest gusts blew clear over her head, leaving her free to trot beneath buildings that would have towered over the little Pomeranian if they weren't hidden by a thick, ethereal gauze. If she'd been any taller, she might have raced home with her tail tucked between her legs—or flown away like a kite, borne aloft by the same winds that banged against stop signs and strained sun-damaged awnings past the point of breaking.

Luckily for Fang, she was the perfect size.

The proud plume of her tail curled over the back of her bomber jacket as she padded up 45th Street, her wide-set eyes trained just beyond her paws as she traced invisible lines in the snow—tracking down the most promising smells she could find with the short nub of her nose. There would have been more on a hot summer day, without the wind to disperse them. On her morning walks around the local park, Fang had stumbled across everything from dusty chicken bones to greasy hot dogs that had slipped their buns. And that wasn't counting the savory exhaust from a thousand restaurant vents, or the sun-warmed garbage in metal trash cans up and down the entire length of the island. But even with the streets frozen down to their rusted grates and the deer long gone, there was so much to smell in Manhattan.

And almost all of it was well within reach.

Even for a Pomeranian.

For a while, she was happy to explore.

Her fur was thick and coarse beneath her bomber jacket, and her body was so warm from her crosstown marathon that she was panting—even with her narrow ankles exposed to the cold above her booties. After a few days on the run, she'd finally gotten used to them, and her tongue lolled from the side of her mouth, her lips curled up in a black-lipped smile as her hot breath clouded and then evaporated in the wind. From her wire cage at the shelter where she'd met her new family for the very first time to the two-bedroom apartment where they lived, Fang hadn't seen much of the world . . . and what she *had* seen had been from the end of a leash.

As much as she loved Ashley, she'd never had a chance to wander.

To chase down every single scent that came her way.

A team of plows trundled across the square in single file, their bright-white headlights cutting through the gloom as Fang sidled farther into the shadows. They'd been working through the night—and for entire *days*—without stopping, ever since the first snowflakes had started to fall. The crews running the trucks worked in shifts so there was always someone clearing a path across the asphalt, even though you wouldn't know it from looking at the streets. No matter how much they cleared, the blizzard just kept blowing—and the more the plows shoveled, the higher the snow piled along the sides of the roads.

At a certain point, there was nowhere else for it to go.

Once soft and airy, it compacted under its own accumulated weight, forming miniature glaciers that locked cars and fire hydrants in solid blocks of snow and ice before overflowing onto the slush of salted sidewalks. While New Yorkers slept, growing snowdrifts quietly claimed the gated stoops of their darkened brownstones, step by slippery step. Like an invading army from the frozen North, they pressed against creaking doors, working their frost-numb fingers into any cracks or crevasses they could find as tireless winds rattled bedroom windows.

By all accounts it was a historic storm.

A "superstorm" is what the newscasters were calling it.

Nobody in the city had watched the evening news to see the winter storm advisories climb from yellow to orange to red, or heard the breathless coverage by red-cheeked reporters in snow-encrusted anoraks. Not on day three of the blackout. But the creaking and wailing just beyond their walls told them every- thing they needed to know. For everyone who still had power, the footage was on every channel from Califor- nia to Connecticut: instantly recognizable streets and tree-lined avenues covered in snow so high you could swim in it. The last official update from the Central Park Weather Station had reported the depth at over fifty inches.

It was the highest they'd ever recorded.

And then the updates had ominously stopped.

Nestled at the foot of Belvedere Castle, a nineteenth- century marvel presiding over the snow-scoured lawns of Central Park, the weather station was less of a station than an assortment of equipment locked in an unassuming chain-link enclosure. Rain gauges and humidity sensors automatically sent readings to the computers at the NCRC in Washington, D.C.—but measuring snowfall wasn't quite so easy. For that, park stewards in dark green anoraks and thermal gloves had to shuffle out from the castle's stony embankments to check the heights on meteorological measuring sticks they'd planted across the park, like wide-ruled flowers.

It wasn't a perfect science.

Earlier in the storm, the rough-hewn footpaths to the west of the castle were barely dusted with a thin layer of powder while the frozen Turtle Pond to the north was hidden under entire feet of it. In an ideal world, averaging and sharing their measurements would have been easy, but in the real world—in the bone-shivering chaos of the superstorm—half of the measuring sticks had been buried beneath gently sloping drifts while the rest had been toppled by the same winds that made the sensors on top of the Belvedere's spires whir so fast that they whistled. Without power, the castle hadn't shared any new readings in hours, and with no new readings, there was no way of knowing exactly how dire the storm had become.

Only one thing was certain.

No matter how many plows were out on the streets, they weren't any match for the snow. If something didn't change, the city was going to be iced under until spring—and, unwilling to wait that long—a team of scrappy orange bulldozers had joined the struggling plows. They trailed behind them on thick steel treads, carting endless piles of snow into what looked like a room-sized cauldron that had been erected in the middle of Times Square. It steamed in the cold-white glow of generator-powered floodlights, melting the snow into a briny, rock-salt soup that was siphoned down through industrial hoses into the sewers below. Fang recoiled at the smell of it, her sensitive nostrils quivering as the dozers unloaded their buckets.

Feeding the mega-melter.

The melter rumbled as water rushed out of its

base and into the bowels of the city, and Fang barked—
unsure of herself—while the dozers beeped and backed
into the darkness, digging up more snow for the sewers. They moved in jerks and starts, their headlights
staring past the little Pomeranian like unblinking eyes.
Fang squared her shoulders for a fight, the curve of
her tiny incisors glinting in their reflected light. Every
mega-melter that had been deployed across Manhattan could thaw a hundred and thirty tons of snow per
hour, and the dozers were working as fast as they possibly could to fill them.

But Fang didn't care.

She'd hated the dozers as soon as she heard them.

Barking her throat dry as she ran from drift to drift,
she circled the bumbling dozers in a wide and wild arc—
much too small for the drivers to even notice from the
comfort of their heated cabs, even if they could have
heard her over the rumbling engines. The farther Fang
strayed from the hardpacked snow, the farther she sank
beneath its glittering surface, and it wasn't long before
she was jumping through deeper channels. Undaunted,
she pushed forward through the slush, bounding up
onto the hood of an ice-locked taxi. Its mustard-yellow
frame was buried in a wind-blown ramp of sparkling
snow that led all the way up its frozen windshield and
onto its yellow roof. The winds were stronger so high
above the ground, and Fang squinted as she turned to
face the steaming melter and the orange dozers that

continued to fill it, undeterred by the little Pom. Now that she was on more equal footing, she was sure she'd be able to get their attention.

To make them know that Times Square was *hers*.

But it was all Fang could do to keep her balance on the slick metal roof.

Her booties scrambled for traction as she crouched behind its lifeless rooftop lights, trying and failing to hide from the freezing cold winds. With the greasy tufts of her fur plastered so tightly against her skin, she looked more and more like the rats she'd been chasing up Madison Avenue: wet and cold, and far too small to be out in a blizzard so big. Fang puffed out her chest and barked at the dozers anyway, giving them one last piece of her mind before she found herself hopelessly caught in a wind so strong that it lifted her up into thin air before tossing her onto the ground. She landed with a sickening thud, her whimpers lost beneath the clang of the dozers and the bellowing storm as a sharp and sudden pain shot through her paw.

She knew as soon as she felt it that her adventure was over.

That it was finally time to go home.

If she could even make it that far.

CONEY ISLAND, BROOKLYN

December 24, 6:25 a.m.

Joy pressed her shoulder against the truck's door while she jiggled its handle, pushing as hard as she could to break the thick rime that had filled its narrow gaps overnight and frozen the heavy door to its frame. When it finally crackled open, she tumbled out onto the ice—along with half a dozen plastic wrappers and a gallon's worth of empty cans that clattered at her feet. Her lunch and dinner and super-caffeinated breakfast, in that order: chocolate bars and gas station jerky and soda for all three. Seeing them laid out in the cold light of day was enough to make her nauseous, and she felt the sour splash of bile rising in her throat as she tossed them back onto the floor of the empty cab that had been her home for the last forty-one hours.

Give or take a couple of minutes.

Joy stretched her arms over her head, cracking her knuckles.

She hadn't even come *close* to making it past New Jersey before nightfall.

The blizzard had made sure of that. What should have been a quick four-hour drive on I-95 had turned into twelve hours of gridlock . . . and that was just the start of her nightmares. There'd been a pileup outside of Trenton and another near New Brunswick, where a semitruck had toppled on its side, its crumpled trailer capsized across three entire lanes of traffic. She was so shocked at the sight of it that she'd pulled onto the shoulder of the highway and wrapped her tires in anti-skid chains as soon as she made it past the first bottleneck.

But chains or no chains, it hadn't felt safe to keep pushing on.

Even with a mini-plow mounted beneath the grille of her truck.

It wasn't the snow so much as the other drivers on the road that worried Joy, anyway. Even the biggest plows would have been helpless against them, so she'd slumped down behind her steering wheel instead of inching back into the molasses-slow stream of traffic, her eyes glazing over as an endless stream of taillights blurred beyond her fogging windshield. She'd sat there all night, snacking her way through a plastic grocery bag full of junk food, her windshield wipers straining as the snow turned to hail. When she'd sensed the deepening snow cocooning around her, she'd braved the elements just long enough to dig her truck out of the ice with a stiff brush and flimsy plastic shovel she'd found wedged beneath the seat.

But she didn't nod off, not even once.

It was too cold for that.

Joy had shivered in the darkened cabin instead, not wanting to keep the engine idling for fear of running out of gas. When the traffic jams finally cleared in the small hours of the morning, she'd twisted her key in the ignition and turned the heater on high before pulling back onto the icy blacktop—just long enough to take the first plowed exit she could find and park beneath the covered entrance of a roadside motel. She didn't remember checking in or passing out on top of the over-starched duvet . . . but she must have, because she'd woken up in the late afternoon of her second day on the road still wearing her winter jacket, with her muddy boots dangling off the end of the bed and her phone ringing through the last of its batteries.

Luckily for Joy, her Motel 6 still had power.

She'd splashed warm water on her face beneath the fluorescent bathroom lights, then charged up her devices enough to check in with the captain of the *Mjölnir*. She was cutting it closer than she'd wanted— but with a little luck, she was still on track to meet the Polar icebreaker off the southern tip of Brooklyn. The deputy director of the Office of Emergency Management in New York had been a lot less optimistic. Urging her not to come over a crackling connection, he'd explained that their twenty-four-hour command center was snowed in so tightly that they were more or less trapped. The arctic blast had hit them even faster and more forcefully than the NCRC's elaborate models had predicted, and the mayor had ordered every bridge and tunnel closed until the plows could catch up with the storm. Until then, the city that never slept was on total lockdown as they pivoted from emergency preparedness to damage control from a makeshift bunker at the foot of the Brooklyn Bridge.

Even if Joy somehow managed to make it all the way to New York...

It wasn't safe there.

Not now that they were in the thick of it.

Hundreds of bright-orange plows and bulldozers had been deployed in the greater metropolitan area, each outfitted with a tracking system that allowed the Office of Emergency Management to monitor the street clearing remotely—for as long as their generators were still chugging, anyway. The roads might have been filling up as soon as they were cleared, but with the blizzard raging beyond anyone's wildest expectations, clearing a path for electricians to work on the blackout was the most they could hope for. In the meantime, all they could do was wait out the storm.

Stay-at-home orders had been issued for anyone who could hear them and shelters and hospitals across the city had been filled with warm cots for anyone in need.

The last thing they needed was one more person to rescue.

And if Joy had a choice, she might've listened to him.

There was nothing she wanted more than to be back at home, watching old monster movies with her niece's cat, but that ship had sailed as soon as she'd pulled out of the parking lot in Washington, D.C. For better or worse, Joy was on the job now—and if conditions were really as bad as they sounded, the best place for her to do that job was on board the *Mjölnir*. The big ship was outfitted to spend entire months trapped in the ice, with satellite linkups and a fully stocked cafeteria, and as tempting as it might have been to turn around and drive back home . . . Joy had a feeling that they hadn't seen the worst of the storm.

And there was no telling how bad it was going to get.

The Eastern Seaboard was already locked in a state of emergency, and setting up a mobile command center on a twelve-ton icebreaker felt like a smarter choice than risking another sleepless night in infinite gridlock. Or spending the holidays all alone in the middle of nowhere, helplessly checking the news on her phone while she waited for the power to go out. With chains wrapped around her tires and the plow lowered and ready for action, the abandoned streets of New York were a more promising option for her over-sized truck.

Especially since Joy had a beast of a boat to catch.

She'd just have to make her way to Coney Island to meet it.

On a clear day, it would've been a quick two-hour trip, but it had taken her another twelve hours in the driver's seat to get there. Peering past the beams of her headlights into the static of oncoming snow, she'd carefully inched through thickening layers of sleet and ice—working her way beneath an iconic skyline that she wouldn't have even known was there if it wasn't for the soft glow of the touch-screen map that was guiding her through the pearly haze. A few hours before dawn, her plow had scraped clear of the asphalt and onto the slick wooden planks of Coney Island's boardwalk. She was too tired to celebrate as she stomped her way past the battened down snack shops and T-shirt stores that lined the beachfront.

But she'd finally made it.

Joy wiped her watch face clear as she scanned the horizon.

She knew it was a long shot, meeting the *Mjölnir* in the middle of a storm, but she didn't have plan B tucked away in her back pocket and she definitely didn't have another drive in her. Not when she was so exhausted that she could barely stand. A graffitied metal gate rattled in the wind, and Joy turned to see the candy-colored spokes of Coney Island's Wonder Wheel glinting reassuringly overhead. At a hundred fifty feet tall and a hundred years old, the steel Ferris wheel towered over the entire boardwalk—including the vintage roller coaster at its feet.

The world-famous Cyclone.

Its sun-bleached wooden frame looked like it could have toppled in a gentle breeze if its trestles hadn't been coated in sea spray and iced firmly into place— but the coaster had seen so many storms since it had been hammered together almost a century before, and it was still standing proudly near the windswept beach, promising bathing suits and hot dogs and warmer days to come while dishwater gray waves slapped against the snow-covered sand.

Joy checked her watch one last time before she heard it.

The sound of the *Mjölnir*'s engine churning in the surf.

It was still just a hum beneath the roaring wind, in a register so low she would have thought she was imagining it if she hadn't seen its shadow looming on the horizon. The ship looked small at first—just a speck in the storm—but the longer she stared, the more she could make out its bright-red bow cutting through the gloom: fresh from the fjords of Greenland and right on time after three long days and nights on the sea. Joy bit her lips to keep them from cracking as she smiled at the sight of it. Accustomed to more frigid waters, the heavy icebreaker barely rocked in the wind, but the smaller Zodiac boats splashing down from its decks were another story. Their outboard motors whined while they crashed across the roiling whitecaps, a fine mist of salt water spraying in their wake as they raced for shore.

There were two of them, black against the waves.

"Over here!" Joy shouted.

She waved her arms above her head as she jogged closer to the shore, her boots crunching through the sand and the snow and the paper-thin crust of ice that had formed just beyond the splash of the tide line. Nobody waved back . . . but as she watched them fight their way past the jagged tips of the rocky jetties, Joy noticed that the scientists' faces were strained and red above the bright-orange blobs of their weatherproof gumbies. As weatherproof as their Arctic expedition gear might have been, none of them looked excited to test it in the frothing wash of the Atlantic. They gripped the bouncing boats for dear life, their arms wrapped through the wet nylon ropes that lined each Zodiac until they'd surfed in past the breakers— pushing in as close to the sand as they could get.

"You made it!" Joy shouted.

A man with a short, snow-encrusted beard finally waved back, then braced himself against the inflatable prow of the Zodiac as he tossed her a slick, waterproof duffel. It fell a few feet short of its mark and floated, half submerged in the sickly gray seafoam. Joy cringed at the cold kiss of salt water on her ankles as she fished it out of the surf.

"Open it!" the man yelled, his voice breaking in the wind.

Joy unpacked the duffel to find a thick neoprene suit.

It was bright orange, like the one-piece gumbies all of the scientists were wearing, and she grinned as she unfolded it—then stepped in without hesitation. The suit was made for someone twice her size, so there was plenty of room for her to pull the rubbery fabric up and over her wet boots and jeans . . . but the arms, with their built-in gloves, were more awkward. Joy spent a long, self-conscious minute trying to figure out how to zip herself in with her bulky rubber fingers. As annoying as it was to suit up with an audience in the middle of a blizzard, the suit was so impervious to the cold that Joy felt suddenly invincible.

She pulled the orange hood over her ears and smiled.

The feeling was so unexpected that—bleary-eyed at the water's edge and struggling to stand upright in the unrelenting wind—she couldn't help but laugh. The man with the short beard reached an orange arm out from his Zodiac, beckoning her to join them. Joy took a deep breath before she stepped forward into the waves, then turned back for one last look at her truck. After everything they'd been through together, it felt wrong to just leave it parked haphazardly in front of the boarded-up storefronts on the deserted boardwalk, beneath the watchful eye of the Wonder Wheel . . . but she didn't have a choice.

She was going to sea.

Or up through the bay and into Manhattan, anyway.

Joy reached for the bearded man's hand, awkwardly hoisting herself up onto the slick inflatable hull of the Zodiac and sliding on her belly to its puddled floor. Overhead, a flock of strange white birds wheeled through the snow. Rolling to her knees, Joy pushed her wet bangs from her eyes and squinted up at them. There was something strange about their glossy black legs and the way they screamed as they skimmed across the whitecaps while the Zodiac raced back to the shadow on the horizon, its engine whining as they bounced over each approaching wave. Joy wrapped her arms through the frayed nylon lifeline, swallowing the bile she felt rising at the back of her throat as the nose of the Zodiac rose and fell with every swell.

The waves were so much taller than they'd looked from shore.

And the wind was so much stronger on the water.

"Ivory gulls," the man with the short beard shouted.

Joy nodded into the ice-cold spray, trying not to barf.

"They followed us down—all the way from Greenland!"

UNION SQUARE, MANHATTAN

December 24, 9:25 a.m.

Ashley stared out the living room window, cocooned in front of the creamy-white curtains that she'd pulled behind her like a veil. She was all alone in her makeshift tent except for the radiator, which gurgled helpfully as steam coursed through its accordion folds. Ashley frowned as it hissed and popped. Earlier in the morning—before anyone else had woken up—she'd made the mistake of propping her feet up on the narrow lip of the windowsill, and her ankles were still tender from where they'd slipped and touched the hot metal of the antique heater . . . but she hadn't moved away from the window.

She hadn't moved an inch.

Not even when she'd started sweating.

Or when her calves had cramped with pins and needles.

Three full hours after they'd stumbled up the stairs, her dad had finally made it home—empty-handed with wind-burnt cheeks and collapsing with relief to find Ashley and her cousins safe and warm. He'd slept on the couch until just before sunrise, when he'd ventured back out into the storm, and Ashley had been sitting in the hard wooden chair ever since: cradling her bruised arm against her chest as waves of anxiety washed over her in fits and starts. Her eyes were bleary from peering down into the murky darkness, but she couldn't make herself look away from the frosted glass even if she wanted to. So she stayed awake instead, hoping and praying for a miracle . . . and waiting for her dad to come running home with her dog wrapped in his arms. As tired as she was, it hadn't felt right to spread out on her bed beneath her cool cotton sheets.

Not when they were both still out there, somewhere.

Lost and alone in the storm.

Ashley hugged her knees to her chest and choked back a sob.

On the other side of the curtains, the rest of the apartment was slowly starting to stir. Exhausted by the storm, without any alarms or clocks to wake them, they'd slept in later than Ashley had expected. Not that anyone could tell. It could have been six o'clock in the morning or seven at night. The storm still hadn't let up and the morning sun was no match for it. Tracking its rise above the cold smudge of the horizon, Ashley had watched it struggle to turn the bruised black sky into a depressingly gray shadow of itself. Elizabeth stifled a yawn as Matty shuffled out of the bathroom, fresh from the shower, and they conferred in hushed voices as Ashley's mom padded around the kitchen, opening cabinets and unstacking plates.

She was making pancakes again.

For the fourth meal in a row.

They didn't have much of a choice: it had been three full days since the power had gone out and they were starting to run out of food, so it was either pancakes or cold cereal . . . and the last of their milk had soured in the slowly warming fridge. Ashley's mom had poured it down the sink as soon as it started to smell, then improvised—mixing tap water, flour, and generous spoonfuls of sugar into a sweet and runny batter that she could bake in the dark without perishables like eggs or dairy. For breakfast they ate them with syrup. For lunch, she'd added slices of overripe bananas to the recipe and they'd smeared the savory cakes with peanut butter and raspberry jelly.

Crisp and golden brown, they tasted better than anyone expected.

But there was only so long they could live off of pancakes.

And they only had so much flour left in their pantry.

As sick as she was of eating pancakes for every meal, with no way and nowhere to shop for fresh groceries, they'd be feasting on stale crackers and refried beans for Christmas dinner if the storm didn't let up soon. Ashley frowned at the thought of it while her mom blended the last of their flour and sugar together with a big wooden spoon ... and then shrieked, her bowl clattering to the tiled floor as the lights flickered overhead. Ashley was more startled by her mother's scream than the unexpected surge. The power had been flickering on and off again all night, staying on *just* long enough for her to get her hopes up as the ceiling fans started spinning—and then inevitably slowed. The excitement was always short-lived and had only dulled as the night turned to morning. Ashley turned her attention back to the blizzard and sighed.

"Everyone saw that, right?" Matty yelled.

Through the curtains, she could hear him frantically searching for his charger—as if the half-second flash was somehow enough to revive his cold brick of a phone. His sister couldn't help but laugh as he unzipped his suitcase and upended it over the couch, scattering his carefully folded shirts across the cushions while Ashley's mom measured more flour and sugar into the bowl. She hummed absentmindedly to herself as she replaced what she'd spilled, then spooned the sweetened batter into the warming pan. Lit by only the dimmest wisps of light, the natural gloom of the living room echoed the heaviness in Ashley's heart, but she could feel the mood in the room brightening as the pancakes sizzled on their burner. The promise of electricity had lifted all of their spirits—all of their spirits except for hers—and it wasn't long before the kitchen was filled with excited conversation.

Like nothing was even wrong.

Ashley scowled as tears welled in her eyes.

For all of the fuss her mom made, Matty had barely even been *bruised* by his fall down the cellar stairs—but something was seriously wrong with her arm. It hurt whenever she moved it and quietly throbbed when she didn't, and Ashley wondered if anyone even realized she was stationed behind the curtains, staring down into the snowdrifts that kept burying their street . . . or if they were all just ignoring her. She wouldn't blame them if they were. Her cousins had given her the widest possible berth ever since they'd trudged back home without Fang—and as bad as it felt to be avoided, it was better to be alone than to lose her temper. Even hiding behind the curtains, she could feel it simmering and threatening to boil. It was either that or the radiator hissing at her feet, but either way, she could feel herself ruining everyone's vacation.

Like it was her fault that Christmas was ruined.

But it wasn't her fault.

And it wasn't fair.

Hot tears ran down Ashley's cheeks and she mashed

her eyes with the heels of her hands, then rubbed them dry on the fuzz of her pajamas. The warm, sweet smell of bubbling batter filled the apartment as her mom flipped pancakes on the gas-powered flame—and Ashley's stomach growled. She wanted nothing more than to get up and join her cousins. To be able to put on a happy face, like everything was going to be okay. But she squinted down into the snow instead, searching for her dad and the telltale plume of her little Pomeranian's tail.

It was all she could do, given the circumstances.

On any other day, she could have texted her dad or taped flyers up and down every single street in Manhattan. She would've called every animal shelter in the phone book and posted Fang's picture on every online forum she could find. She would have been out on the sidewalks, shouting Fang's name until her voice was raw and rasping . . . but there was no one but the deer to hear her now—and in the ice and endless wind, her flyers would have only blown away. Ashley wasn't even allowed outside in the snow anymore, not alone. Not after they'd straggled home with torn clothes and running noses, so exhausted they could barely stand. The muscles in her legs were still screaming from the effort, and even if she broke the rules and braved the storm again, there was too much ground to cover.

The city was so big . . .

And Fang was so very, *very* small.

"*C'mon,*" Ashley hissed, gritting her teeth.

Wiping the fogging window clear, she stared through her own warped reflection at the narrow strip of street below—calling out to her dad and to her dog in her thoughts, as if she could guide them home through sheer force of will. It was silly, she knew, but that didn't stop Ashley from trying. She squeezed the arms of her chair until her knuckles whitened, so focused that she didn't even notice her mom joining her behind the curtains until her arms were wrapped around her shoulders. Blinking resolutely into the storm, she tried her hardest not to cry as her mom pulled her into a hug so tight she gasped for air . . . but her mom didn't let go, and—relaxing her grip on the chair—Ashley couldn't stop herself: her tears flowed freely, salting her chapped lips as her mom tucked a strand of sweaty hair behind her ear.

"You have to eat," she whispered.

Ashley twitched in her chair.

But she didn't get up.

"You listen to me," her mom said, looking Ashley square in the eyes. "Your dad is more than capable of taking care of himself, and Fang might be small . . . but she's a fighter. She has a built-in coat and she knows where she lives." Her voice was soft and low, so Ashley's cousins wouldn't hear, but it was stern—and she frowned as she smudged a tear from Ashley's face. "You *know* she knows where we live from the way she drags us home on her leash, and she's going to come back when she's ready." Shaking her head, Ashley tried her best to pull free from the hug—but her arm twinged at her side, and her mom only hugged her tighter. "We'll keep looking for her, Ash, but the best thing you can do for Fang *and* your father is eat."

"And then we'll go look for them?" Ashley asked.

Her mom stood up and parted the curtains.

"We'll talk about it," she said.

Without the loose linen screen to hide behind, a flush of embarrassment crept up Ashley's neck and settled uncomfortably beneath her ears. The apartment was so suddenly quiet, as if Matty and Elizabeth had been listening in the entire time, on the edge of their seats. Even the radiator had stopped clanging, and Ashley could feel her cousins' eyes boring into the back of her head, just waiting for her to turn around. She knew she'd look tear-streaked and splotchy when she finally did, and she would have given anything to slink off to the bathroom without everyone feeling sorry for her. All Ashley wanted was to splash water on her face. . . .

And to start the day fresh.

With Fang in her lap and a smile in her heart.

"We're going to be okay," her mom said. "Okay?"

Ashley nodded as she rubbed her sniffling nose in the crook of her arm, bracing herself for another rib-crushing hug . . . but it never came. Instead, her mom's shins knocked against the legs of Ashley's chair as she raced to flip a pancake she'd forgotten on the stove. Left to its own devices, it had started to char, and as soon as her mom tossed the entire pan into the sink—beneath the running faucet—a greasy black smoke filled the room. Laughing through her tears, Ashley opened the window she'd been staring through all morning and leaned into the sluggish dawn. The air was so freezing that it dried her tears on contact, and the curtains billowed out behind her as whirls of snow danced over her shoulders and landed on the floor.

"It's too cold!" Matty shouted.

But Ashley ignored him.

And so did the wind.

It tore past her into the living room, then whipped into the kitchen, riffling through recipes pinned by magnets to the fridge. Napkins flew as place mats shifted, and somewhere, outside—in the darkest, grayest depths of the blizzard—Ashley heard an unmistakable yapping. It was sharp and insistent, and it cut through the storm like a fuzzy knife through melting butter. At the same time, a hard and emphatic knock against the door threw the entire apartment into a frenzy.

"Hurry down!" her dad shouted.

Not waiting to be let inside.

"She's too hard to catch on my own!"

Without stopping to close the window, Ashley

sprinted to her bedroom and pulled her still-damp snow pants up over her pajamas, then zipped into the first warm jacket she could find. As hurt and as tired as she was, her heart was racing. Determined not to let Fang slip through her fingers a second time, she was halfway down the narrow stairwell before she heard the rest of her family tumbling behind her. Half dressed with untied boots, they joined her on the landing—their arms full of coats and heavy sweaters that they rushed to pull over their heads as Ashley kicked open the creaking metal door and stepped into the wailing nightmare of the storm. Elizabeth handed her two floppy pancakes as she joined her in the wind.

"In case you're hungry," she said.

Ashley stuffed them into a fleece-lined pocket.

She'd eat them later, when she had the time.

For now . . . they had a dog to catch.

HUDSON RIVER PARK, MANHATTAN

December 24, 9:55 a.m.

"Wait up!" Matty yelled, grimacing as he pulled his brand-new winter gloves over sticky fingers. He'd been picking his way through his second pancake of the morning when Uncle Jack had pounded on the door, and the syrup was *just* tacky enough on the tips of his fingers that the soft innards of his gloves clung unpleasantly to his skin as he thudded down the middle of the street with his arms pumping at his sides, racing to keep up with his cousin. As annoying as it was, sticky fingers weren't even close to the worst of Matty's problems.

Not when his entire body was sore.

From his ankles to his eyebrows, it felt like he'd been run over by a train—and the hot, steaming shower his aunt had told him to take wasn't helping. If anything, it only made things worse: his hair was still wet and freezing against the backs of his ears, and his long woolen socks had started to sag almost as soon as he'd tugged them up around his drip-dried calves. Matty could feel them bunching at his toes as he crunched through the hardening crust of snow and ice, but he didn't have a second to stop and pull himself together.

He was lagging too far behind as it was.

Even if Ashley could hear him shouting above the storm, Fang was finally in her sights—and she hadn't even noticed when he'd stopped to adjust his heavy boots. Even Aunt Charley was crashing through the snow, in red-faced pursuit of the filthy caramel streak that was Ashley's dog. Only his sister stopped sprinting long enough for him to catch up. She peered over her shoulder, into the storm, as she called out to him. High-pitched with a nervous edge that pierced the rising wind, her voice was like a lifeline that Matty clung to as he stumbled into the curdling fog, feeling his way toward her outstretched hand.

"Do you want to go back?" she shouted.

Matty shook his head.

Surprising himself.

His cheeks were already starting to numb from the cold and every aching muscle in his body had perked up at the thought of jogging up the stairs to his cousin's overheated apartment. But it was already the day before Christmas, and Matty couldn't bear to think about how sad the next morning would be if Ashley didn't catch Fang. *Or if his cousin somehow didn't make it home at all.* There were a million things that could go wrong in the storm . . . and it was bad enough already, living on pancakes without their mom and dad. With no way to even let them know they were okay. As much as Matty hated the idea of spending another frozen minute fighting his way through the blizzard, he couldn't let his family run into danger without him. Not when worrying himself sick on the couch would have felt a million times worse.

Swallowing his fears, he pulled his sister forward.

Into the fog.

"Are you sure?" she asked.

Matty nodded as he squeezed her hand.

Not that Elizabeth could see him, anyway: the haze was so solid and milky-white that they could hardly make out their own hands in front of their faces—and the farther they jogged, the more it felt like they were pushing their way into a cloud. It didn't make any difference to Matty. Or at least, that's what he told himself as he wiped the lenses of his glasses with the smooth nylon thumbs of his gloves. No matter how often he cleaned them, they were so constantly smudged in the storm that he could barely make out the slogans on billboards that were fifteen feet tall, much less the tiny metal street signs that were clanging and shuddering in the wind.

Crossing Eighth Avenue, he'd stopped long enough to try.

But by the time he and Elizabeth trudged beneath the clumps of jagged icicles that were clinging to the rusted metal bridge over Tenth Avenue, they were as good as blindfolded. Matty took what he'd hoped would be a deep and calming breath, but the air was so very cold that he coughed and sputtered instead. Less than a block away, an avalanche of heavy ice and snow slid free from the slick glass of a tapered skyscraper, and he flinched as it crashed onto the street—setting off a chain of car alarms that blared into the void of the storm. His sister screamed at the sound of them, squeezing his hand so tightly that he started to seriously second-guess his decision not to run straight home to Ashley's apartment.

Fang had seemed *so* close.

When everyone was running and falling down the stairs, Matty was sure that they'd be snatching her off the sidewalk and finishing breakfast with big, happy smiles on their faces . . . but it was seeming less and less likely that they were even going to catch up with Fang, much less *catch* her. Matty had only glimpsed her for a second before the fog. A bedraggled flash of brown, she was favoring one limp and muddy paw, and her fancy bomber jacket was ripped at the shoulder after a long weekend out on the streets in the city that never sleeps.

But even on three legs, she was fast.

Too fast to keep up with when Matty was struggling just to stand upright in the wind. As small as she was, Fang left a deep, snaking trough of a track through the snow—so spotting her as she galloped after the shadow of a greasy black rat had been easy enough before the fog had descended, even with sleet slapping sharply against their faces. But now that the blizzard had worked itself up into a blinding white rage, Matty and his sister were back to chasing echoes.

And the gusts were only getting stronger with every block they passed.

"Fang!" Aunt Charley yelled. "C'mere, girl!"

"Come *on*, Fang!" Ashley screamed.

Their voices bounced skyward, ping-ponging between darkened apartment buildings and guiding the way . . . until they suddenly went quiet, buried by the roar of the storm. Matty's heart pounded so loudly that it was all he could hear as he changed direction, tacking toward the ghost of his cousin's muffled shouts and yelling back into the blizzard. Running as fast as they dared, he and Elizabeth dropped each other's hands so they could sprint through the whiteout, shouting Ashley's name until their throats were raw. And even then, they kept on shouting until the street narrowed into a cobblestone alley that dead-ended at concrete banks of Manhattan. No match for the misty plains of the Hudson River, the fog dispersed on the edges of the island, carried away by the same strong winds that had tried their very best to knock Matty to his knees.

The frozen river looked almost peaceful despite the storm.

Or it would've been, if Fang wasn't barking her head off.

Matty could hear her racing farther and farther away, into the distance, but his sister had stopped running. Now that the haze had cleared, he could finally see her. Not quite clearly, but clear enough through the blur of his glasses. She was standing at a metal fence that was dripping with icicles and staring out at the icy expanse of the river beyond. Except for a thin liquid line that had been carved through its center by the bright-red prow of a massive ship, the Hudson was so solid and scoured by the wind that it glistened like a polished diamond beneath a fine dusting of snow. The ship itself seemed to tower over the muted skyline of New Jersey, so big and unexpected that Matty felt almost dizzy just looking at it. Gray smoke billowed out from its grimy black stacks as its foghorn sounded, so deep and so resonant that the air itself seemed to shimmer in its wake while a flock of the strange white birds circled overhead.

Wheeling down into the watery path of the ship.

And screeching bloody murder.

Matty covered his ears as he joined his sister at the railing.

"Where . . . is . . . everyone?" he asked, pausing between words to catch his breath.

He'd managed to warm up while he was running, but it was so bitterly cold on the shores of the Hudson that he almost longed for the open shelter of the cellar stairs—and with the back of his neck dripping with sweat, Matty was even colder still. Almost as soon as he stopped running, he felt his entire body starting to shiver. Even with his socks tangled up in the toes of his boots, it was better to keep moving, so he bounced on his heels as his sister pointed down the lines of the railing. Squinting through his broken glasses, beyond the squalling snow, he saw Ashley and Aunt Charley trying to corner the little Pomeranian at the end of the very long pier while Uncle Jack squatted behind them with his arms spread wide.

"We should wait here," Matty said. "In case she doubles back."

But Fang wasn't doubling back.

Galloping into the wind with her purple tongue lolling out of the side of her mouth, Fang's booties kicked up clouds of fresh powder as she chased after what Matty could only assume was the same poor subway rat she'd been after all morning—from the East Village all the way to the piers. The snow was blowing so fiercely across the frozen river that it had piled up against the docks, forming a steep and roughshod ramp down onto the ice, and Matty's eyes jumped in and out of focus as the wet, black smear of rat scampered to its peak and leapt with a surprisingly balletic grace onto the frozen ice. The leap was more graceful than the landing: its pink paws splayed as it rolled head over tail across the slick river ice.

Fang wasn't far behind.

Matty leaned over the railing, so caught up in the stress of the moment that he was holding his breath. It was one thing to lose a dog on an island, but now that they'd run out of streets to chase her through, they were running out of time. New Jersey was less than a mile across the ice, and if Fang kept on racing toward Hoboken, there was nothing they could do to stop her. Not in the middle of a superstorm, when they could barely even walk—much less drive. Adrenaline coursed through Matty's veins, warming him from the inside out as every instinct in his body converged on one simple truth.

It was now or never.

But as badly as he wanted to help, Matty was too far away.

He could only watch, his teeth chattering above his double-wrapped scarf as Aunt Charley and Ashley shouted, pleading with the Pomeranian to slow down as she scaled the small mountain of snow and barked furiously from its peak. Matty was shouting, too, he realized. He yelled Fang's name at the top of his lungs, hoping to distract her long enough for someone to wrangle her away from the ledge—but the little dog was determined. She was already charging onto the ice by the time Ashley dove headfirst into the snow, making one last heroic grasp for her dog's filthy, knotted ruff . . . and coming up empty-handed. Matty stared openmouthed as Fang took off across the Hudson, her ears flattening in the wind as she ran.

Even with Fang's new limp, his cousin wasn't even close.

But that didn't mean she was lost forever.

Not yet, anyway.

Squinting through the sleet and swirling snow, Matty stared out at the big red ship that was moored in the middle of the Hudson. It seemed to be anchored in place, with a long and narrow gangplank feeding down to the glistening ice from its deck. Halfway between the pier and the slurry of broken ice at the base of the big ship's reinforced hull, a group of sailors in bright-orange survival suits were milling around on the surface. They blurred in and out of focus, looking strange and otherworldly—like astronauts on a mission to Mars—and Matty waved and shouted, trying to get their attention as Fang streaked toward them. But they were too far away to hear anything but the rush of cold, arctic winds and a distant bellowing thunder.

Matty blinked, rubbing his glasses clear for the thousandth time.

It wasn't rocket science.

There wasn't any reason to stop running now, just because the land had stopped: if the ice was thick enough for the sailors, it had to be thick enough for him. His cousin was still crying after Fang from the end of the pier when he made up his mind. Even without the heaps of windswept snow piling up against the docks, the railing was low enough that it took hardly any effort at all for him grasp it with his bulky gloves and lower himself down onto the snow. It crunched reassuringly underfoot, as solid as the blacktop on Fifth Avenue in the sunshine. Or close enough, anyway. His sister was too preoccupied tracking Fang's mad dash across the Hudson to see Matty's drop, but she started screaming almost as soon as she heard his boots hit the ice.

"What are you *doing*?!" she shouted, the color draining from her cheeks.

"It's okay," Matty said. "I'm okay."

He meant it, too.

Even if his sister didn't believe him.

Fang and the subway rat were still bolting across the ice, circling each other in widening loops and arabesques, but there was nowhere for them to hide on the vast expanse of the frozen river. Matty held his breath as he took one exploratory step out onto the

Hudson . . . and then another. The snow was thinner on the ice, but it was deep enough that he didn't slip, and his pulse quickened as he started to jog—hesitantly at first, and then breaking out into a full-fledged run. Elizabeth was still shouting at him from the promenade, but the blizzard was even stronger on water, and even the shrieks of the ivory gulls sounded faint over the roar of the wind in his ears and the laboriously chugging engine of his own ragged exhalations.

PIER 62 AT HUDSON RIVER PARK, MANHATTAN

December 24, 10:20 a.m.

"Matty!" Elizabeth shouted.

Her voice cracked and faded in the wind as she watched her brother lower his narrow shoulders against the storm and sprint across the ice—toward Fang and the big red ship that was looming above the haze. If he could even hear her, he didn't show it . . . and their aunt and uncle were so far down the pier that they were tiny smudges in the snow. Elizabeth took a deep breath and shivered as she gripped the slippery iron railing, leaning so far over it that she nearly flipped off the promenade and onto the river as she shouted after her brother.

"Come back!" she yelled. "I mean it!"

But he was too far gone already.

She stared into the wind for ten long Mississippi

seconds, biting her wind-chapped lips as she watched the red blur of Matty's parka fade into the blizzard. And weighed her options. On the eleventh second, Elizabeth took a deep breath and lifted her leg over the railing. Her scaredy-cat genius of a brother had chosen the worst possible time to run straight into danger, and there was no one *else* around to stop him. She was so mad at Matty—and so terrified—that she was actually shaking, but she'd already lost track of him once already and she wasn't about to let that happen again.

Not when she'd promised to look out for him.

And definitely not on Christmas.

But perched on top of the ice-cold railing with New York City behind her and the frozen river at her feet, Elizabeth was overwhelmed by a sudden, self-preserving fear. Her overtired arms and legs locked into place at the thought of falling, and she clutched the railing for dear life—shouting her brother's name into the churning storm. It wasn't any use. His red jacket was only getting smaller and smaller as he raced beneath the roiling clouds and into the shadow of the massive ship, and before Elizabeth had a chance to work up the courage to climb down from the railing and chase after him, her balance shifted in the wind.

Dropping down onto the ice was easy enough.

With over four feet of hardened snowpack rising to meet her heavy boots, the fall was short and fast—but she hadn't been ready for it, and she landed much harder than she'd intended. As soon as she hit the ground, her legs gave out beneath her and Elizabeth rolled topsy-turvy onto the Hudson, the folds of her scarf filling with wet clumps of snow as she scrambled to dig her heels into the slush. *To keep herself from sliding all the way to New Jersey.* Panicking, Elizabeth ran her hands across the ice in a wide and frantic arc, checking for cracks in its surface—but the snow on the river was thick, and the ice beneath it felt firm. . . .

And much harder than she'd expected.

Elizabeth sighed, her breath condensing into little clouds of mist as she pushed herself up onto her feet and took off running after her brother. As much as she'd been looking forward to a big city adventure, it was so far from what she'd had in mind that she almost had to laugh. If she'd known that she was going to be spending the holidays chasing her brother across a frozen river—through a blizzard, in the middle of the Biggest Winter Storm in the History of New York City—she never would have boarded their plane back in Tampa. But none of that mattered anymore. All Elizabeth cared about now was the crunch of her boots on the ice and Matty. He was already halfway out to the big red ship, and it was only looking bigger and bigger with every toe-numbingly cold step she put between herself and the safety of shore.

Elizabeth stared up at its towering silhouette while she ran.

Wondering what it could possibly be doing there.

Anchored in the ice beside Manhattan's jagged skyline.

Its deck was so high above the frozen water that she had to strain her neck just to read the unfamiliar string of consonants that were stenciled across its prow in blocky white letters: *M-J-Ö-L-N-I-R*, with two square dots above the *o*. Whatever it meant, it was even farther from home than Elizabeth and Matty—and Elizabeth got a twist in her stomach just thinking about it. And about her parents, who were a thousand miles away in the Florida sunshine. An ivory gull screeched as it swooped low across the Hudson, its black feet skimming the drifting snow as plumes of smoke billowed from the *Mjölnir*'s twin smokestacks. Even from so far away, Elizabeth could sense a rush of activity on board the big ship.

Her brother could, too.

She could tell by the way he slowed to a jog, watching as sailors in puffy orange suits spilled down its aluminum gangplank and onto the ice. Elizabeth shouted Matty's name as she picked up her pace. She knew he wouldn't hear her—except for the wind rushing into her hood, Elizabeth couldn't hear anything, either . . . not even the sound of her own voice in the storm—but she couldn't help herself. Matty was so close to catching Fang, and she was so close to catching up to Matty, and together they were all so close to a happy ending for *once* in their lives that Elizabeth was actually smiling as she sprinted across the ice.

"I'm right behind you!" she shouted.

She waved her hands above her head as she ran—and then abruptly stopped, her smile souring into a sickening frown as she felt the river shifting beneath the tread of her boots. Steadying herself as best she could, Elizabeth knelt carefully onto the trembling river and wiped a window into the snow so she could peer down into the murky darkness. There was nothing to see beneath the ice, not through the clouded sheet of a river. But between the promenade and the *Mjölnir*, something had changed. She could feel it with every fresh footfall: a vibration working its way from the soles of her feet up to her quivering knees.

Matty and Fang felt it, too, she could tell.

It's why they had stopped running.

Even the Pomeranian was standing as still as a statue, her ears pricked forward as she whimpered at the ice. Beneath her paws, an otherworldly chorus had started singing. Or twanging, Elizabeth realized. Like a rubber band plucked to the point of breaking and then released, the ice reverberated with every step. "It's okay," Elizabeth muttered, forcing herself to keep moving while the ominous twanging grew louder and louder—splitting into an inevitable fracture that swallowed half of her footprints as it spiderwebbed behind her.

You're going to be okay.

But Elizabeth was so far out from shore that she couldn't even see their cousin on the waterfront—and there was no way she was going to make it all the way back to Ashley, not now that the ice had started to shift beneath her boots. And not without Matty. They were both so much closer to the sailors in their strange orange suits, and Elizabeth's stomach dropped as she turned away from the safety of the piers and sprinted for the *Mjölnir.*

"Matty, Fang!" she yelled. "Hurry!"

Fang cocked her head as Elizabeth shouted into the wind, sounding so much braver than she felt as narrow fissures chased her across the razor-thin ice. She was so convincing that for one long and hopeful moment, she thought she might actually make it. That she had a chance at reaching the long aluminum gangplank that was hanging down from the big ship's deck. The wind was at her back for once, and she looked like she was flying as she tore across the Hudson—her heavy boots barely touching the river long enough to make any marks in the snow as she waved wildly at the orange suits, screaming at the top of her burning lungs.

And pitching unexpectedly forward.

Time didn't slow as Elizabeth fell.

She didn't see a movie montage of her entire life as she crashed to the ice in a tangle of arms and kicking legs. She only saw Matty, zipped up tightly in his bright-red jacket and looking impossibly small in the shadow of the big red ship. Elizabeth tried to shout his name as the frozen river hissed and cracked beneath her, giving way to the subzero soup of the Hudson . . . but the water was so very cold that she felt her lungs tighten in her chest on impact. Gasping for air, she grasped wildly for traction—but there was only ice and windswept snow in reach, and neither did her any good as she sank beneath the sparkling surface.

Elizabeth tried her best to tread water.

To keep her head above the ice.

But she could barely even breathe, much less fight the currents that were tugging at her legs, pulling her farther and farther into their icy depths. Every single muscle in Elizabeth's body shivered and cramped at once as she struggled to claw at the crumbling ice. To pull herself up and out of the Hudson. Her warm winter clothes—waterlogged and heavy as a hundred rocks—were hindering more than helping. She tried to shout, to scream for Matty or the sailors from the *Mjölnir,* as snow and endless hail spiraled down from the frothing gray sky . . . but the air was too thin in her chest to make a sound, and she panicked as her cries for help were muffled by her own frantic splashing and the chattering of her teeth.

THE HUDSON RIVER, MANHATTAN

December 24, 10:23 a.m.

Fang's haunches quivered as she bounded across the frozen skin of the river.

It groaned and trembled beneath her, and—balancing on three tired legs instead of four—she staggered as she backtracked past the boy in the bright-red jacket, zigzagging against the sleet and the vicious wind that carried it. She could feel it pulling at the nape of her neck, like an invisible leash dragging her across the ice, and it would have been easier to just give in. To let it blow her all the way down the Hudson and out into the choppy whitecaps of Gravesend Bay. But giving in wasn't in the little Pomeranian's nature. Her long tongue lolled between her jaws as she squared her shoulders against the storm: too small to fight the winds forever, but just light enough on her paws to cross the cloudy river without stomping through its surface.

The same couldn't be said of the girl who'd been chasing her.

Fang's ears flattened against her fur.

The girl was thrashing so loudly in the water that her first instinct was to run, but hearing the girl sputter her own name as she splashed, Fang took one tentative step toward her, and then another, trotting cautiously toward the wet and crumbling lip of the hole with her hurt paw hanging limply from her shoulder. The girl had fallen so hard that the thin river ice had splintered beneath her chin. The girl's chin had split open, too, streaking the soft white snow with a sickening shade of red. Fang danced around the hole, yelping helplessly at the girl while she clutched at its slippery surface with an outstretched hand.

Fang *wanted* to help her.

To fish her out of the water and onto dry land.

But she was far too small to even know where to start.

From the darkened shoulders of her river-wet jacket all the way down to the soles of her boots, the girl was almost completely submerged in a thick and chunky slush. It looked as if it might freeze over any second, trapping the girl in its watery embrace, and Fang barked encouragingly as she struggled to crawl

up onto her elbows and kick her way free from the
Hudson. But the fractured ice was too weak to hold
her, and it only cracked beneath her weight, plunging her back down into the heart-stopping chill of the
widening hole.

"F-F-Fang," the girl whispered. "Get help!"

Fang whimpered as the girl slowly sank.

Unsure of what to do.

Even with her lips contorted in a strangled panic,
the girl's face was so familiar . . . and the smell of her
wet and tangled hair reminded Fang of home. But the
cold was starting to catch up with the little Pomeranian, too. The longer she stood on the windswept
river, watching the girl try and fail to climb onto the
ice, the more she could feel her own muscles starting to shiver and cramp. To keep herself warm, Fang
needed to move. She barked impatiently into the
storm, circling the hole one last time as a flock of ivory
gulls screeched overhead. Searching for an easy meal
to scavenge after their long flight to New York, they
swooped so low over the Hudson that the tips of their
wings sketched faint lines across its surface.

Fang growled as they dove.

She was tempted to chase them.

But—shaking a thick layer of snow from her matted
fur—Fang launched herself into the seething white
heart of the blizzard instead, dashing past a terrified
boy who was struggling to balance on the wobbling

ice and careening toward a group of scientists in bright-orange suits. Fang's hackles rippled across her narrow shoulders as she neared them, then worked their way down to her tail, which wagged on its own accord as one of the scientists looked up with alarm. Shuffling through the mist, they'd been so busy taking measurements on the frozen Hudson that they didn't even see her before they heard her barking. Running with the wind again, instead of against it, Fang was flying so fast that her neoprene booties slipped across the ice.

Unable to stop her from crashing headfirst into a pair of orange legs.

"What are *you* doing out here?" a woman asked.

Kneeling to inspect the little Pomeranian, she patted Fang's head with a thick rubber glove—then tried to pick her up to shield her from the snow. But as cold as Fang was, she just shrugged herself free. Pointing the wind-burned nub of her nose back toward the city and the swelling hole in the ice, she barked and snapped at the woman's hands until the woman dropped her to the ice, then nipped and dragged at her ankles until she finally followed Fang away from the safety of the gangplank and out past the shadow of the big red ship. Spotting the girl who was bobbing in the ice, the woman broke out into a sprint.

"There's someone in the water!" she shouted.

Chasing Fang into the storm.

IN THE SHADOW OF THE *MJÖLNIR*, MANHATTAN

December 24, 10:25 a.m.

"Someone grab a medic!" Joy shouted.

Nobody moved, so she yelled it again—pointing randomly at one of the orange-suited scientists who were huddled behind her, drawn by the commotion. Ducking his head against the wind, he peeled away from the group, and Joy watched just long enough to make sure he made it all the way back to the subtly swaying ramp that led all the way up to the icebreaker's deck. She couldn't do anything but hope that he'd find some help within its thick steel hull.

Until then, it was up to *her* to save the girl.

And she didn't have much time.

The rest of the group shuffled across the thinning river ice as quickly as they could, dragging a black

Zodiac boat behind them like a sled. The standard-issue survival suits were so bulky that it was hard to walk in them, much less run—and the inflatable boat was their safety net. It coasted behind them, so light that it nearly fluttered in the wind as the little dog weaved excitedly between their legs, barking and jumping as they marched across the Hudson.

"Hurry!" Joy shouted. "She's in shock."

Joy was in shock, too.

When the scientists on board the *Mjölnir* had invited her to join them on the ice of the Hudson River—to take stock of the city in the historic storm—the last thing she'd expected to see was a fancy little lap dog galloping out of the fog in a torn and muddied bomber jacket. Now, less than a minute after it had nipped through the lining of her thick neoprene gloves, Joy was racing across ice so thin that it sang beneath her boots with every heavy step. One wrong move away from falling in herself. She swore she could even feel the rush of the river running beneath her, through the snow and clouded ice and the soles of her shoes, but Joy didn't have time to worry or try to play it safe. Purple-lipped and shaking, the girl was barely holding her head above the water . . . and there was no telling how long she'd been waiting.

"It's okay," Joy shouted. "You're going to be okay!"

The girl could only sputter in response.

It wasn't much to go on, but at least she was still breathing.

That was all that mattered, even if her breaths were quick and ragged. It was a minor miracle that the girl was still holding her head above the water. She'd been down long enough for a thin layer of snow to gather on the soaking wet fringe of her woolen scarf, and a thin sheen of frost had formed on her dripping hairline. Even in her waterproof gumby suit, Joy was shivering . . . *and she was dry*. But she didn't have a choice. Step by anxious step, she puzzled her way across the fractured ice, stretching her hand out as far as she dared.

"Can you reach me?" she shouted.

Then cursed beneath her breath.

Even lying completely flat on the ice—with her face pressed up against the frigid belly of the Hudson—and stretched with *all* of her might, she barely even grazed the girl's shoulder with the very tips of her fingers. If she'd had just ten or twelve more inches, Joy could've grabbed the hood of her jacket and pulled her to shore, but she might as well have been a mile away for all the good it did her. The girl was struggling just to breathe and if Joy didn't move fast, she was going to lose her beneath the ice.

New plan, Joy thought.

She climbed to her feet as the girl gasped, spitting

river water down her bloodied chin. There wasn't time to wait for help or think before she acted. The girl was drowning, in slow motion and right in front of Joy's eyes. Freezing or not, Joy wasn't about to let that happen. The frantic barks of the little dog echoed in the storm as she took one terrifying step forward and—pinching her nose closed before her plunge—splashed down into the thickening slush.

Her heart nearly stopped on impact.

Even through her gumby suit, the shock of the cold was enough to knock the wind out of her, and Joy counted down from ten to one—concentrating on every deep and steady breath—before she had enough air in her lungs to push forward through the slush. The girl's frightened eyes flashed with surprise and relief as Joy paddled awkwardly toward her, buoyed by her bulky suit, and Joy did her best to swallow the worry she felt rising in her chest. It was the exact opposite of the kinds of emergency evacuation she planned for the NCRC: Joy didn't have a clue what she was doing, and she was just as scared as the girl in the water.

But she was also determined.

"B-b-boat!" she shouted. "Now!"

It only took a moment for the startled scientists to slide the Zodiac across the ice and into the puddle, but it felt like hours as Joy kicked her heavy boots through the black waters of the Hudson—treading freezing water until the Zodiac was close enough for her to grab the nylon safety rope that lined its rubber tubes. Tethering herself to the boat with one arm, she wrapped the other around the trembling girl and shouted for the scientists to pull.

To yank them free from the river.

"Harder!" Joy yelled, tightening her grip.

Tangled in the nylon line, her arm nearly ripped free from its socket as they dragged her—dripping and screaming—out of the water and then pulled her even farther still, towing Joy and the girl across the crumbling ice until they skidded to a halting stop in the shadow of the *Mjölnir*. The thin river ice crumbled and settled behind them, its cracks spiderwebbing so wildly in the wake of the Zodiac that they sounded like a hundred different roller coasters racing down a hundred different tracks. Joy held her breath as she stared up into the roiling clouds and writhing snow, her face so cold from where the Hudson splashed her that it was numb.

Waiting for the cracks to catch up with them.

But the ice was firm beneath her back.

Joy slapped it twice for confirmation.

It wasn't until she finally exhaled that Joy noticed that the girl was screaming bloody murder at her side. Joy felt like screaming, too. She couldn't help it. An entire week of living on nothing but Cherry Coke and Christmas cookies mixed with the sudden rush of the unexpected rescue, and the sugar and adrenaline coursed through her veins as she jumped, whooping, to her feet—and into a shiny mylar blanket the scientists had fished out of a bright-orange safety chest. They wrapped her and the girl in their matching blankets, settling them down into the shallow well of the boat as they dragged them across the ice—toward the massive icebreaker and its aluminum ramp. The little dog chased them just long enough to leap over the thin plastic transom.

Catching a free ride all the way back to the *Mjölnir*.

Joy blinked into the wind as the Pomeranian made her body as small and compact as possible at the girl's trembling feet. Burying her snout between her neoprene booties, she barely seemed to notice the storm whistling and howling over her tiny head. It broke unhappily against the icebreaker's salty steel hull, sounding for all the world like the pounding hammer the big ship was named after, but curling up into a tiny ball, the brave little dog hardly seemed to notice. Just watching her drift to sleep made Joy tired, too, and she blinked her eyes closed—dreaming of her couch back home—as the scientists hauled them across the ice.

"M-my b-b-brother," the girl said, fighting to get the words out.

Joy squinted down at the girl.

Nothing was ever easy in a storm.

"He's . . . s-s-still out there," she stuttered.

"Don't worry, kid," Joy said. "We'll find him."

She pulled the girl even tighter into her arms, warming her beneath the crinkling, windproof blanket as she peered into the blizzard. For all they knew, he was underwater, too. Blue-cheeked and shaking. Joy shivered at the thought as she scanned the fog for any signs of life. But as tired as she was, she didn't have a choice. She'd find the girl's brother. She'd find her entire family, too—even if it meant jumping into the Hudson fifty more times. State of emergency or not, it was Christmas Eve, and the *Mjölnir* had enough extra bunks to house an army.

"Where's that medic?" Joy shouted.

Her voice breaking in the bitter wind.

ANCHORED ON THE HUDSON RIVER

December 25, 5:30 a.m.

No matter how hard he tried, Matty couldn't fall asleep.

He'd spent hours kicking his legs free from tangled sheets and tucking himself back in again, but he was always either way too cold or sweating through his shirt. At first he blamed the *Mjölnir* and the dusty vents above his head. It was an old and musty ship, after all, with rusted rings around its drains and clanging pipes lining every cramped and flickering passage. But Ashley had pulled herself up onto the top bunk and drifted off to sleep without batting an eye, and her entire forearm was wrapped in an itchy new cast after a quick visit to the icebreaker's infirmary. Matty could hear her softly breathing, two feet above his head, as he punched his pillow in half and rolled over to the far side of the narrow bed.

Trying to make himself comfortable.

For the thousandth time.

It didn't help that his thin and somehow lumpy mattress crinkled every time he moved, but it wasn't the bottom bunk that kept Matty twisting and turning through the smallest hours of the morning. He was so tired he could've slept on the floor—and he would've tried that, too, if he thought it would've helped—but the scuffed linoleum tiles wouldn't have stopped his mind from racing. His heart was still pounding in his chest from the terror of the day, and even though his sister was safe—even though they were *all* as safe as they could possibly be in the impenetrable warmth of the big red ship—a lingering fear hung like a fog from the corners of the cramped and stifling cabin as he stared up at the double-paned porthole.

Its glass was so thick with frost that it was useless.

Even if he could somehow scrape it clean, there was nothing but darkness on the other side of the boat. Matty rolled over again, his plastic mattress crackling in protest as he pressed his pillow against the hot tears that were forming at the corners of his eyes. It felt so wrong, spending Christmas without their parents. Even with the blackout and the blizzard—after *everything* they'd been through—at the back of his mind, he'd always thought his parents would find a way to make it up in spite of the storm. That his mom and dad would drive through the snow on Christmas morning, tired but smiling . . . like a happy ending in a made-for-TV movie.

But real life wasn't like a movie.

Matty sat up and sighed.

There wasn't any point in pretending he was going to fall asleep when he'd been fidgeting for six of the past eight hours in bed, so he wrapped a rough woolen blanket around his shoulders like a cape and padded out of the room instead—gently securing the rounded door behind him so he wouldn't wake his cousin. *If that was even possible.* Outside of their cabin, the ship was bright with a cold fluorescent light, and Matty trailed his hands against the bulkhead as he snuck through its narrow passageways, working his way down to the stern of the *Mjölnir*—past the hand-painted signs that pointed to the galley and all the way up to an observation lounge he remembered from their first anxious hours on board the massive icebreaker.

When every single one of his fears had finally come true.

And his sister was still in the sick bay.

Featuring a shiny brass telescope and wide, weatherproof windows, the lounge would have offered a sweeping view of the city if there was anything to see—but Matty didn't even bother to look outside as he collapsed into the waiting arms of a long orange couch. Like his bunk bed, it had been worn down to its seams through decades of use, and he burrowed into its sagging cushions as he surveyed the room. The crew had tried their best to decorate, draping strands of twinkling lights across the ceiling and duct-taping a silver tinsel tree onto the floor. The plastic tree was short and sparse—no more than three feet tall with-out an ornament in sight—and the spangled lights cast long shadows on the walls....

But at least there was power.

Matty reached for his phone.

It was right where he'd left it: charging in the only outlet on the ship that wouldn't fry it to a crisp. The *Mjölnir* had crossed entire oceans before it found Elizabeth in the Hudson—sailing all the way from Swe-den by way of the North Pole, is what one of the crew-members had told him, explaining the strange circular plugs that didn't even come close to fitting his phone. The bright-yellow adaptor that was zip-tied to a cof-fee table at his feet was just another reminder of how very far he was from home, but Matty was so relieved to swipe his screen to life that he was actually smiling as he wedged his bare feet beneath the cushions of the couch, his face shining blue in its reflected light.

"Couldn't sleep?"

Matty nearly dropped his phone mid-scroll.

After just one second staring into its screen, the

observation deck looked even darker than when he'd
first walked through its doors, and it took a long moment for his eyes to adjust enough to see the silhouette of a woman sitting cross-legged in a threadbare
recliner. Blinking through the murky twilight, Matty
surprised himself by recognizing her. The boat was so
big that there were hundreds of people on board, but
Joy had saved his sister from the ice . . . then trekked
all the way back to the piers: across the wobbling ice,
through the wind and the sleet, dragging a big black
boat behind her as she shouted their names into the
storm.

Like some kind of superhero on the Hudson.

In a bright-orange suit two sizes too big for her.

"I couldn't sleep either," Joy said, not waiting for
an answer as Matty's phone buzzed to life in his lap.
It had taken forever to link up with the ship's sluggish
satellites, but now that it was connected, four days'
worth of missed calls and messages flashed across
his screen as Joy happily snacked her way through a
packaged tray of cookies. Aunt Charley had filled his
parents in as soon as she could call them from the captain's bridge—but even if he only answered his friends
back home in Tampa, it was going to take an entire
week just to catch up. Exhausted at the thought of it,
Matty fell back into the faded couch as Fang curled up
in a tight little ball at Joy's side, her tail wagging while
Joy scratched the soft fur between her ears with one

hand and worked her way through an entire row of gingersnaps with the other.

All Matty wanted to do was call his mom.

But it wasn't even six in the morning yet.

"Merry Christmas, kid," Joy said.

She waited for Matty to look up, then slid the plastic tray across the table. A single snickerdoodle tumbled free, and Matty popped it into his mouth before it had a chance to bounce onto the carpet. He was sure that he was still too nervous to eat, but the snickerdoodle was so soft and sweet—with thick dollops of icing coating its cracked cinnamon crust—that he could feel the pit in his stomach starting to melt as he reached for another one, getting up and pacing toward the big wall of windows as he ate. The skyline was still shrouded in mist, but a patchwork of skyscrapers were starting to light up like Christmas trees in the night, and Matty swore that he saw more tiny windows sparking to life every second he spent staring at the view.

"The power's coming back?" he asked, turning to the couch.

But Joy's attention was elsewhere.

And so was Fang's.

She was growling astride Joy's lap, her nose working overtime as the limbs of the little, plastic tree rattled ominously in the corner of the room. Behind its sparkling tinsel and twinkling Christmas lights, a pair of narrowed eyes glinted from the shadows. They were small and sharp and laser-focused, and the skin on Matty's arms crawled as Fang scrambled to the floor—unable to contain her excitement. The tree was no match for his cousin's Pomeranian. Her entire body trembled with frenzied expectation as she charged beneath its flimsy boughs, ripping its flickering lights from the wall as the tree toppled in a flash of fur and gnashing teeth.

A single panicked yelp echoed in the sudden darkness.

Followed by an angry snarl.

Without stopping to think, Matty leapt up onto the coffee table—then rolled forward onto the weathered arm of the sun-bleached couch, keeping off the floors. The old couch groaned beneath the bruised weight of his knees as Fang chased a prey that Matty couldn't even see in widening circles around the empty observation deck, knocking against the legs of chairs and tables as she scampered underfoot. *Another rat,* Matty guessed, cringing at the thought of its yellowed teeth and hairless tail while Fang nipped and yapped her way across the lounge.

Chasing the strange and ghostly blur.

"Watch your feet!" Joy shouted.

Matty stumbled backward, his smudged glasses clattering to the floor as the rat rocketed across the couch with Fang hot on its heels. But even squinting through the darkness, Matty could tell that Fang

wasn't chasing a rat after all. It was something bigger. With teeth that glinted as it darted across his feet.
It wasn't until the blinding overhead lights switched
on that Matty realized he was yelling, and so loudly
that he hadn't even heard his phone. He silenced it
without thinking—just to stop its endless ringing—as
a small, white-furred fox pranced beneath a droop-
ing garland. With Fang awkwardly bumbling on three
good legs, the fox could have easily outrun her . . . but
it waited while she caught her breath, then bounded
over the fallen tree. Matty stared openmouthed as
Fang barreled her way through its branches.

Scattering a long trail of silver needles behind her.

"A stowaway!" Joy shouted, grinning ear to ear.

Drawn by the commotion, a bleary-eyed deckhand
joined them at the threshold of the lounge and—one
by one, as Fang yelped into the night—the rest of the
Mjölnir's crew crowded in behind him. They stood
on the tips of their toes, taking in the festive wreckage of the room while the little Pomeranian ripped her
way across the threadbare carpet and bounded up
onto the coffee table, her claws scrambling for traction
as she knocked Joy's Christmas cookies to the floor. In
the seconds it took Matty to wipe his broken glasses
clean and prop them on his nose, she'd sown enough
destruction—with so much shredded tinsel and hundreds of buttercream pawprints—that it looked like
Santa's workshop had exploded right in front of him.

"Comin' through!" Ashley shouted.

She squeezed past the *Mjölnir*'s crew, pushing her way into the lounge with her hard, white cast. A lop-sided smile broke out across her face as she surveyed the room, and Matty couldn't help but smile, too. His sister was right behind his cousin. The last time he'd seen her she'd been resting in the sick bay . . . and she looked a little worse for wear with a big, fluffy blanket wrapped around her shoulders and a Band-Aid plastered on her chin—but she was alive and she was dry, and she was laughing at Fang and the sprightly arctic fox as her aunt and uncle staggered in behind her, rubbing the sleep from their eyes.

Matty's smile widened at the sight of them.

None of them had expected to spend the night on board the icebreaker.

Matty hadn't even known what an icebreaker *was* until one of the scientists had explained it to him. They'd all only carried the clothes on their backs when they'd climbed up its long and swaying gangplank—leaving the storm and the sleet and the frozen expanse of the city behind them—but here they all were, wearing the matching red long johns they'd borrowed from the onboard laundry. Like they'd planned it on purpose, for some corny group photo. The little fox sprinted across the lounge, chirping playfully over her shoulder, and Fang skittered between Matty's legs while his freshly charged phone buzzed in the palm of his hand. Matty was laughing so hard that he had to stop and catch his breath before he finally answered it.

"Hey," he said, covering his ears to block out the noise.

And jogging away from the ruckus.

It was the first time he'd heard his mom's voice since the power went out, and she sounded so breathless and panicked on the other end of the line that he waved for his sister to join him as he stepped over the battered Christmas tree and made his way to the relative quiet of the *Mjölnir*'s wide windows. His mom talked a mile a minute about Tampa and how Matty and Elizabeth weren't ever going anywhere without them, *not ever again,* and Matty could only nod as the blizzard pounded against the weatherproof glass.

He hadn't been wrong about the power.

There were more lights winking back at him from the skyline than there had been even five minutes before. It was like the entire city was slowly switching on while he watched, and it was glowing so warmly through the snow that Matty shivered as his sister leaned her head against his shoulder, close enough to hear their mother worry in his ear.

"We miss you *so* much!" Elizabeth shouted.

She plucked the phone from Matty's hand and squeezed him in a sudden, one-armed hug as she told her mom how much they loved and missed her.

It wasn't until Matty heard the tremor in his sister's voice that his knees started to weaken beneath him. He'd stayed strong the entire trip. Even on their long march home—and at the bottom of the cellar stairs, pinned down by fifty-pound boxes full of soda and dusty cans of soup. With so much danger swirling all around them and all the challenges they'd faced, spending Christmas morning in the safest place in New York City should've been *easy*. Matty didn't even care that there weren't any presents under the tree, or that Fang and her wild new friend were dragging what was left of it across the lounge.

But it just wasn't the same without their parents.

Matty sighed as he stared out across the river.

Tall black clouds hung so heavily over the jagged shadow of the skyline that they looked like they might crush it, and the snow was still so thick that the entire world looked soft and hazy at the edges—but somewhere behind the island of Manhattan, so dim and far away that he could barely see it, the rosy pink rays of a distant sun were rising through the gloom. Matty's pulse quickened as he reached for his phone, to check and see if the front was *finally* passing, but his sister and their mom were only getting started. He cupped his hands against the windows and stared into the twisting gales instead, listening to Elizabeth recount their Park Avenue adventure and her death-defying rescue on the ice and smiling as he spotted the bright-red reflections of three matching sets of pajamas in the darkened glass.

Matty couldn't help himself.

While Fang and the arctic fox led Joy and the rest of the crew on a predawn chase through the creaking maze of the *Mjölnir,* Aunt Charley and Uncle Jack were hugging his cousin so tightly that she nearly disappeared between their arms. Only Ashley's head peeked out between them, and Matty could see her smile as clear as day in the shimmering mirror of the night, shining as brightly as the Rockefeller Christmas tree before it collapsed. Alone in the lounge with nothing to do but wait for the sun to rise and start melting the ice, Matty paced to the big brass telescope at the prow of the ship and swiveled its focus from the pointed spire of the Empire State Building to the torch that was blazing atop the Statue of Liberty, its golden flame lit up so brightly that it looked like a comet burning through the storm.

Author's Note

"Is this real?"

That's the question I get asked more than any other, by readers of all ages (including adults!). Almost everything I've written has been about natural disasters—which can be heartbreakingly real to the people who've been unlucky enough to have been affected by them, myself included—so it can be a hard question to answer, especially because most of the time what readers are *really* asking is: Should I add some of the stuff that happened in this book to the list of things I'm actually worried about in the real world . . . or is this just a story?

The truth is somewhere in between.

If you read my book *Storm Blown,* you'll know that I spend a lot of time thinking and reading about extreme weather events. It's hard not to when they're always in the news, or when you live in an area where they're more or less expected. That expectation of disaster was my experience growing up on Louisiana's Gulf Coast, where hurricanes were grudgingly accepted as a part of life—like mosquitos in the summer or the ankle-deep floods that filled the streets after an exceptionally hard rain. We usually think of them as sudden and unexpected, but for a lot of people who live in commonly affected areas, the threat of natural disaster is such a low-level hum at the back of their minds that it dulls over time.

We get used to it and we get on with our lives.

That's just human nature.

But a quick glance at a hazard map like the one created by the National Center for Disaster Preparedness (NCDP) at the Earth Institute shows that the places where natural disasters are "normal" aren't as few and far between as we'd like to think. Whether it's flooding or wildfires, hurricanes or avalanches—or even earthquakes and volcanoes—there's a chance that wherever you may be reading this, you live near an area that's experienced some kind natural disaster or extreme weather event in the past few years. You may have even seen a tornado or a blizzard firsthand . . . and if you haven't, you probably know someone who has.

Either way, you wouldn't be alone!

I'm writing this note during the dog days of summer,

just as Hurricane Hanna is making landfall in South Texas. Three other named storms have formed in the Atlantic so far this month—but I wrote the bulk of this book in snowier times, when at least three major blizzards struck North America (all of which were rapidly evolving systems called "bomb cyclones"). If that sounds like a lot, it's because it is. There are some people who say that one year isn't any better or worse than the next when it comes to the weather, but the National Centers for Environmental Information (NCEI) keeps an ongoing tally of weather and climate-related disasters in the United States, and all their historical data—free to access on their very cool website—shows an increase in the number of billion-dollar disasters over time.

It's hard to argue with the numbers.

In the United States, for example, we averaged roughly fifteen billion-dollar disasters every year from 2016 to 2019. That's more than double the previous average, which was in place well before I was even born—and big winter storms like the one in *Snow Struck* are following the same general trends. According to the National Oceanic and Atmospheric Administration (NOAA), "The frequency of extreme snowstorms in the eastern two-thirds of the contiguous United States has increased over the past century. Approximately twice as many extreme U.S. snowstorms occurred in the latter half of the 20th century than the first." With all this information at their fingertips, analysts at the NOAA are calling the past ten years "a landmark decade of U.S. billion-dollar weather and climate disasters."

But as far as blizzards go, I hadn't seen any until relatively recently.

In fact, I spent most of my younger years sweating in the sunshine.

I was born and raised in New Orleans, and mine wasn't a family that chased the snow in winter. I had relatives in New York, where my great-grandfather and his sons ran a shoe-repair shop (and later, law offices) on Mermaid Avenue in Coney Island for decades . . . but I never made the trip up to see them. Instead, my mom would drive us to Florida for longer holidays—all the way down to her childhood home, near Miami Beach—and on shorter day trips we'd take a ferry to a barrier island off the coast of Mississippi, where I'd get sunburned looking for dolphins from the glossy white deck. After a surprise move to the southern hemisphere, I graduated from high school in Jakarta, Indonesia . . . which is a long way of saying that when I finally moved north after a lifetime of blinking sunscreen out of my eyes, the winters took a *lot* of getting used to. I was so nervous about my first snow in Boston that I bought the biggest coat I could find, an enormous parka with neon-orange lining that could double as a sleeping bag.

By the time I moved to Brooklyn, I'd finally learned how to layer.

But I've never really gotten used to the cold.

I was working full-time—for a book publisher, on the nineteenth floor of the Flatiron building (where Ashley and her cousins spot the herd of deer, across from Madison Square Park)—when I experienced my first real-life blizzard. It was a big one: the newspapers called it a "snowicane" because of its hurricane-force winds, and it dropped over two feet of sleet and snow while I watched from my office desk, wondering how I was going to get home. I'll never forget trudging back to my apartment from the subway station, past the red-copper domes of a Russian Orthodox Church and a baseball diamond with stadium lighting that cast the park in a strangely purple glow. The snow was up to my knees and soaking through my jeans, but I wasn't in a rush to get inside. Not when the entire city seemed so eerily empty and timeless, with every snow-covered lamppost reminding me of C. S. Lewis and his mythical kingdom of Narnia.

Two years later, Superstorm Sandy hit the Eastern Seaboard.

I thought I'd seen the last of those kinds of big, life-altering storms once I moved to New York, a thousand miles away from the Gulf of Mexico and Hurricane Alley . . . but, as Matty and Elizabeth learn (the hard way) in *Snow Struck,* extreme weather can find you no matter where you are. Superstorm Sandy was a typical hurricane at first: it had been weakening into a post-tropical storm as it worked its way up the coast and into cooler Atlantic waters, when—all of a sudden, surprising even the most seasoned meteorologists—a cold front from the Arctic transformed it into an unexpected snowstorm. Reporters gave it all sorts of names like "Blizzicane" and "Frankenstorm" to try to explain what was happening, but no matter what they called it, it was one of the most destructive weather events on record in the United States.

A state of emergency was declared.

Evacuations were ordered and school was canceled.

Hundreds of thousands of New Yorkers lost power for weeks.

A few months after the storm, when recovery efforts were well under way, I bicycled the twenty miles from my apartment to the boardwalk on Rockaway Beach to survey the damage. I wasn't sure what I expected to see, but the wide wooden boardwalk was completely gone: blasted from the beach by furious winds and waves I couldn't even begin to imagine. While *Snow Struck* is a book about a historic blizzard (and not a hurricane), I always think about those frozen, gale-force winds when—every year, like clockwork—snowpalypses, snowmaggedons, and other "snowstorms of the century" are inevitably reported.

It's always with the same breathless excitement.

Bordering on hyperbole.

But these kinds of extreme weather events *are* real, and—as oceans warm and sea levels continue to rise—they're increasingly a part of our lives. Global weather systems are so complex that it's hard to say how exactly climate change is going to affect the weather from year to year: sometimes the winters are warmer and sometimes they're colder. Sometimes abnormally warm weather paves the way for extremely low temperatures, like in *Snow Struck*. As a planet, we're in a period of flux, and that instability has created a less predictable environment where extreme weather events and natural disasters—from drought-driven wildfires to frigid bomb cyclones and seasonal flooding—thrive. Which sounds a little scary, I know . . .

But there's a silver lining.

Scientists will be studying the long-term effects of accelerated climate change for years to come, but tens of thousands of studies and papers have already been published on the subject, and consensus has been reached on at least one major point: our climate is changing more quickly than it should be because of human activities, like burning fossil fuels for electricity and transportation. A lot of people don't like to hear that because it makes them feel guilty for something they didn't even know they were doing wrong. It might not seem fair, but if you tilt your head and consider the problem from a slightly different angle, it's easy to feel optimistic.

If humans are the root of the problem . . .

It's in our power to fix it!

You may have seen bumper stickers that say "Stop Climate Change," and that isn't *really* possible—the Earth's climate was changing millions of years before the first cars were even invented. But there are a lot of things we can and should be doing—as kids and adults, and as a planet—to slow that change and minimize our effect on the weather. Small, everyday things like recycling and riding a bike instead of driving (or planting a tree and trying not to use single-use plastics) can make a huge difference. But the absolute *best* thing we can do to slow climate change is to learn about and care for our environment—and to convince our parents and loved ones to care about it, too.

We only have one planet, after all.

And it's in our own best interest to look out for it!

Acknowledgments

Snow Struck wouldn't exist without the endless encouragement and enthusiasm of Rachel Ekstrom Courage, my fearless wife and literary agent. That was her in the dedication, snowboarding off a French alp on a hang glider. We met in the Flatiron Building in New York, where we both worked in publishing (my first job was in the mailroom, sending advanced reader's copies of novels to booksellers all across the country), and the earliest seeds of this story were formed during our many walks home from the subway through knee-deep snow.

I feel like I won the lottery, having Wendy Loggia as an editor on this and my previous book. The process of working with her on *Storm Blown* made me a much stronger writer—and *Snow Struck* is so much bigger and better thanks to her editorial vision and insight. Thanks also to Hannah Hill for her editorial notes on an earlier version of this story, to Carrie Andrews for helping me shine my sentences to a polish with her copyedits, to Alison Romig, and to the entire team at Delacorte Press and Random House Children's Books, from the library marketing department to the sales force, for getting this book out into the world. The cover of *Snow Struck* looks like the blockbuster movie poster of my dreams thanks to designers Larsson McSwain and April Ward (and to the amazing Mike Heath at Magnus Creative, who I didn't have a chance to thank last time!).

To all the parents, teachers, booksellers, festival organizers, friends, and librarians who've helped spread the word about my books: *thank you*. It's such an incredible privilege to be able to write these kinds of stories for young readers, and I wouldn't be able to do it without you. Very special thanks to Ryan Labay of Akron-Summit County Public Library (Patron Saint of Authors), to Carnegie Library of Pittsburgh (where I do most of my writing and research), and—last but not least—to my loving (and book-loving!) family: Adrienne Petrosini, Rich and Sandy Ekstrom, Maria and Paul Bryant, and the Henrys (Ella, Ben, Donata, and René).

ABOUT THE AUTHOR

NICK COURAGE is a New Orleans–born writer (and aspiring baker and skateboarder) who lives in Pittsburgh with his wife and cat. He is the author of the middle-grade novel *Storm Blown,* and his work has appeared in the *Paris Review* and *Writer's Digest.* When he's not writing (or skating behind the library), Nick likes to ride his bike as far as he can—past the city, to the woods or the beach.

nickcourage.com